ONCE TRAPPED

(A RILEY PAIGE MYSTERY—BOOK 13)

BLAKE PIERCE

BOOKS BY BLAKE PIERCE

THE MAKING OF RILEY PAIGE SERIES
WATCHING (Book #1)
WAITING (Book #2)

RILEY PAIGE MYSTERY SERIES
ONCE GONE (Book #1)
ONCE TAKEN (Book #2)
ONCE CRAVED (Book #3)
ONCE LURED (Book #4)
ONCE HUNTED (Book #5)
ONCE PINED (Book #6)
ONCE FORSAKEN (Book #7)
ONCE COLD (Book #8)
ONCE STALKED (Book #9)
ONCE LOST (Book #10)
ONCE BURIED (Book #11)
ONCE BOUND (Book #12)
ONCE TRAPPED (Book #13)
ONCE DORMANT (Book #14)

MACKENZIE WHITE MYSTERY SERIES
BEFORE HE KILLS (Book #1)
BEFORE HE SEES (Book #2)
BEFORE HE COVETS (Book #3)
BEFORE HE TAKES (Book #4)
BEFORE HE NEEDS (Book #5)
BEFORE HE FEELS (Book #6)
BEFORE HE SINS (Book #7)
BEFORE HE HUNTS (Book #8)
BEFORE HE PREYS (Book #9)

AVERY BLACK MYSTERY SERIES
CAUSE TO KILL (Book #1)
CAUSE TO RUN (Book #2)
CAUSE TO HIDE (Book #3)
CAUSE TO FEAR (Book #4)
CAUSE TO SAVE (Book #5)

CAUSE TO DREAD (Book #6)

KERI LOCKE MYSTERY SERIES
A TRACE OF DEATH (Book #1)
A TRACE OF MUDER (Book #2)
A TRACE OF VICE (Book #3)
A TRACE OF CRIME (Book #4)
A TRACE OF HOPE (Book #5)

PROLOGUE

Morgan Farrell had no idea where she was or where she had just come from. She felt as if she were stepping out of a deep, thick fog. Something or someone was right there in front of her.

She leaned forward, staring, and saw a woman's face staring back at her. The woman looked just as lost and confused as Morgan felt.

"Who are you?" she asked the woman.

The face mouthed the words in unison with her, and then Morgan realized …

My reflection.

She was looking at her own face in a mirror.

She felt stupid not to have recognized herself right away, but not completely surprised.

My reflection.

She knew she was looking at her own face in a mirror, but it felt like looking at a stranger. This was the face she'd always had, the face that people called elegant and beautiful. Now it looked artificial to her.

The face in the mirror didn't look quite … alive.

For a few moments, Morgan wondered if she had died. But she could feel her slightly ragged breathing. She felt her heart beating a little fast.

No, she wasn't dead. But she seemed to be lost.

She tried to pull her thoughts together.

Where am I?

What was I doing before I got here?

Weird as she felt about not knowing, it was a familiar problem. This wasn't the first time she'd found herself in some part of the huge house without knowing how she'd gotten there. Her sleepwalking spells were caused by the multiple tranquilizers the doctor had prescribed, plus too much scotch.

Morgan only knew one thing—Andrew had better not see her looking like she looked right now. She had no makeup on, and her hair was a mess. She lifted a hand to push a strand of hair off her forehead, then saw …

My hand.

It's red.

1

It's covered with blood.

She watched as the mouth on the reflected face dropped open with shock.

Then she lifted her other hand.

It was also red with blood.

With a shudder of revulsion, she impulsively wiped her hands on the front of her clothing.

Then her horror mounted. She had just smeared blood on her extremely expensive silk nightgown.

Andrew would be furious if he found out.

But how was she going to clean herself up?

She glanced around, then hastily reached for a hand towel hanging next to the mirror. As she tried to clean her hands with it, she saw the monogram …

AF

This was her husband's towel.

She forced herself to focus on her surroundings … the plush monogrammed towels … the shimmering gold-colored walls.

She was in her husband's bathroom.

Morgan sighed with despair.

Her nighttime wanderings had taken her into her husband's bedroom a few times before. If she woke him up, he was always furious at her for violating his privacy.

And now she had wandered all the way through his bedroom into his adjoining bathroom.

She shivered. Her husband's punishments were always cruel.

What's he going to do to me this time? she thought.

Morgan shook her head, trying to pull herself out of her mental fog. Her head was splitting and she felt nauseous. Obviously she'd had a lot to drink on top of too many tranquilizers. And now, not only had she gotten blood all over one of Andrew's precious towels, she saw that she had made prints all over the white bathroom counter. There was even blood on the marble floor.

Where did all this blood come from? she asked herself.

A strange possibility occurred to her …

Did I try to kill myself?

She couldn't remember doing that, but it certainly seemed possible. She'd contemplated suicide more than once since she'd been married to Andrew. And if she ever did die by her own hand, she wouldn't be the first to do so in this house.

2

Mimi, Andrew's wife before Morgan, had committed suicide.

So had his son Kirk, just last November.

She almost smiled with bitter irony …

Did I just try to continue the family tradition?

She stepped back to get a better look at herself.

All this blood …

But she didn't seem to be wounded anywhere.

So where had the blood come from?

She turned and saw that the door leading into Andrew's bedroom was wide open.

Is he in there? she wondered.

Had he slept through whatever had happened?

She breathed a little easier at the possibility. If he was sleeping that soundly, maybe she could get away without him noticing that she'd been here.

But then she stifled a groan as she realized it wasn't going to be that easy. There was still all this blood to deal with.

If Andrew came into his bathroom and found this terrible mess, of course he'd know that she was somehow to blame.

She was always to blame for everything as far as he was concerned.

Her panic rising, she began to wipe the counter with the towel. But that was no good. All she was doing was smearing the blood all over the place. She needed water to clean things up.

She almost turned on the faucet in the sink when she realized the sound of running water would surely wake Andrew up. She thought maybe she could softly close the bathroom door and run the water as quietly as she could.

She crept on tiptoe across the enormous bathroom toward the door. When she got there, she cautiously peeked out into the bedroom.

She gasped aloud at what she saw.

The lights were turned low, but there was no mistaking Andrew lying there in bed.

He was covered with blood. The sheets were covered in blood. There was even blood on the carpeted floor.

Morgan rushed over to the bed.

Her husband's eyes were wide open in an expression of frozen terror.

He's dead, she realized. She hadn't died, but Andrew had.

Had *he* committed suicide?

No, that was impossible. Andrew had nothing but contempt for people who took their own lives—including his wife and son.

"Not serious people," he'd often said about them.

And Andrew had always prided himself on being a serious person.

And he'd always raised that issue with Morgan …

"Are you a serious person?"

As she looked more carefully, she could see that Andrew had bled from many different wounds all over his body. And nestled among the blood-soaked sheets beside his body she saw a large kitchen knife.

Who could have done this? Morgan wondered.

Then a weird, euphoric calm fell over her as she realized …

I finally did it.

I killed him.

She'd done it in her dreams many times.

And now, at long last, she'd done it for real.

She smiled and said aloud to the corpse …

"Who's a serious person *now*?"

But she knew better than to bask in this warm and pleasant feeling. Murder was murder, and she knew that she had to accept the consequences.

But instead of fear or guilt, she felt a deep sense of contentment.

He was a horrible man. And he was dead. Whatever happened now, this was well worth it.

She picked up the phone next to his bed with her sticky hand and almost dialed 911 before she thought …

No.

There's someone else I want to tell first.

It was a kindly woman who had shown concern about her welfare some time ago.

Before she did anything else, she needed to call that woman and tell her that she needn't worry about Morgan anymore.

Everything was just fine at last.

CHAPTER ONE

Riley noticed that Jilly was twitching a little in her sleep. The fourteen-year-old was in the adjoining seat, with her head resting on Riley's shoulder. Their plane had been in the air for about three hours now, and it would be another couple of hours before they would land in Phoenix.

Is she dreaming? Riley wondered.

If so, Riley hoped that the dreams weren't bad.

Jilly had lived through horrific experiences during her short life, and she still had lots of nightmares. She'd seemed especially anxious since that letter from social services in Phoenix had arrived, informing them that Jilly's father wanted his daughter back. Now they were flying to Phoenix for a court date that would settle the matter once and for all.

Riley couldn't help but worry as well. What would become of Jilly if the judge didn't allow her to stay with Riley?

The social worker had said she didn't expect that to happen.

But what if she was wrong? Riley wondered.

Jilly's whole body started twitching more sharply. She began moaning quietly.

Riley shook her gently and said, "Wake up, sweetheart. You're having a bad dream."

Jilly sat bolt upright and stared straight ahead for a moment. Then she burst into tears.

Riley put her arm around Jilly and reached into her purse for a tissue.

She asked, "What is it? What were you dreaming about?"

Jilly sobbed wordlessly for a few moments. Then she said, "It was nothing. Don't worry."

Riley sighed. She knew that Jilly harbored secrets that she didn't like to talk about.

She stroked the girl's dark hair and said, "You can tell me anything, Jilly. You know that."

Jilly wiped her eyes and blew her nose.

Finally she said, "I was dreaming about something that really happened. A few years ago. My dad was on one of his serious drunks and he was blaming me as usual—for my mother leaving, for his not being able to keep a job. For everything. He told me he

5

wanted me out of his life. He dragged me by the arm to a closet and threw me inside and locked the door and …"

Jilly fell silent and closed her eyes.

"Please tell me," Riley said.

Jilly shook herself a little and said, "I was afraid to scream at first, because I thought he'd drag me back out and beat me. He just left me in there, like he'd forgotten all about me. And then …"

Jilly choked back a sob.

"I don't know how many hours passed, but everything got real quiet. I thought maybe he'd just passed out or gone to bed or something. But it was like that for a long, long time, and everything stayed so quiet. Finally I realized that he must have left the house. He did that sometimes. He'd go away for days and I'd never know when he was coming back, or *if* he was coming back."

Riley shuddered as she tried to imagine the poor girl's horror.

Jilly continued, "Finally I started screaming and banging on the door, but of course nobody could hear me, and I couldn't get out. I was alone in that closet for … I still don't know how long. Several days, probably. I had nothing to eat, and I sure couldn't sleep, and I was so hungry and afraid. I even had to go to the bathroom in there and I had to clean that up later. I started seeing and hearing weird things in the dark—I guess they must have been hallucinations. I guess I kind of lost my mind."

Small wonder, Riley thought with horror.

Jilly said, "When I heard noises in the house again, I thought maybe I was just hearing things. I yelled out, and Dad came to the closet and unlocked it. He was stone cold sober now, and he looked surprised to see me. 'How'd you get in there?' he said. He acted all upset that I'd gotten myself into such a mess and treated me OK for a little while after that."

Jilly's voice had faded to a near whisper, and she added, "Do you think he's going to get custody of me?"

Riley gulped down a knot of anxiety. Should she share her own fears with the girl she still hoped to adopt as her own daughter?

She couldn't bring herself to do that.

Instead she said …

"I'm sure he won't."

"He'd better not," Jilly said. "Because if he does, I'll run away for good. Nobody will ever find me."

Riley felt a deep chill as she realized …

She really means it.

Jilly had a history of running away from places she didn't like.

Riley remembered all too well how she'd found Jilly in the first place. Riley had been working on a case involving dead prostitutes in Phoenix, and she'd found Jilly in the cab of a truck in a parking lot where prostitutes worked. Jilly had decided to become a prostitute and sell her body to the owner of the truck.

Would she do anything that desperate again? Riley wondered.

Riley was horrified by the idea.

Meanwhile, Jilly had calmed down and was drifting back to sleep. Riley nestled the girl's head against her shoulder again. She tried to stop worrying about the upcoming court date. But she couldn't shake off her fear of losing Jilly.

Would Jilly even survive if that happened?

And if she did survive, what kind of life would she have?

*

When the plane landed, four people were waiting to greet Riley and Jilly. One was a familiar face—Brenda Fitch, the social worker who had put Jilly into Riley's care in the first place. Brenda was a slender, nervous woman with a warm and caring smile.

Riley didn't recognize the three other people. Brenda hugged Riley and Jilly and made introductions, starting with a middle-aged married couple, both of them stout and smiling.

Brenda said, "Riley, I don't believe you've met Bonnie and Arnold Flaxman. They were Jilly's foster parents for a short while after you rescued her."

Riley nodded, remembering how Jilly had soon run away from the well-meaning couple. Jilly had been determined to live with no one except Riley. Riley hoped that the Flaxmans didn't harbor any hard feelings about that. But they seemed kind and welcoming.

Brenda then introduced Riley to a tall man with a long, oddly shaped head and a somewhat vacuous smile.

Brenda said, "This is Delbert Kaul, who is serving as our attorney. Come on, let's go somewhere to sit down and talk things over."

The group hurried through the concourse to the nearest coffee shop. The adults ordered coffee and Jilly got a soft drink. As they all sat down, Riley remembered that Bonnie Flaxman's brother was Garrett Holbrook, an FBI agent stationed here in Phoenix.

Riley asked, "How's Garrett these days?"

Bonnie shrugged and smiled. "Oh, you know. Garrett is Garrett."

Riley nodded. She remembered the agent as a rather taciturn man with a cold demeanor. But then, she'd been investigating the murder of Garrett's estranged half-sister. He had been grateful when she solved the murder, and had helped put Jilly into foster care with the Flaxmans. Riley knew that he was a good man beneath his frosty exterior.

Brenda said to Riley, "I'm glad you and Jilly could get here on such short notice. I'd really hoped we'd be finalizing the adoption by now, but as I wrote to you in my letter, we've run into a snag. Jilly's father claims he made the decision to give up Jilly under duress. Not only is he contesting the adoption, he's threatening to charge you with kidnapping—and me as an accomplice."

Looking through some legal papers, Delbert Kaul added, "His case is pretty flimsy, but he is making a nuisance of himself. But don't worry about it. I'm sure we can fix all this tomorrow."

Somehow, Kaul's smile didn't strike Riley as very reassuring. There was something weak and uncertain about him. She found herself wondering just how he'd gotten assigned the case.

Riley noticed that Brenda and Kaul seemed to have an easy rapport. They didn't appear to be a romantic couple, but they did seem to be good friends. Maybe that was why Brenda had hired him.

Not necessarily a good reason, Riley thought.

"Who is the judge?" Riley asked him.

Kaul's smile faded a little as he said, "Owen Heller. Not exactly my first choice, but the best we could get under the circumstances."

Riley suppressed a sigh. She was feeling less and less assured. She hoped Jilly wasn't getting the same feeling.

Kaul then discussed what the group should expect at the hearing. Bonnie and Arnold Flaxman were going to testify about their own experience with Jilly. They would emphasize the girl's need for a stable home environment, which she emphatically could not have with her father.

Kaul said he wished he could get Jilly's older brother to testify, but he had long since disappeared and Kaul hadn't been able to track him down.

Riley was supposed to testify about the kind of life she was able to give Jilly. She had come to Phoenix armed with all sorts of documentation to back up her claims, including financial information.

Kaul tapped his pencil against the table and added, "Now Jilly, you don't *have* to testify—"

Jilly interrupted. "I want to. I'm going to."

Kaul looked a little surprised by the note of determination in Jilly's voice. Riley wished the lawyer seemed as determined as Jilly did.

"Well," Kaul said, "let's consider that settled."

When the meeting ended, Brenda, Kaul, and the Flaxmans left together. Riley and Jilly went to rent a car, and then they drove to a nearby hotel and checked in.

*

Once they got settled into their hotel room, Riley and Jilly ordered a pizza. The TV played a movie they'd both seen before and didn't pay much attention to. To Riley's relief, Jilly didn't seem the least bit anxious now. They chatted pleasantly about little things, like Jilly's upcoming school year, clothes and shoes, and celebrities in the news.

Riley found it hard to believe that Jilly had been in her life for such a short time. Things seemed so natural and easy between them.

Like she's always been my daughter, Riley thought. She realized that was exactly how she felt, but it brought on a renewed burst of anxiety.

Was it all going to end tomorrow?

Riley couldn't bring herself to consider how that would feel.

They were almost finished with their pizza when they were interrupted by a loud signal from Riley's laptop computer.

"Oh, that must be April!" Jilly said. "She promised we'd do a video chat."

Riley smiled and let Jilly take the call from her older daughter. Riley listened idly from across the room as the two girls chattered away like the sisters they'd truly become.

When the girls finished talking, Riley spoke to April while Jilly plopped down on the bed to watch TV. April's face looked serious and concerned.

She asked, "How are things looking for tomorrow, Mom?"

Glancing across the room, Riley saw that Jilly had gotten interested in the movie again. Riley didn't think she was really listening to what she and April were saying, but she still wanted to be careful.

"We'll see," Riley said.

April spoke in a low voice so Jilly couldn't hear.

"You look worried, Mom."

"I guess so," Riley said, speaking quietly herself.

"You can do this, Mom. I know you can."

Riley gulped hard.

"I hope so," she said.

Still speaking softly, April's voice shook with emotion.

"We can't lose her, Mom. She can't go back to that kind of life."

"I know," Riley said. "Don't worry."

Riley and April stared at each other in silence for a few moments. Riley suddenly felt deeply moved by how mature her fifteen-year-old seemed right now.

She's really growing up, Riley thought proudly.

April finally said, "Well, I'll let you go. Call me as soon as you know anything."

"I'll do that," Riley said.

She ended the video call and went back to sit on the bed with Jilly. They were just getting to the end of the movie when the phone rang. Riley felt another wave of worry.

Phone calls hadn't brought good news lately.

She picked up the phone and heard a woman's voice.

"Agent Paige, I'm calling from the Quantico switchboard. We just got a call from a woman in Atlanta and ... well, I'm not sure how to handle this, but she wants to talk directly to you."

"Atlanta?" Riley asked. "Who is it?"

"Her name is Morgan Farrell."

Riley felt a chill of alarm.

She remembered the woman from a case she'd worked on back in February. Morgan's wealthy husband, Andrew, had briefly been a suspect in a murder case. Riley and her partner, Bill Jeffreys, had interviewed Andrew Farrell at home and had determined that he wasn't the killer she was looking for. Nevertheless, Riley had seen the signs that the man was abusing his wife.

She had silently slipped Morgan an FBI card, but had never heard from her.

I guess she finally wants help, Riley thought, picturing the thin, elegant, but timid woman she'd seen in Andrew Farrell's mansion.

But Riley wondered—what was she going to be able to do for anybody under her present circumstances?

In fact, the last thing in the world Riley needed right now was another problem to solve.

The waiting operator asked, "Do you want me to put the call

through?"

Riley hesitated for a second, then said, "Yes, please."

In a moment, she heard the sound of a woman's voice.

"Hello, is this Special Agent Riley Paige?"

Now it occurred to her—she couldn't remember Morgan having said a single word while she'd been there. She'd seemed too terrified of her husband to even speak.

But she didn't sound terrified right now.

In fact, she sounded rather happy.

Is this just a social call? Riley wondered.

"Yes, this is Riley Paige," she said.

"Well, I just thought I owed you a call. You were very kind to me that day when you visited our home, and you left me your card, and you seemed to be anxious about me. I just wanted to let you know, you don't need to worry about me anymore. Everything is going to be fine now."

Riley breathed a little easier.

"I'm glad to hear that," she said. "Did you leave him? Are you getting a divorce?"

"No," Morgan said cheerfully. "I killed the bastard."

CHAPTER TWO

Riley sat down in the nearest chair, her mind reeling as the woman's words echoed in her mind.

"I killed the bastard."

Had Morgan really just said that?

Then Morgan asked, "Agent Paige, are you still there?"

"I'm still here," Riley said. "Tell me what happened."

Morgan still sounded eerily calm.

"The thing is, I'm not sure exactly. I've been rather doped up lately, and I tend not to remember things I do. But I killed him, all right. I'm looking right down at his body lying in bed, and he's got knife wounds all over him, and he bled a lot. It looks like I did it with a sharp kitchen knife. The knife is lying right next to him."

Riley struggled to make sense of what she was hearing.

She remembered how unhealthily thin Morgan had looked. Riley had been sure that she was anorexic. Riley knew better than most people how hard it was to stab a person to death. Was Morgan even physically capable of doing such a thing?

She heard Morgan sigh.

"I hate to impose, but I honestly don't know what to do next. I wonder if you could help me."

"Have you told anybody else? Have you called the police?"

"No."

Riley stammered, "I'll ... I'll get right on it."

"Oh, thank you so much."

Riley was about to tell Morgan to stay on the line while she made a separate call on her own cell phone. But Morgan hung up.

Riley sat there staring into space for a moment. She heard Jilly ask, "Mom, is something wrong?"

Riley looked and saw that Jilly seemed deeply concerned.

She said, "Nothing to concern yourself about, honey."

Then she grabbed her cell phone and called the police in Atlanta.

*

Officer Jared Ruhl felt bored and restless as he rode in the passenger seat next to Sergeant Dylan Petrie. It was night, and they were patrolling one of the richest neighborhoods in Atlanta—an area where there was seldom any criminal activity. Ruhl was new to the force, and he was hungry for a taste of action.

Ruhl had all the respect in the world for his African-American partner and mentor. Sergeant Petrie had been on the force for twenty years or more, and he was one of the most seasoned and experienced cops around.

So why are they wasting us on this beat? Ruhl wondered.

As if in reply to his unspoken question, a female voice sputtered over the scanner …

"Four-Frank-thirteen, do you copy?"

Ruhl's senses sharpened to hear their own vehicle's identification.

Petrie answered, "Copy, go ahead."

The dispatcher hesitated, as if she didn't quite believe what she was about to say.

Then she said, "We have a possible one-eighty-seven in the Farrell home. Go to the scene."

Ruhl's mouth dropped open, and he saw Petrie's eyes widen with surprise. Ruhl knew that 187 was the code for a homicide.

At Andrew Farrell's place? Ruhl wondered.

He couldn't believe his ears, and Petrie looked as though he couldn't either.

"Say again," Petrie said.

"A possible 187 in the Farrell home. Can you get there?"

Ruhl saw Petrie squint with perplexity.

"Yeah," Petrie said. "Who is the suspect?"

The dispatcher hesitated again, then said, "Mrs. Farrell."

Petrie gasped aloud and shook his head.

"Uh … is this a joke?" he said.

"No joke."

"Who's my RP?" Petrie asked.

What does that mean? Ruhl asked himself.

Oh, yeah …

It meant, "Who reported the crime?"

The dispatcher replied, "A BAU agent called it in from Phoenix, Arizona. I know how strange that sounds, but …"

The dispatcher fell silent.

Petrie said, "Code Three response?"

Ruhl knew that Petrie was asking whether to use flashing lights and a siren.

The dispatcher asked, "How close are you to the location?"

"Less than a minute," Petrie said.

"Better keep quiet then. This whole thing is …"

Her voice faded away again. Ruhl guessed she was concerned that they not draw too much attention to themselves. Whatever was really going on in this luxurious and privileged neighborhood, it was surely best to keep the media out of the loop for as long as they could.

Finally the dispatcher said, "Look, just check it out, OK?"

"Copy," Petrie said. "We're on our way."

Petrie pushed the accelerator and they sped along the quiet street.

Ruhl stared in astonishment as they approached the Farrell mansion. This was the closest he'd ever been to it. The house sprawled in all directions, and it looked to him more like a country club than anybody's home. The exterior was carefully lit—for protection, no doubt, but also probably to show off its arches and columns and great windows.

Petrie parked the car in the circular drive and stopped the engine. He and Ruhl got out and strode up to the huge front entrance. Petrie rang the doorbell.

After a few moments, a tall, lean man opened the door. Ruhl guessed from his fancy tuxedo-like outfit and his stern, officious expression that he was the family butler.

He looked surprised to see the two police officers—and not at all pleased.

"May I ask what this is all about?" he asked.

The butler didn't seem to have any idea that there might be trouble inside that mansion.

Petrie glanced at Ruhl, who sensed what his mentor was thinking …

Just a false alarm.

Probably a prank call.

Petrie said to the butler, "Could we speak with Mr. Farrell, please?"

The butler smiled in a supercilious manner.

"I'm afraid that's impossible," he said. "The master is fast asleep, and I have very strict orders—"

Petrie interrupted, "We have reason to be worried about his safety."

The butler's eyebrows rose.

"Really?" he said. "I'll look in on him, if you insist. I'll try not to waken him. I assure you, he would complain quite vociferously."

Petrie didn't ask permission for him and Ruhl to follow the butler into the house. The place was vast inside, with rows of marble columns that eventually led to a red-carpeted staircase with curved, fancy banisters. Ruhl found it harder and harder to believe that anybody could actually live here. It seemed more like a movie set.

Ruhl and Petrie followed the butler on up the stairs and through a wide hallway to a pair of double doors.

"The master suite," the butler said. "Wait right here for a moment."

The butler passed on through the doors.

Then they heard him let out a yelp of horror inside.

Ruhl and Petrie rushed through the doors into a sitting room, and from there into an enormous bedroom.

The butler had already switched on the lights. Ruhl's eyes almost hurt for a moment from the brightness of the enormous room. Then his eyes fell upon a canopied bed. Like everything else in the house, it too was huge, like something out of a movie. But as big as it was, it was dwarfed by the sheer size of the rest of the room.

Everything in the master bedroom was gold and white—except for the blood all over the bed.

CHAPTER THREE

The butler was slumped against the wall, staring with a glazed expression. Ruhl himself felt as though the wind had been knocked out of his lungs.

There the man was, lying on the bed—the rich and famous Andrew Farrell, dead and extremely bloody. Ruhl recognized him from seeing him on TV many times.

Ruhl had never seen a murdered corpse before. He'd never expected the sight to seem so weird and unreal.

What made the scene especially bizarre was the woman sitting in an ornate upholstered chair right next to the bed. Ruhl recognized her, too. She was Morgan Farrell—formerly Morgan Chartier, a now-retired famous model. The dead man had turned their marriage into a media event, and he liked to parade her around in public.

She was wearing a flimsy, expensive-looking gown that was streaked with blood. She sat there unmoving, holding a large carving knife. Its blade was bloody, and so was her hand.

"Shit," murmured Petrie in a stunned voice.

Then Petrie spoke into his microphone.

"Dispatch, this is four-Frank-thirteen calling from the Farrell house. We've got a one-eighty-seven here for real. Send three units, including a homicide unit. Also contact the medical examiner. Better tell Chief Stiles to get over here as well."

Petrie listened to the dispatcher on his earpiece, then seemed to think for a moment.

"No, don't make this a Code Three. We need to keep this as quiet as we can for as long as we can."

During this exchange, Ruhl couldn't take his eyes off the woman. He'd thought she was beautiful when he'd seen her on TV. Weirdly enough, she seemed just as beautiful to him even now. Even holding a bloody knife in her hand, she looked as delicate and fragile as a china figurine.

She was also as still as if she were made of china—as motionless as the corpse, and apparently unaware that anyone had entered the room. Even her eyes didn't move as she kept staring at the knife in her hand.

As Ruhl followed Petrie toward the woman, it occurred to him that the scene no longer reminded him of a movie set.

It's more like an exhibit in a wax museum, he thought.

Petrie gently touched the woman on the shoulder and said, "Mrs. Farrell …"

The woman didn't seem the least bit startled as she looked up at him.

She smiled and said, "Oh, hello, Officer. I wondered when the police were going to get here."

Petrie put on a pair of plastic gloves. Ruhl didn't need to be told to do the same. Then Petrie delicately took the knife out of the woman's hand and handed it to Ruhl, who carefully bagged the weapon.

As they were doing this, Petrie said to the woman, "Please tell me what happened here."

The woman let out a rather musical chuckle.

"Well, that's a silly question. I killed Andrew. Isn't that obvious?"

Petrie turned to look at Ruhl, as if to ask …

Is it obvious?

On one hand, there didn't seem to be any other explanation for this bizarre scene. On the other hand …

She looks so weak and helpless, Ruhl thought.

He couldn't begin to imagine her doing such a thing.

Petrie said to Ruhl, "Go talk to the butler. Find out what he knows."

While Petrie examined the body, Ruhl went over to the butler, who was still crouched against the wall.

Ruhl said to him, "Sir, could you tell me what happened here?"

The butler opened his mouth, but no words came out.

"Sir," Ruhl repeated.

The butler squinted as if in deep confusion. He said, "I don't know. You arrived and …"

He fell silent again.

Ruhl wondered …

Does he really not know anything at all?

Maybe the butler was faking his shock and perplexity.

Maybe he was actually the killer.

The possibility reminded Ruhl of the old cliché …

"The butler did it."

The idea might even be funny under different circumstances.

But certainly not right now.

Ruhl thought fast, trying to decide what questions to ask the man.

He said, "Is there anybody else in the house?"

The butler replied in a dull voice, "Just the live-in help. Six servants in all aside from myself, three men and three women. Certainly you don't think …?"

Ruhl had no idea what to think, at least not yet.

He asked the butler, "Is it possible that anyone else is in the house somewhere? An intruder, maybe?"

The butler shook his head.

"I don't see how," he said. "Our security system is of the very best."

That's not a no, Ruhl thought. Suddenly he felt quite alarmed.

If the killer was an intruder, might he still be in the house somewhere?

Or might he be slipping away at this very moment?

Then Ruhl heard Petrie talking into his microphone, giving someone instructions on how to find the bedroom in the huge mansion.

It seemed like only seconds until the room was swarming with cops. Among them was Chief Elmo Stiles, a bulky and imposing man. Ruhl was also surprised to see the county District Attorney, Seth Musil.

The normally smooth and polished DA looked disheveled and disoriented, as if he had just been roused out of bed. Ruhl guessed that the chief had contacted the DA as soon as he'd heard the news, then picked him up and brought him here.

The DA gasped with horror at what he saw and rushed toward the woman.

"Morgan!" he said.

"Hello, Seth," the woman said, as if pleasantly surprised by his arrival. Ruhl wasn't especially surprised that Morgan Farrell and a high-ranking politician like the DA knew each other. The woman still didn't seem to be aware of much of anything else that was going on around her.

Smiling, the woman said to Musil, "Well, I suppose it's obvious what happened. And I'm sure you're not surprised that—"

Musil hastily interrupted.

"No, Morgan. Don't say anything. Not just yet. Not until we get you a lawyer."

Sergeant Petrie was already organizing the people in the room.

He said to the butler, "Tell them the layout of the house, every nook and cranny."

Then he said to the cops, "I want the whole place searched for any intruders or any sign of a break-in. And check in with the live-in staff, make sure they can account for their actions during the last few hours."

The cops gathered around the butler, who was on his feet now. The butler gave them directions, and the cops left the room. Not knowing what else to do, Ruhl stood next to Sergeant Petrie, looking over the grisly scene. The DA was now standing protectively over the smiling, blood-spattered woman.

Ruhl was still struggling to come to terms with what he was seeing. He reminded himself that this was his first homicide. He wondered …

Will I ever be involved in one weirder than this?

He also hoped that the cops searching the house wouldn't return empty-handed. Maybe they'd come back with the real culprit. Ruhl hated the thought that this delicate, lovely woman was really capable of murder.

Long minutes passed before the cops and the butler returned.

They said they hadn't found any intruders or any sign that anyone had broken into the house. They'd found the live-in staff asleep in their beds and had no reason to think that any of them were responsible.

The medical examiner and his team arrived and began to attend to the body. The huge room was really quite crowded now. At long last, the bloodstained woman of the house seemed to be aware of the bustle of activity.

She got up from her chair and said to the butler, "Maurice, where are your manners? Ask these good people if they'd like anything to eat or drink."

Petrie walked toward her, taking out his handcuffs.

He said to her, "That's very kind of you, ma'am, but it won't be necessary."

Then, in an extremely polite and considerate tone, he began to read Morgan Farrell her rights.

CHAPTER FOUR

Riley couldn't help but worry as the court session unfolded.

So far, everything seemed to be going smoothly. Riley herself had testified about the kind of home she was trying to make for Jilly, and Bonnie and Arnold Flaxman had testified to Jilly's desperate need for a stable family.

Even so, Riley felt uneasy about Jilly's father, Albert Scarlatti.

She'd never actually seen the man before today. Judging from what Jilly had told her about him, she had pictured a grotesque ogre of a man.

But his actual appearance surprised her.

His once-black hair was heavily streaked with gray, and his dark features were, as she'd expected, ravaged from years of alcoholism. Even so, he seemed perfectly sober right now. He was dressed well but not expensively, and he was kindly and charming with everyone he talked to.

Riley also wondered about the woman sitting at Scarlatti's side and holding his hand. She, too, looked as though she'd lived a hard life. Otherwise, her expression was difficult for Riley to read.

Who is she? Riley wondered.

All Riley knew about Scarlatti's wife and Jilly's mother was that she had disappeared many years ago. Scarlatti had often told Jilly that she'd probably died.

This couldn't be her after all these years. Jilly had shown no sign of even knowing this woman. So who was she?

Now it was time for Jilly to speak.

Riley squeezed Jilly's hand reassuringly, and the young teenager took the stand.

Jilly looked small in the big witness chair. Her eyes darted around the courtroom nervously, glancing at the judge, then making eye contact with her father.

The man smiled with what appeared to be sincere affection, but Jilly hastily averted her gaze.

Riley's attorney, Delbert Kaul, asked Jilly how she felt about the adoption.

Riley could see Jilly's whole body shake with emotion.

"I want it more than anything I've ever wanted in my life," Jilly said in an unsteady voice. "I've been so, so happy living with my mom—"

"You mean Ms. Paige," Kaul said, gently interrupting.

"Well, she's my mom now as far as I'm concerned, and that's what I call her. And her daughter, April, is my big sister. Until I started living with them, I had no idea what it would be like—having a real family to love me and care for me."

Jilly seemed to be bravely fighting back her tears.

Riley wasn't sure that she was going to be able to do the same.

Then Kaul asked, "Can you tell the judge a little about what it was like living with your father?"

Jilly looked at her father.

Then she looked at the judge and said, "It was awful."

She went on to tell the court what she had told Riley yesterday—how her father had locked her in a closet for days. Riley shuddered as she listened to the story all over again. Most of the people in the courtroom seemed to be deeply affected by it. Even her father hung his head.

When she was finished, Jilly was truly in tears.

"Until my new mom came into my life, everyone I loved ended up leaving sooner or later. They couldn't stand living with Dad because he was so awful to them. My mother, my older brother—even my little puppy, Darby, ran away."

Riley's throat tightened. She remembered Jilly crying when she spoke of the puppy she'd lost so many months ago. Jilly still worried about what had become of Darby.

"Please," she said to the judge. "Please don't send me back to that. I'm so happy with my new family. Don't take me away from them."

Jilly then came back and sat next to Riley again.

Riley squeezed her hand and whispered to her, "You did really well. I'm proud of you."

Jilly nodded and wiped away her tears.

Then Riley's attorney, Delbert Kaul, presented the judge with all the necessary papers to finalize the adoption. He was especially emphasizing the consent form signed by Jilly's father.

As far as Riley could tell, Kaul was doing a reasonably thorough job with the presentation. But his voice and manner were hardly inspiring, and the judge, a beefy, scowling man with small, beady eyes, didn't seem to be at all impressed.

For a moment, Riley's mind drifted back to the bizarre phone call she'd gotten yesterday from Morgan Farrell. Of course Riley had contacted the police in Atlanta right away. If what the woman had said was true, then surely she was in custody by now. Riley couldn't help wondering what had really happened.

Was it really possible that the fragile woman she'd met in Atlanta had committed murder?

This is no time to think about all that, she reminded herself.

When Kaul finished his presentation, Scarlatti's lawyer stood up.

Jolene Paget was a keen-eyed woman in her thirties whose lips seemed to be shaped in a slight but perpetual smirk.

She said to the lawyer, "My client wishes to contest this adoption."

The judge nodded and growled, "I know he does, Ms. Paget. Your client had better have a good reason for wanting change his own decision."

Riley immediately noticed that, unlike her own lawyer, Paget wasn't referring to any notes. Also unlike Kaul, her voice and demeanor exuded self-confidence.

She said, "Mr. Scarlatti has very good reason, your honor. He gave his consent under duress. He was going through an especially hard time and didn't have a job. And yes, he was drinking back then. And he was depressed."

Paget nodded toward Brenda Fitch, who was also sitting in the courtroom, and added, "He was easy prey to pressure from social services personnel, especially this woman. Brenda Fitch threatened to bring him up on charges for entirely made-up crimes and offenses."

Brenda let out a sharp gasp of outrage. She said to Paget, "That's not true and you know it."

Paget's smirk broadened as she said, "Your honor, would you kindly tell Ms. Fitch not to interrupt?"

"Please keep quiet, Ms. Fitch," the judge said.

Paget added, "My client also wishes to bring charges of kidnapping against Ms. Paige—with Ms. Fitch as an accessory."

Brenda let out an audible groan of disgust, but Riley forced herself to keep quiet. She'd known all along that Paget was going to pursue this issue.

The judge said, "Ms. Paget, you've presented no evidence of kidnapping by anybody. As for the duress and threats you mentioned, you've offered no proof or evidence. You've said nothing to persuade me that your client's initial consent shouldn't still stand."

Albert Scarlatti then got to his feet.

"May I say a few words on my own behalf, your honor?" he begged.

When the judge nodded his approval, Riley felt a new jolt of concern.

Scarlatti hung his head and spoke in a low, quiet voice.

"What Jilly told you just now about what I did to her—I know it sounds awful. And Jilly, I'm awfully sorry. But the truth is, that's not exactly how it happened."

Riley had to stop herself from interrupting him. She was sure that Jilly hadn't lied about this.

Albert Scarlatti chuckled a bit sadly. A warm smile spread across his worn features.

"Jilly, surely you'll admit that you've been a handful to raise. You can be a challenge, little daughter. You've got a temper, and you'd get completely out of control sometimes, and I just didn't know what to do that day. The way I remember it, I was just plain desperate when I put you in that closet."

He shrugged a little and continued, "But it wasn't like you said. I'd never have put you through something like that for days. Not even for a few hours. I'm not saying you're not telling the truth, just that your imagination sometimes runs away with you. And I understand that."

Then Scarlatti turned his attention to the others in the courtroom.

He said, "A lot has happened since I lost my little Jilly. I've cleaned myself up. I've been in rehab and I go to AA regularly, and I haven't had a drink in months. I hope never to have a drink again for the rest of my life. And I've got a steady job—nothing really impressive, just janitorial work, but it's a good job, and I can give you a reference from my employer that I'm doing just fine."

Then he touched the mysterious woman he'd been sitting next to on the shoulder.

"But there's been another big change in my life. I met Barbara Long here, the most wonderful woman in the world, and she's the best thing that ever happened to me. We're engaged to be married later this month."

The woman smiled at him with glistening eyes.

Scarlatti spoke directly to Jilly now.

"That's right, Jilly. No more single-parent family. You're going to have a father and a mother—a real mother after all these years."

Riley felt like a knife had been plunged in her chest.

Jilly just said that I'm *her real mom,* she thought. But what could she say about that single-parent crack? Her divorce from Ryan had been final even before she found Jilly.

Scarlatti then directed his attention to Brenda Fitch.

He said, "Ms. Fitch, my lawyer just said some pretty tough things about you just now. I just want you to know that I don't have any hard feelings. You've been doing your job, and I know that. I just want you to know how much I've changed."

Then he looked Riley straight in the eye.

"Ms. Paige, I've got no hard feelings toward you either. In fact, I'm grateful for everything you did to take care of Jilly while I was trying to get myself together. I know it couldn't have been easy for you, being single and all. And with a teenager of your own to take care of."

Riley opened her mouth to protest, but Albert went on speaking warmly. "I know you care about her, and you needn't worry. I'll be a good father to Jilly from now on. And I'll want you to keep on being a part of Jilly's life."

Riley was stunned. She now realized why his lawyer had threatened to bring charges of kidnapping in the first place.

It's classic good cop, bad cop.

Jolene Paget had presented herself as a cutthroat attorney prepared to go to any lengths to win her case. She'd cleared the way for Scarlatti to come across as the nicest guy in the world.

And he was very convincing. Riley couldn't help but wonder …

Is he really a nice guy after all?

Was he really just going through a bad stretch?

Worst of all—might she be wrong in trying to take Jilly away from him? Was she doing nothing except adding unnecessary trauma to Jilly's life?

Finally Scarlatti looked pleadingly at the judge.

"Your honor, I beg you, please let me have my daughter back. She is my flesh and blood. You won't regret your decision. I promise."

A tear trickled down his cheek as he sat back down.

His lawyer stood up, looking more smug and confident than ever.

She spoke to Jilly with a tone of oily, fake sincerity.

"Jilly, I hope you understand that your father wants only what's best for you. I know you've had troubles with him in the past, but tell me the truth now—isn't that a pattern with you?"

24

Jilly looked puzzled.

Paget continued, "I'm sure you won't deny that you ran away from your father, and that's how Riley Paige found you in the first place."

Jilly said, "I know, but that was because—"

Paget interrupted, pointing to the Flaxmans.

"And didn't you also run away from this nice couple when they took you in?"

Jilly's eyes widened and she nodded silently.

Riley swallowed hard. She knew what Paget was going to say next.

"And didn't you once even run away from Ms. Paige and her family?"

Jilly nodded and hung her head miserably.

And of course it was true. Riley remembered all too well how hard it had been for Jilly to adjust to life in her home—and especially how she'd struggled with feelings of unworthiness. In an especially weak moment, Jilly had run off to another truck stop, thinking that selling her body was all she was good for.

"I'm nobody," Jilly had told Riley when the police brought her back.

The lawyer had done her research well, but Jilly had changed so much since then. Riley was sure that those days of insecurity were over.

Still maintaining a tone of deep concern, Paget said to Jilly …

"Sooner or later, dear, you've got to accept the help of people who care about you. And right now, your father wants more than anything else to give you a good life. I think you owe it to him to give him a chance to do that."

Turning to the judge, Paget added, "Your honor, I leave the matter to you."

For the first time, the judge seemed to be genuinely moved.

He said, "Mr. Scarlatti, your eloquent comments have forced me to reconsider my decision."

Riley gasped aloud.

Is this really happening?

The judge continued, "Arizona statute is very clear on the matter of severance. The first consideration is the fitness of the parents. The second consideration is the best interests of the child. Only if the parent is deemed unfit can the second consideration be brought into question."

He paused to think for a moment.

"Mr. Scarlatti's unfitness has not been established here today. I think rather to the contrary, he seems to be doing everything he can to become an excellent father."

Looking alarmed, Kaul stood up and spoke sharply.

"Your honor, I object. Mr. Scarlatti gave up his rights voluntarily, and this is completely unexpected. The agency had no reason to bring evidence to establish his unfitness."

The judge spoke with a note of finality and rapped his gavel.

"Then I have no reason to consider anything further. Custody is granted to the father, effective immediately."

Riley couldn't help letting out a cry of despair.

This is real, she thought.

I'm losing Jilly.

CHAPTER FIVE

Riley was almost hyperventilating as she tried to grasp what was happening.

Surely I can contest this decision, she thought.

The agency and the lawyer could easily put together some solid evidence of Scarlatti's abusive behavior.

But what would happen in the meantime?

Jilly would never stay with her father. She would run away again—and this time she might really disappear.

Riley might never see her youngest daughter again.

Still sitting at the bench, the judge said to Jilly, "Young lady, I think you should go to your father now."

To Riley's surprise, Jilly looked utterly calm.

She squeezed Riley's hand and whispered …

"Don't worry, Mom. This is going to be all right."

She walked over to where Scarlatti and his fiancée were now standing. Albert Scarlatti's smile seemed warm and welcoming.

Just as her father held out his arms to hug her, Jilly said, "I've got something to say to you."

A curious expression crossed Scarlatti's face.

Jilly said, "You killed my brother."

"Wh-what?" Scarlatti stammered. "No, that's not true, and you know it. Your brother Norbert ran away. I've told you lots of times—"

Jilly interrupted him.

"No, I'm not talking about my big brother. I don't even remember him. I'm talking about my little brother."

"But you never had a—"

"No, I never had a little brother. Because you killed him."

Scarlatti's mouth dropped open and his face reddened.

Her voice shaking with anger, Jilly continued, "I guess you think I don't remember my mother, because I was so little when she left. But I do remember. I remember she was pregnant. I remember you yelling at her. You hit her in the stomach. I saw you do it, again and again. Then she was sick. And then she wasn't pregnant anymore. She told me it was a boy, and he would have been my little brother, but you killed him."

Riley was staggered by what Jilly was saying. She had no

27

doubt that every word of it was true.

I wish she could have told me, she thought.

But of course, Jilly must have found it too painful to talk about—until this very moment.

Jilly was sobbing now. She said, "Mommy cried a lot when she told me. She said she had to go away, or you'd kill her sooner or later. And she did go away. And I never saw her again."

Scarlatti's face was knotting up in an ugly expression. Riley could see that he was struggling with his rage.

He growled, "Girl, you don't know what you're talking about. You're imagining the whole thing."

Jilly said, "She was wearing her pretty blue dress that day. The one she really liked. See, I do remember. I saw the whole thing."

Jilly's words were pouring out in a desperate torrent.

"You kill everything and everybody sooner or later. You can't help it. I'll bet you even lied when you told me my puppy ran away. You probably killed Darby too."

Scarlatti was shaking all over now.

Jilly's words kept flowing out, "My mother did the right thing by running away, and I hope she's happy, wherever she is. And if she's dead—well, she's still better off than she would be with you."

Scarlatti let out a roar of fury. "Shut up, you little bitch!"

He grabbed Jilly by the shoulder with one hand and slapped her across the face with the other.

Jilly cried out and tried to pull away from him.

Riley was on her feet, rushing toward Scarlatti. Before she got there, two security officers had grabbed the man by the arms.

Jilly broke free and ran to Riley.

The judge pounded his gavel and everything got quiet. He looked around the courtroom as if he couldn't believe what had just happened.

For a moment, he just sat there, breathing heavily.

Then he looked at Riley and said, "Ms. Paige, I think I owe you an apology. I made the wrong decision just now, and I rescind it."

He glared at Scarlatti and added, "Another sound from you and I'll put you under arrest."

Looking at the others in the room, the judge said firmly, "There will be no further hearings. This is my final determination on this adoption. Custody is awarded to the adoptive mother."

He rapped his gavel again and got up and left the courtroom without another word.

Riley turned and looked at Scarlatti. His dark eyes were

furious, but the two security officers were still standing beside him. He glanced at his fiancée, who was looking on in horror. Then Scarlatti hung his head and just stood there quietly.

Jilly threw herself into Riley's arms, sobbing.

Riley held her close and said, "You're a brave girl, Jilly. I'm never going to let you go, no matter what happens. You can count on it."

*

Jilly's cheek was still stinging as Riley wrapped up a few details with Brenda and the lawyer. But it seemed like a good kind of hurting and she knew it would soon go away. She'd told the truth about something she'd kept to herself for much too long. As a result, she was free from her father forever.

Riley—her new mom—drove her back to their hotel room, where they packed up quickly and drove to the airport. They arrived in plenty of time for their flight home and checked their bags so they wouldn't have to lug them around. Then they went together to a restroom.

Jilly stood looking in a mirror while her mom was in a nearby stall.

A slight bruise was forming on the side of her face where her father had hit her. But it was going to be OK now.

Her father could never hurt her again. And all because she'd come out and told the truth about her little lost brother at last. That was all it had taken to turn everything around.

She smiled a little as she remembered Mom saying to her …

"You're a brave girl, Jilly."

Yes, Jilly thought. *I guess I am pretty brave.*

CHAPTER SIX

When Riley came out of the restroom, she didn't see Jilly anywhere.

The first thing she felt was a flash of anger.

She remembered telling Jilly clearly …

"Wait right outside the door. Don't go anywhere."

And now she was nowhere in sight.

That girl, Riley thought.

She wasn't worried about missing their flight. They had plenty of time before boarding. But she had hoped to take things slow and easy after such a hard day. She'd planned for them to go on through security, find their gate, and then find a nice place to eat.

Riley sighed with discouragement.

Even after Jilly's courageous actions in the courtroom, Riley couldn't help but be disappointed by this new display of immaturity.

She knew that if she went searching for Jilly in the big terminal, they'd probably go on missing each other time and time again. She looked for a place to sit and wait for Jilly to come back, which she surely would do sooner or later.

But as Riley gazed around the big, open terminal building, she caught a glimpse of Jilly going through one of the glass doors that led outside.

Or at least she *thought* it was Jilly—it was hard to be sure from where Riley was standing.

And who was that woman that the girl seemed to be with?

It looked like Barbara Long, Albert Scarlatti's fiancée.

But the two people disappeared quickly among the travelers milling about outside.

Riley felt a tingle of apprehension. Had her eyes been playing tricks on her?

No, she was now pretty sure of what she'd seen.

But what was going on? Why would Jilly be going anywhere with that woman?

Riley got moving. She knew there was no time to make sense of this. Breaking into a trot, she instinctively reached under her lightweight jacket and patted the gun she wore in her shoulder holster.

30

She was stopped by a uniformed security guard who stepped in front of her.

He spoke in a calm, professional voice. "Are you drawing a weapon, ma'am?"

Riley let out a groan of frustration.

She said, "Sir, I don't have time for this."

She could tell by the guard's expression that she'd only confirmed his suspicion.

He drew his own weapon and moved toward her. Out of the corner of her eye, Riley saw that another guard had spotted the activity and was also approaching.

"Let me by," Riley snapped, showing both of her hands. "I'm an FBI agent."

The guard with the gun didn't reply. Riley guessed that he didn't believe her. And she knew he was trained not to believe her. He was just doing his job.

The second guard looked like he was now about to frisk her.

Riley was losing precious time. Given her superior training, she calculated that she could probably disarm the guard with the gun before he could fire. But the last thing she needed right now was to get into a needless hassle with a pair of well-meaning security guards.

Forcing herself to stand still, she said, "Look, just let me show you my ID."

The two guards glanced at each other warily.

"OK," the guard with the gun said. "But slowly."

Riley carefully pulled out her badge and showed it to them.

Their mouths dropped open.

"I'm in a hurry," Riley said.

The guard standing in front of her nodded and holstered his gun.

Gratefully, she broke into a run across the terminal and dashed through the glass doors to the outside.

Riley looked all around. Neither Jilly nor the woman were anywhere in sight.

But then she spotted her daughter's face in the back window of an SUV. Jilly looked alarmed, and her hands were pressing against the glass.

Even worse, the vehicle was starting to pull away.

Riley broke into a desperate run.

Luckily, the SUV bounced to a halt. A vehicle ahead of it had stopped for pedestrians and the SUV was trapped behind it.

Riley reached the driver's side before the SUV could pull away again.

And there was Albert Scarlatti in the driver's seat.

She pulled out her gun and pointed it through the window, directly at his head.

"It's over, Scarlatti," she yelled at the top of her lungs.

But before she knew it, Scarlatti swung his door open, slamming it into her. The gun fell out of her hand and clattered to the pavement.

Riley was furious now—not just at Scarlatti, but at herself for misjudging the distance between herself and the door. For once she'd let her panic get the best of her.

But she recovered her wits in a split-second.

This man was not going to get away with Jilly.

Before Scarlatti could slam the door shut again, Riley jammed her arm inside to block it. Although the door hit her arm painfully, it couldn't close.

Riley yanked the door wide open and saw that Scarlatti hadn't bothered to fasten his seat belt.

She grabbed him by the arm and dragged him, cursing and struggling, out of the car.

He was a big man, and stronger than she'd expected. He pulled loose from her and raised his fist to punch her in the face. But Riley was faster. She hit him hard in the solar plexus and heard the wind burst out of his lungs as he buckled forward. Then she hit him in the back of the head.

He fell flat on his face on the pavement.

Riley retrieved her gun from where it had fallen and put it back into her holster.

By then, several security guards were scurrying around her. Fortunately, one of them was the man she'd faced inside the terminal.

"It's OK," the man yelled to the other guards. "She's FBI."

The worried guards obediently kept their distance.

Now Riley heard Jilly yell from inside the car …

"Mom! Open the back!"

When Riley stepped over to the vehicle, she saw that the woman, Barbara Long, was sitting in the front passenger seat, looking terrified.

Without a word, Riley touched the unlock switch that controlled all the doors.

Jilly threw the hatch open and climbed out of the car.

Barbara Long opened the door on her side, looking as if she hoped to slip away. But one of the guards stopped her before she could take two steps.

Looking utterly defeated, Scarlatti was trying to crawl back to his feet.

Riley wondered …

What should I do with this guy? Arrest him? And her?

It seemed like a waste of time and energy. Besides, she and Jilly might be stuck here in Phoenix for days pressing charges against him.

While she was trying to make up her mind, she heard Jilly's voice behind her …

"Mom, look!"

Riley turned around and saw Jilly holding a small, big-eared dog in her arms.

"You could just let that old ex-dad go," Jilly said, with a mischievous grin. "After all, he *did* bring my dog back. Wasn't that nice of him?"

"That's …" Riley sputtered in astonishment, trying to remember the name of the puppy Jilly had talked about.

"This is Darby," Jilly said proudly. "Now she can go home with us."

Riley hesitated for a long moment, then felt her face break out into a smile.

She looked around at the guards and said, "Deal with this guy however you like. And his girlfriend too. My daughter and I have got a plane to catch."

Riley led Jilly and the dog away from the perplexed-looking guards.

"Come on," she said to Jilly. "We've got to find ourselves a pet carrier. And explain this to the airline."

CHAPTER SEVEN

As their plane descended into DC, Riley sat with Jilly snuggled against her shoulder, napping. Even the little dog, nervous and whiny at the beginning of the flight, had settled down quickly. Darby was curled up and sleeping quietly in the carrier they'd hastily bought from the airline. Jilly had explained to Riley that Barbara Long had approached her outside the restroom and convinced her to go with her to get Darby, claiming she hated dogs and wanted Jilly to have her. When she got to the car, Barbara shoved her inside and locked the doors, and they took off.

Now that the whole ordeal was over, Riley found herself thinking again about that weird phone call from Morgan Farrell last night …

"I killed the bastard," Morgan had said.

Riley had called the Atlanta police right away, but she hadn't heard any news since from them, and she hadn't had time to check back and find out what had happened.

She wondered—had Morgan been telling the truth, or had Riley sent the cops on a false alarm?

Was Morgan now in custody?

The whole idea of the fragile-looking woman killing anybody at all still struck Riley as very hard to believe.

But Morgan had been most insistent.

Riley remembered her saying …

"I'm looking right down at his body lying in bed, and he's got knife wounds all over him, and he bled a lot."

Riley knew all too well that even the mildest and unlikeliest people could be driven to violent extremes. It usually happened because of some twist in their own makeup, something repressed and hidden that burst forth under extreme circumstances, causing them to commit seemingly inhuman acts.

Morgan had also told her, *"I've been rather doped up lately."*

Maybe Morgan had just fantasized or hallucinated the whole thing.

Riley reminded herself …

Whatever happened, it's none of my concern.

It was time for her to focus on her own family, which now included two daughters—and to Riley's own surprise, a dog.

And wasn't it also time for her to get back to work?

But Riley couldn't help thinking that after today's courtroom and airport dramas, maybe she deserved a good rest break. Shouldn't she take another day of leave before returning to Quantico?

Riley sighed as she realized …

Probably not.

Her work was important to her. She thought it might be important to the world at large. But then, thinking that way worried her. What kind of parent worked day in and day out pursuing the most vicious monsters alive, sometimes finding more than a little of a monster in herself in the process?

She knew that she sometimes couldn't help bringing her grim work home with her, at times even in the direst possible way. Her cases had sometimes put the lives of people she loved in danger.

But it's what I do, she thought.

And deep down, she knew that it was good work that had to be done. Somehow, she owed it even to her daughters to keep doing it—not only to protect them from monsters, but to show them how monsters could be defeated.

She needed to keep on being an example to them.

It's best this way, she thought.

As the plane came to a stop at the concourse, Riley gave Jilly a little shake.

"Wake up, sleepyhead," she said. "We're here."

Jilly grumbled and groaned a little, and then her face broke into a grin as she saw the dog in its case. Darby had just woken up herself and was looking at Jilly and wagging her tail happily.

Then Jilly looked at Riley with joy in her eyes.

"We really did it, didn't we, Mom?" she said. "We won."

Riley hugged Jilly tightly and said, "We sure did, dear. You're really and truly my daughter now, and I'm your mom. And nothing's ever going to change that."

*

When Riley, Jilly, and the dog arrived at their townhouse, April was waiting for them right at the door. Just inside were Blaine, Riley's divorced boyfriend, and his fifteen-year-old daughter, Crystal, who was also April's best friend. The family's Guatemalan housekeeper, Gabriela, stood watching nearby.

Riley and Jilly had reported their good news from Phoenix and they had called again when they had landed and were on the way home, but she hadn't mentioned the puppy. The whole crowd was there to welcome Jilly, but after a moment April leaned over to look at the carrier that Riley had put on the floor.

"What's that?" she asked.

Jilly just giggled.

"It's something alive," Crystal said.

Jilly opened the top of the carrier and there was Darby, looking wide-eyed and a little worried at all the faces surrounding her.

"Omigod, omigod, omigod!" Crystal yelled.

"We've got a dog!" April squealed. "We've got a dog!"

Riley laughed as she remembered how calm and collected April had seemed when they'd talked just the night before. Now all that adult maturity had suddenly vanished, and April was acting like a little girl again. It was wonderful to see.

Jilly lifted Darby out of the carrier. It didn't take the little dog very long to begin enjoying all the attention.

As the girls continued fussing noisily over the dog, Blaine asked Riley, "How did things go? Is everything really all settled?"

"Yes," Riley told him, smiling. "It's really over. Jilly is legally mine."

Everybody else was too excited about the dog to talk about the adoption at the moment.

"What's her name?" April said, holding up the dog.

"Darby," Jilly told April.

"Where did you get her?" Crystal asked.

Riley chuckled and said, "Well, that's quite a story. Give us a few minutes to settle in before we tell it."

"What breed is she?" April asked.

"Part Chihuahua, I think," Jilly said.

Gabriela took the dog out of April's hands and examined it carefully.

"Yes, some Chihuahua, and she's got some other kinds of dog in her," the stout woman said. "What is the word in English for a mix of dogs?"

"A mutt," Blaine said.

Gabriela nodded sagely and said, "Yes, you've got a real mutt here—*auténtico,* the real thing. A mutt is the best kind of dog. This one still has a little growing to do, but she will stay pretty small. *¡Bienvenidos!* Darby. *¡Nuestra casa es tuya también!* This is your home too!"

She handed the puppy to Jilly and said, "She'll need some

water now, and food after everything calms down. I have some leftover chicken we can give her later, but we'll have to buy some real dog food soon."

Following Gabriela's instructions on how to set up a place for Darby, the girls hurried upstairs to Jilly's room to make a bed and put down old newspapers in case she had to go to the bathroom during the night.

Meanwhile, Gabriela put food on the table—a delicious Guatemalan dish called *pollo encebollado,* chicken in onion sauce. Soon everybody sat down to eat.

Himself a chef and restaurant owner, Blaine praised the meal and asked Gabriela all kinds of questions about it. Then the conversation turned to all that had happened in Phoenix. Jilly insisted on telling the whole story herself. Blaine, Crystal, April, and Gabriela all sat with their mouths agape as they heard about the wild scene in the courtroom, and then the still wilder adventure at the airport.

And of course, everybody was delighted to hear about the new dog that had come into their lives.

We're a family now, Riley thought. *And it's great to be home.*

It was also going to be great to get back to work tomorrow.

After dessert, Blaine and Crystal went home, and April and Jilly went to the kitchen to feed Darby. Riley poured herself a drink and sat down in the living room.

She felt herself relaxing more and more. It really had been a crazy day, but now it was over.

Her phone rang, and she saw that the call was from Atlanta.

Riley felt a jolt. Could this be Morgan again? Who else would be calling from Atlanta?

She picked up the phone and heard a man's voice. "Agent Paige? My name is Jared Ruhl, and I'm a police officer here in Atlanta. I got your number from the Quantico switchboard."

"What can I do for you, Officer Ruhl?" Riley said.

In a tentative voice, Ruhl said, "Well, I'm not just sure, but … I guess you know that we arrested a woman for the murder of Andrew Farrell last night. It was his wife, Morgan. In fact, weren't you the person who called in about it?"

Riley was feeling edgy now.

"I was," she said.

"I also heard that Morgan Farrell called you right after the killing, before she called anybody else."

"That's right."

A silence fell. Riley sensed that Ruhl was struggling with what he wanted to say.

Finally he said, "Agent Paige, what do you know about Morgan Farrell?"

Riley squinted with concern. She said, "Officer Ruhl, I'm not sure it's proper for me to comment. I really don't know anything about what happened, and it's not an FBI case."

"I understand that. I'm sorry, I guess I shouldn't have called …"

His voice trailed off.

Then he added, "But Agent Paige, I don't think Morgan Farrell did it. Murdered her husband, I mean. I'm kind of new to this job, and I know I've got a lot to learn … but I just don't think she's the type who could do that."

Riley was startled at those words.

She certainly didn't *remember* Morgan Farrell as being the "type" who might commit murder. But she had to be careful what she said to Ruhl. She wasn't at all sure she ought to be having this conversation at all.

She asked Ruhl, "Has she confessed?"

"They tell me she has. And everybody believes her confession. My partner, the police chief, the DA—absolutely everybody. Except me. And I can't help but wonder, do you …?"

He didn't finish his question, but Riley knew what it was.

He wanted to know whether Riley believed Morgan to be capable of murder.

Slowly and cautiously, she said, "Officer Ruhl, I appreciate your concern. But it's really not appropriate for me to speculate on any of this. I assume that it's a local case, and unless the FBI is called in to help in the investigation, well … frankly, it's none of my business."

"Of course, my apologies," said Ruhl politely. "I should have known better. Anyway, thanks for taking my call. I won't bother you again."

He ended the call, and Riley sat staring at the telephone, sipping from her drink.

The girls clattered past her, closely followed by the little dog. They were all on the way to the family room to play, and Darby was looking quite happy now.

Riley watched them go by, with a deep feeling of satisfaction. But then memories of Morgan Farrell began to intrude on her mind.

She and her partner, Bill Jeffreys, had gone to the Farrells' mansion to interview Morgan's husband regarding the death of his own son.

She remembered how Morgan had seemed almost too weak to stand, clinging to the banister of the huge staircase for support while her husband presided over her as if she were some sort of trophy.

She remembered the look of vacant terror in the woman's eyes.

She also remembered what Andrew Farrell had said about her as soon as she was out of earshot ...

"A rather famous model when I married her—perhaps you've seen her on magazine covers."

And regarding how much younger Morgan had been than himself, he'd added ...

"A stepmother should never be older than her husband's oldest children. I've made sure of that with all my wives."

Riley now felt the same chill she'd felt back then.

Morgan had obviously been nothing more than a costly trinket for Andrew Farrell to show off in public—not a human being at all.

Finally Riley remembered what had happened to Andrew Farrell's wife before Morgan.

She had committed suicide.

When Riley had given Morgan her FBI card, she'd been worried that the woman might meet the same fate—or die under other sinister circumstances. The last thing she had imagined was that Morgan would kill her husband—or anybody else for that matter.

Riley began to feel a familiar tingle—the kind of tingle she got whenever her instincts told her that things were not what they seemed.

Normally, that tingle was a signal for her to probe the matter more deeply.

But now?

No, it's really none of my business, she told herself.

Or was it?

While she was puzzling things over, her phone rang again. This time she saw that the call was from Bill. She'd texted him that everything was all right and she'd be home tonight.

"Hi, Riley," he said when she answered. "Just checking in. So everything went all right in Phoenix?"

"Thanks for calling, Bill," she replied. "Yes, the adoption is final now."

"Everything was thoroughly uneventful, I hope," Bill asked.

Riley couldn't help but laugh.

"Not exactly," she said. "In fact, far from it. There was, uh, some violence involved. And a dog."

She heard Bill chuckle as well.

"Violence and a dog? I'm intrigued! Tell me more!"

"I will when we see each other," Riley said. "It'll be a better story if I can tell you face to face."

"I'm looking forward to it. I guess I'll see you tomorrow in Quantico, then."

Riley fell silent for a moment as she felt on the brink of a strange decision.

She said to Bill, "I don't think so. I think maybe I'll take a couple more days off."

"Well, you certainly deserve it. Congratulations again."

They ended the call, and Riley headed upstairs to her room. She turned on her computer.

Then she booked a flight to Atlanta for tomorrow morning.

CHAPTER EIGHT

By early afternoon the next day, Riley was sitting in the office of Atlanta's police chief, Elmo Stiles. The large, gruff man didn't seem at all happy with what Riley had been telling him.

He finally growled, "Let me get this straight, Agent Paige. You've come here all the way from Quantico to privately interview Morgan Farrell, who we're holding in custody for the murder of her husband. But we didn't ask for the FBI's help. In fact, the case is now open and shut. We've got a confession and everything. Morgan is guilty, and that's pretty much that. So what's your business here?"

Riley tried to project an air of confidence.

"I told you before," she said. "I need to talk to her about a completely separate matter—a different case altogether."

Stiles squinted skeptically and said, "A different case that you can't tell me anything about."

"That's right," Riley said.

It was a lie, of course. For the thousandth time since she'd flown out of DC this morning, she wondered just what the hell she thought she was doing. She was used to bending the rules, but she was seriously crossing a line by pretending to be here on official FBI business.

Just why had she ever thought this might be a good idea?

"What if I say no?" Stiles said.

Riley knew perfectly well that this was the chief's prerogative, and if he did say no, she'd have to comply. But she didn't want to say so. She had to gear herself up for some serious bluffing.

She said, "Chief Stiles, believe me, I wouldn't be here if it weren't a matter of utmost importance and urgency. I'm just not at liberty to say what it is."

Chief Stiles drummed his fingers on his desk for a few moments.

Then he said, "Your reputation precedes you, Agent Paige."

Riley cringed a little inside.

That could be a good thing or a bad thing, she thought.

She was well-known and respected throughout the law enforcement profession for her keen instincts, her ability to get into a killer's mind, and her knack for solving seemingly unsolvable cases.

She was also known for sometimes being a nuisance and a loose cannon, and local authorities who had to work with her often took a dislike to her.

She didn't know which of those reputations Chief Stiles might be referring to.

She wished she could read his expression better, but he had one of those faces that probably never looked pleased about much of anything.

What Riley really dreaded at this moment was the possibility that Stiles might do the most logical thing—pick up the phone and call Quantico to confirm that she was here on FBI business. If he did, nobody there would cover for her. In fact, she'd wind up in a good bit of trouble.

Well, it wouldn't be the first time, she thought.

Finally Chief Stiles stopped drumming his fingers and got up from his desk.

He grumbled, "Well, far be it from me to stand in the way of FBI business. Come on, I'll take you to Morgan Farrell's jail cell."

Suppressing a sigh of relief, Riley got up and followed Stiles out of his office. As he led her through the bustling police station, Riley wondered whether any of the cops around her might happen to be Jared Ruhl, the officer who had called her last night. She wouldn't recognize him if she saw him. But might he know who she was?

Riley hoped not, for his sake as much as for her own. She remembered telling him over the phone about Morgan Farrell's death …

"Frankly, it's none of my business."

It had been exactly the right thing for her to say, and it would be best for Ruhl if he thought Riley was sticking by her decision. It could be a big problem for him if Chief Stiles found out that he'd been making queries outside the department.

As Stiles led her into the women's part of the jail, Riley was nearly deafened by the noise. Prisoners were pounding on bars and loudly arguing with one another, and now they started yelling at Riley as she walked past their cells.

Finally Stiles ordered a guard to open the cell occupied by Morgan Farrell, and Riley walked inside. The woman was sitting on the bed staring at the floor, seemingly unaware that anyone had arrived.

Riley was shocked by her appearance. Morgan was, as Riley

remembered, extremely thin and fragile-looking. She looked even more so now, clad in an orange jumpsuit that looked way too big for her.

She also appeared to be deeply exhausted. The last time Riley had seen her, she'd been fully made up and looking like the model she had been before marrying Andrew Farrell. Without makeup, she looked shockingly waiflike. Riley thought that somebody who didn't know anything about her might take her for a homeless woman.

In a rather polite tone, Chief Stiles said to Morgan, "Ma'am, there's a visitor here to see you. Special Agent Riley Paige of the FBI."

Morgan looked up at Riley and stared at her, as if she wasn't sure whether she might be dreaming.

Chief Stiles then turned to Riley and said, "Check in with me when you're through."

Stiles left the cell and told the guard to shut the door behind him. Riley glanced around to see what kind of surveillance the cell might have. She wasn't surprised to see a camera. She hoped that there weren't any audio devices as well. The last thing she wanted right now was for Stiles or anyone else to eavesdrop on her conversation with Morgan Farrell. But now that she was here, she had to take that chance.

As Riley sat down on the bed next to her, Morgan continued to squint at her in near disbelief.

In a tired voice, she said, "Agent Paige. I hadn't expected you. It's kind of you to come see me, but really, it wasn't at all necessary."

Riley said, "I just wanted to …"

Her voice trailed off as she found herself wondering …

What do *I want exactly?*

Did she really have any clear idea of just what she was doing here?

Finally Riley said, "Could you tell me what happened?"

Morgan sighed deeply.

"There's not much to tell, is there? I killed my husband. I'm not sorry I did, believe me. But now that it's done … well, I'd really like to go home now."

Riley was shocked by her words. Didn't the woman understand what a terrible situation she was in?

Didn't she know that Georgia was a death penalty state?

Morgan seemed to be having trouble holding her head up. She

shuddered at the sound of a woman's shrill shouting in a nearby cell.

She said, "I thought I'd be able to get some sleep here in jail. But listen to all that racket! It goes on all the time, twenty-four hours a day."

Riley studied the woman's weary face.

She asked, "You've not gotten much sleep, have you? Maybe not for a long time?"

Morgan shook her head.

"It's been two or three weeks now—even before I got here. Andrew got into one of his sadistic moods and decided not to leave me alone or let me sleep, night or day. It's easy for him to do …"

She paused, apparently noticing her mistake, then said, "It *was* easy for him to do. He had some kind of trick metabolism that some high-powered men have. He could get by on three or four hours of sleep every day. And lately he'd been home a lot of the time. So he hounded me everywhere in the house, never giving me any privacy, coming into my bedroom at all hours, making me do … all kinds of things …"

Riley felt a little ill at the thought of what those unspoken "things" might be. She was sure that Andrew had sexually tormented Morgan.

Morgan shrugged her shoulders.

"I finally snapped, I guess," she said. "And I killed him. From what I hear, I stabbed him a good twelve or thirteen times."

"From what you hear?" asked Riley. "Don't you remember?"

Morgan let out a quiet groan of despair.

"Do we have to get into what I remember and don't remember? I'd been drinking and taking pills before it happened and it's all a fog. The police asked me questions until I didn't know which end was up. If you want to know the details, I'm sure they'll let you read my confession."

Riley felt an odd tingle at those words. She wasn't yet sure just why.

"I really wish you'd tell me," Riley said.

Morgan wrinkled her brow in thought for a moment.

Then she said, "I guess I made up my mind … that I had to do *something.* I waited until he went to his room that night. Even then, I wasn't sure whether he was asleep. I knocked on his door lightly, and he didn't answer. I opened the door and looked inside, and there he was in his bed, fast asleep."

She seemed to be thinking harder.

"I guess I must have looked around for something to do it with—kill him, I mean. I guess I didn't see anything. So I guess I went down the kitchen and I got that knife. Then I came back up and—well, I guess I went a little crazy stabbing him, because I wound up with blood everywhere, including all over me."

Riley took note of how often she was saying those words …

"I guess."

Then Morgan let out a sigh of annoyance.

"What a mess that was! I do hope the live-in help has cleaned it all up by now. I tried to do it myself, but of course I'm no good at that kind of thing under the best of circumstances."

Then Morgan took a long, slow breath.

"And then I called you. And you called the police. Thanks for taking care of that for me."

Then she smiled curiously at Riley and added, "And thanks again for coming by to see you. It was very sweet of you. I still don't understand what this is all about, though."

Riley was feeling more and more troubled by Morgan's description of her own actions.

Something's not right here, she thought.

Riley paused to think for a moment and then asked …

"Morgan, what kind of knife was it?"

Morgan wrinkled her brow.

"Just a knife, I guess," she said. "I don't know much about kitchen utensils. I think the police said it was a carving knife. It was long and sharp."

Riley was feeling more and more uneasy about all the things that Morgan didn't know or wasn't sure of.

As for herself, Riley didn't do much of her family's cooking anymore, but she certainly knew everything that was in her kitchen and exactly where everything was. Everything was kept in its special place, especially since Gabriela had been in charge. Her own carving knife was kept in a wooden stand with other sharp knives.

Riley asked, "Where exactly did you find the knife?"

Morgan let out an uneasy laugh.

"Didn't I just tell you? In the kitchen."

"No, I mean *where* in the kitchen?"

Morgan's eyes clouded over.

"Why are you asking me that?" she said in a soft, pleading voice.

"Can't you tell me?" Riley asked with gentle insistence.

Morgan was starting to look distressed now.

"Why are you asking me these questions? Like I told you, it's all in my confession. You can read it if you haven't already. Really, Agent Paige, this isn't kind of you. And I'd really like to know what you're doing here. Somehow I don't think it's just out of kindness."

Morgan's voice shook with quiet anger. "I've already had to answer all kinds of questions—more than I can count. I don't deserve any more of this, and I can't say I like it."

She drew herself upright and added, "I did what had to be done. Mimi, his wife before me, committed suicide, you know. It was all over the media. So did his son. All the rest of his wives—I'm not even sure how many they were—just waited around suffering until they got a few wrinkles and he decided they weren't any good for showing off anymore, and then he got rid of them. What kind of a woman puts up with that? What kind of woman thinks she deserves it?"

Then with a low snarl she added …

"I'm not that kind of woman. And I think Andrew knows that now."

Then her face clouded with confusion again.

"I don't like this," she whispered. "I think you'd better leave."

"Morgan—"

"I said I want you to leave right now."

"Who is your lawyer? Have you been examined by a psychiatrist?"

Morgan almost shouted, "I mean it. Go."

Riley wished she could ask a lot more questions. But she could see there was no use in trying. She called for a guard, who let her out of the cell. Then she made her way back to Chief Stiles's office and looked inside the open door.

Stiles looked up at her from his paperwork with a suspicious expression.

"Did you find out what you needed to know?" he asked Riley.

For a moment, Riley didn't know what to say.

She wanted to keep open the possibility of talking to Morgan again.

She was tempted to say …

"No, and I'll need to come back and talk to her some more."

But that might trigger Stiles skepticism to a breaking point, and he might end up calling Quantico after all.

Instead she said …

"Thanks for your cooperation, sir. I'll show myself out."

As she headed out of the station, she recalled the strange conversation she'd just had with Morgan about the knife, and how defensive the woman had gotten about it …

"Why are you asking me these questions?"

Riley was sure of one thing. Morgan had no idea where the knife had been kept in the kitchen. And if she'd had to go to the trouble of finding it, she'd have been able to tell Riley where she'd found it.

She also remembered what Morgan had told her on the phone …

"The knife is lying right next to him."

At that moment, Morgan surely hadn't known where it had come from.

She's not guilty, Riley realized as she climbed into her rented car.

She knew it in her gut, even if Morgan herself didn't believe it.

And no one else was going to question her guilt. They were all happy to have the matter settled.

It was up to Riley to set things right.

CHAPTER NINE

As she took a sip of coffee, Riley wondered …

What do I do now?

Her head buzzing with questions, she'd driven to a fast food restaurant and ordered a hamburger and coffee. She had found a place to sit away from the other customers so she could think about her next move.

Riley was used to bending rules and working in strange circumstances. But this situation was new even to her. She was in uncharted territory.

She wished she could call Bill, her longtime partner. Or that she could talk things over with Jenn Roston, the young agent who'd also partnered with her on recent cases. But that would mean getting them involved in a situation that even she wasn't supposed to be working on.

Was there anyone she could talk to locally?

I can't very well ask Chief Stiles anything, Riley thought.

Of course there were a few people in other places that she sometimes turned to in unconventional situations. One was Mike Nevins, a forensic psychologist in DC who worked as an independent consultant on some FBI cases. Riley had asked Mike for help on many cases, including a few that she hadn't exactly handled by the book. He'd also helped both her and Bill through bouts with PTSD. Mike had always been discreet, and he was also a good friend.

She flipped open her laptop, put in her earpieces, opened her video chat program, and called Mike's office. Right away he appeared on her screen—a dapper, rather fussy-looking man wearing an expensive shirt with a vest.

"Riley Paige!" Mike said in his smooth and soothing baritone. "How nice to see you. It's been a while. How can I help you?"

Riley was happy to see his face. Even so, she suddenly wondered …

How can *he help me?*

What should she tell him?

"Mike, what can you tell me about false confessions?" she asked.

Mike tilted his head curiously.

"Um—could you perhaps be more specific?" he asked.

"I don't mean the ones who just show up after a murder and confess for the publicity. I mean the ones who really believe they're guilty."

"Are you on an interesting new case?"

Riley hesitated, and Mike chuckled.

"Oh, dear," he said. "You've gone rogue again, haven't you?"

Riley laughed nervously.

"I'm afraid so, Mike," she replied.

"Are you actually breaking the law this time?"

Riley thought for a second. She was a little surprised to realize that she hadn't broken any actual laws—at least not yet.

She said, "No, not really."

Mike smiled a comforting smile.

"Well, in that case, I don't see why you shouldn't tell me all about it. If you're bending FBI rules again, that's neither here nor there as far as I'm concerned. I'm not your boss, you know. I can't very well fire you. And I don't have any particular desire to tell on you."

Greatly relieved, Riley filled him in on the whole story, starting with when she had first encountered Morgan Farrell back in February. She described how strongly she'd felt back then that the woman was being abused by her husband. Finally she told Mike about her trip to Atlanta and the conversation she had just had with Morgan.

After listening attentively, Mike asked, "And you're sure Morgan is really innocent?"

"I feel it deep down in my gut," Riley said.

Mike chuckled again.

"Well, you've got one of the most reliable guts in the business. I'm inclined to believe you. But still … I can't say I've ever heard of a situation exactly like this. It's rather atypical. A false confession usually unfolds rather differently."

"How?" Riley asked.

Mike thought for a moment.

Then he said, "For one thing, Morgan Farrell seems to have been eager to confess right when she called you, before the police had even arrived. Suspects usually make false confessions after being put under considerable coercion and great duress."

Riley understood what Mike was getting at.

Morgan had confessed with no coercion at all.

Mike continued, "For example, the average police interrogation lasts for thirty to sixty minutes. To provoke a false confession, cops usually have to hammer away relentlessly at a suspect for a long time—as long as fourteen hours. They have to wear down the suspect's will. The suspect confesses just to get it over with, figuring they can straighten things out later. The circumstances don't exactly fit your case ... however ..."

Mike paused for a moment, then said, "You mentioned that Morgan complained about not being allowed to sleep."

"That's right," she said. "Her husband had been tormenting her by keeping her awake. She said it had been going on two or three weeks."

Mike stroked his chin and said, "You probably already know that sleep disruption is a common torture technique—or as folks like to call it nowadays, 'enhanced interrogation.' That can lead to terrible confusion, even hallucinations. The subject winds up having no idea what's real or what's imaginary. They'll say whatever they're expected to say and might come to believe it themselves. They might even harbor some delusion that they'll get to go free if they just confess."

Riley flashed back to something that Morgan had said ...

"I'd really like to go home now."

As weird as it had seemed to Riley at the time, that comment made sense now.

Riley said, "What you're saying is that Morgan was subjected to procedures often used to get to a confession, even though it wasn't for that purpose."

Mike nodded and said, "That's right. The drugs and alcohol she'd been consuming surely added to her confusion. You said she told you to read her confession if you wanted to know what happened. To make that confession, she probably got a lot of coaching from cops who didn't realize they were coaching her at all. They were just talking her through a plausible series of events. By the time she signed it, *everybody* believed it was true, including her."

Riley also remembered Morgan saying ...

"The police asked me questions until I didn't know which end was up."

Her mind was reeling now.

"Mike, what am I going to do about this?" she asked. "Even Morgan thinks she's guilty. So does everybody else. Besides, I'm not even supposed to be here doing all this."

Mike shrugged.

"If I were you, I'd start by talking to her lawyer. If he's good at his job, he won't care that you're not exactly playing by the rules. All he'll care about is doing his best for his client."

Riley thanked Mike for his help and ended the chat.

She remembered Morgan refusing to say who her lawyer was. Well, it wouldn't be hard to find out.

She got online and looked over the media coverage concerning Andrew Farrell's murder. The killing had caused a predictable public sensation, and there was a lot of tabloid speculation about *why* Morgan had gone crazy and killed her husband. So far, Morgan's lawyer hadn't stepped forward to say anything about his client.

But his name was there in the news: Chet Morris, a partner in the Atlanta law firm of Gurney, Dunn, and Morris. Riley took out her cell phone called the firm's number. When a receptionist answered, Riley asked to speak with Chet Morris.

"May I ask what this is about?" the receptionist asked.

For a second, Riley wasn't sure what to say. After all, she wasn't here on official FBI business.

But then she reminded herself of what Mike had said about Morgan's lawyer …

"If he's good at his job, he won't care that you're not exactly playing by the rules."

She said, "I'm Agent Riley Paige with the FBI. I've got some urgent information for him about his client, Morgan Farrell."

The receptionist put Riley on hold, and a few moments later she heard a man's voice.

"This is Chet Morris. How may I help you?"

Riley introduced herself again.

Morris said in a bland voice, "Oh, yes. The name is familiar. Didn't my client call you right after she killed her husband? I believe you were the person who first contacted the police."

Riley said, "I've got very good reason to believe that your client is innocent of murder."

A silence fell. For a moment Riley wondered if the call had gotten disconnected.

Finally Morris said, "I really don't understand what this is all about, Agent Paige. I'm sure you're aware that my client confessed. Due to her cooperation alone, I'm confident that I can keep her from getting the death penalty."

Riley was puzzled.

Doesn't he understand what I'm saying?

She decided to be more forthright.

She said, "I met Morgan last February at her home when her husband was still alive. I suspected at the time that he was abusing her, and I offered my help if she wanted it. As you know, she called me right after her husband was killed. Then last night I got a call from an Atlanta cop. I'd rather not mention his name, but he was part of the team that showed up at the crime scene. He told me that he didn't believe Morgan had killed her husband."

"And you believed him?" Morris asked.

"I didn't know what to believe. I came to Atlanta—I'm here right now. I have just visited Morgan in her cell and talked with her."

Morris let out a grunt of dismay.

He said, "Agent Paige, I'd really rather you hadn't done that without checking in with me first. Frankly, I wouldn't have allowed it if I'd known."

Riley felt another flash of confusion.

She said, "Mr. Morris, I'm not sure you understand. I'm all but certain that she's innocent."

"Is that what she told you?" Morris asked.

"No, but—"

"Then why do you think so?"

Riley was truly perplexed now. This call wasn't going at all like she'd expected.

She said, "I just talked to an expert forensic psychologist. He explained all the reasons why she might have given a false confession. Look, if I could just come by your office, we could discuss—"

Morris interrupted, "I think not, Agent Paige. And I really don't appreciate your harassing my client and further confusing her. She's already traumatized enough by what she's done. I'll thank you not to meddle in this matter any further. If you do, I'll have no other recourse but to report you and perhaps even press charges."

Before Riley could say another word, Morris ended the call.

Riley sat staring at the phone, flabbergasted.

She remembered something else Mike had said about Morgan's lawyer …

"All he'll care about is doing his best for his client."

But that didn't seem to be true at all.

Chet Morris seemed to be completely indifferent to the possibility that his client was innocent.

What's going on here? she wondered.

All she knew for sure was that she needed someone else's help. She reminded herself that she couldn't involve any of her usual allies at Quantico. But it occurred to her that she knew someone she could turn to in situations like this.

Last January, when she was on a case in Seattle, she'd met a very intelligent FBI technical analyst. Since then, he'd been willing to help her again, and under somewhat unorthodox circumstances.

She looked up the number and dialed, and soon heard Van Roff's gruff, husky voice.

"Agent Riley Paige, as I live and breathe. What kind of trouble are you going to make for me today?"

Riley smiled as she imagined the overweight, socially inept technician noticing her name on his caller ID.

"I need your help, Van," she said.

"Nothing to do with the fiend I will not name?"

Riley was startled. The only research Roff had ever refused to do for her had involved a criminal mastermind named Shane Hatcher.

"No, he's still in prison."

"Is it something legitimate?"

"Not exactly, I'm afraid."

Van Roff let out a snort of approval.

"Then count me in," he said. "Things have been pretty boring out here lately."

Riley filled him in on the whole story so far. When she finished telling him about her conversation with the lawyer he said, "Wait a minute. Are you sure you didn't call the prosecuting attorney by mistake?"

"I'm sure," Riley said.

"What's wrong with that guy?"

"I was hoping you could help me figure that out. There must be some reason why Chet Morris is acting this way."

Van Roff fell silent for a moment. Then Riley heard his fingers rattling over his keyboard.

Finally he said, "Huh. This is kind of interesting."

"What have you got?" Riley asked.

"Chet Morris's law firm—Gurney, Dunn, and Morris—represented Andrew Farrell when he was alive. All three of the lawyers used to work on cases for him. What do you make of that?"

Riley felt a sharp prickle of interest.

She said, "So Morgan Farrell's defending attorney used to represent the murdered man himself. That's kind of weird."

Riley heard Roff's fingers rattle some more.

Then he said, "Here's something else. The Atlanta DA, Seth Musil, is prosecuting the case. He also used to work with Gurney, Dunn, and Morris. While he was there he also worked on cases for Andrew Farrell. So the prosecuting attorney had a cozy professional relationship with the defending lawyer. How suspicious is that? Do you think maybe we're looking at some kind of conspiracy?"

Riley thought for a moment.

"No, I doubt that," she said. "It's not completely surprising that Morgan would use the same law firm as her husband. It's not at all smart of her, though. There might be plenty of reasons why Gurney, Dunn, and Morris want to wrap up this case without a lot of fuss. They have reason to be perfectly happy with Morgan's confession."

Her mind boggled at the whole idea. Morgan Farrell's fate lay in the hands of a bunch of her husband's cronies. And a misogynist like Farrell might very well have vented to them about the frustrations of his current marriage. They weren't likely to be the most sympathetic people in Morgan's life.

Roff said, "It sounds like we're dealing with some serious professional incompetence, if not malpractice."

"It sure does," Riley said. "The thing is, what am I going to do about it? I'm not exactly in a position to set things right."

Roff let out a low rumbling chuckle.

"Heh. I wouldn't say that. Just fix things the old-fashioned way. Catch the real killer. So what if you don't have permission? That's never stopped you in the past."

Riley was pleased. She'd definitely called just the right guy for help.

She thought for a moment, then said, "Van, I've got an idea—"

Roff interrupted, "Yeah, and I think I've got the same idea. Give me just a minute."

She heard his fingers rattling again.

Riley smiled.

It felt good to be working with someone so completely on her own wavelength.

Just a few minutes later, she heard Van Roff's triumphant chuckle.

CHAPTER TEN

"Bingo!" Roff said.

Riley was thrilled by his triumphant tone. As his typing continued, she waited impatiently to find out more.

She knew exactly what Roff was up to. He'd been looking for other recent crimes of a similar nature. Possibly—just possibly—Andrew Farrell's murder was part of an ongoing pattern. And it sure sounded as though Van Roff had found something interesting.

Riley finally interrupted him. "Tell me what you've got," she said.

"There was a knife murder in Birmingham just last Friday—another rich guy, although not as high-profile as Andrew Farrell. This one was Julian Morse, an heir to a family that made its fortune back in Birmingham's big steel days. He wound up in banking."

"So he was also stabbed to death?" Riley asked.

"More than to death, just like Farrell. Multiple wounds. Copious blood. The cops there are treating it as a local matter. But it sounds like kind of a coincidence, don't you think? Two rich dudes getting offed in exactly the same way a hundred fifty miles apart and within just a few days?"

Riley was thoroughly intrigued.

No, it doesn't sound like a coincidence at all, she thought.

She asked Van Roff to send her the details, thanked him for his help, and ended the call. Then she sat at the table wondering what to do next. Was it time to call her team chief, Brent Meredith, and see if he'd make this an official FBI case?

No, not yet, she thought. She needed to find out more about this second case.

Meredith was a sympathetic ally at the BAU, but he was also rigorous. What little she knew at the moment was still too flimsy to persuade him. All she'd accomplish would be getting herself called back to Quantico for a sharp scolding.

As she sat trying to decide what else to do, her cell phone rang. She saw that the call was from the Quantico switchboard. When she took the call, the operator said …

"Agent Paige, we've got a call for you from Officer Jared Ruhl of the Atlanta police. I believe we've connected him with you before. Will you take his call this time?"

Riley suppressed a sigh. She remembered looking around the police station a little while ago and wondering whether Officer Ruhl was anywhere nearby. She hadn't wanted him to know that she was here in Atlanta—and she still didn't. But she thought she'd better find out why he was calling now.

"I'll talk to him," she said to the operator.

A moment later she heard Ruhl's voice. He didn't sound the least bit happy.

"Agent Paige, where are you right now?"

"Um … in a fast food place," Riley said.

"No, I mean what *city*."

Riley gulped hard and said, "Atlanta."

She heard Ruhl let out a snort of dismay.

"That's what I thought," he said. "A buddy of mine told me that he'd seen a BAU agent at the station talking to the chief. He said he recognized Riley Paige from pictures in the media. You're kind of famous among cops, you know. He was wondering what you're doing here. So am I. Would you mind telling me just what's going on?"

"It's nothing that need concern you," Riley said.

"Like hell. This is about the Farrell murder, isn't it? It's about what I told you—that I didn't think his wife killed him. You told me it wasn't an FBI case, and anyway you weren't interested, it was none of your business. I really don't appreciate getting lied to."

"I didn't lie to you, Officer Ruhl," Riley said.

And of course it was true that she hadn't lied. Farrell's murder hadn't been an FBI case at the time, and it still wasn't one now.

Ruhl continued, "I called in the tip to you. You ought to have kept me in the loop."

Riley couldn't help admiring the chutzpah of this young local cop for chewing out a respected FBI agent. Still, she felt completely unprepared for this.

What can I tell him now? she wondered.

She asked, "Have you talked to anyone else about what you told me? I mean, your idea that Morgan Farrell isn't the killer?"

She heard him let out a discouraged sigh.

"Yeah, I've mentioned it to some of my buddies. They just laugh at me. Everybody thinks it's an open-and-shut case, and they say I'm an idiot for thinking otherwise."

Now Riley was starting to understand why Ruhl sounded so angry. Nobody liked being ridiculed by their peers. Still, for his own sake, she didn't want to get him mixed up in this.

She said, "Officer Ruhl, I'm afraid I'm not at liberty to discuss this matter."

"I don't buy that," Ruhl snapped. "And if you won't tell me, I know someone who will. I'll go talk to Chief Stiles. Since you met with him, he must know what's going on. Whatever it is, I'm going to ask him to put me on the case."

Riley felt a tingle of alarm.

The last thing she needed right now was for Ruhl to alert Stiles as to what she was really doing. And although Ruhl didn't seem to know it, it would be bad for him too. Stiles wasn't going to be pleased with the rookie for having gone behind his back to contact her in the first place.

Maybe a little honesty is in order, Riley thought. She paused to consider her words carefully.

Then she said, "Officer Ruhl, you seem to know quite a bit about me. Like you said, I'm kind of famous in the law enforcement world. What exactly do you know about me?"

Ruhl spoke slowly, "Well … they say you're brilliant, and you've got great intuition, and you can really get into a killer's head, and …"

"And?"

"And you've got your own way of doing things. You like to bend the rules. Sometimes you even break them."

Riley breathed a little easier.

He seems to be catching on, she thought.

Now she could hear a sort of unspoken "a-ha" in his voice.

"Oh. So right now you're—"

Riley interrupted, "Officer Ruhl, the less I tell you about any of this, the better for both of us."

A silence fell.

Riley waited, wondering what she could say to turn the young cop off from this … this situation that wasn't actually a case.

Finally he said, "Agent Paige, I'm sorry about the way I talked to you before. It was rude and I should have shown more respect. And now I'm just asking you, please …"

He fell silent. Riley knew what he was going to ask, and she didn't much like it.

He continued, "I'm not working any other cases right now. I can get away for the rest of today at least. I want to work on this with you."

Riley fought down an impulse to just say no.

But it really didn't seem fair.

After all, he *had* called in to alert her to his suspicions. And she was sure that his instincts had been right about Morgan not being the killer.

And so far, the only thanks he'd gotten for it was the ridicule of his colleagues.

She said, "Look, I'm going to be honest with you. This is liable to end badly for me. As I guess you already know, I'm kind of used to dealing with the consequences of being a loose cannon. But I'd hate to get you into trouble. And that's likely to happen, believe me."

"That's OK," Ruhl said. "Count me in. What do we do next?"

Riley thought for a moment, then said, "I'm driving to Birmingham right now to check out a lead. Where can I pick you up?"

She could hear excitement in Ruhl's voice.

"Right outside the station. I'll be there waiting."

He ended the call without another word.

Riley sat staring at the phone for a moment.

I guess I've got a new partner, she thought as she headed out to her car.

But was that going to be a good thing or a bad thing?

She didn't know. The truth was, she didn't have any idea what she might be getting herself and Ruhl into.

As she climbed into her car she thought with a sigh …

It's business as usual, I guess.

CHAPTER ELEVEN

As Riley approached the police station in her rented car, she wondered …

Did I just make a serious mistake?

Shouldn't she have just told Officer Jared Ruhl to stay off the case and to keep quiet about it? Instead, here she was about to partner up with an unfamiliar young cop.

In fact, she worried, how would she even recognize him among the various people she could see going in and out of the brick building?

But that didn't turn out to be a problem. There he was—a slight, scrawny-looking guy in a police uniform, his hands in his pockets, obviously on the watch for her car.

Riley didn't like the looks of him. It wasn't so much his sharply sloping caveman-like brow or his underdeveloped chin. It didn't matter to her whether he was pleasant to look at. But there was something off-putting in his body language—a palpable defensiveness in his hunched posture and his shuffling feet. She sensed at a glance that he didn't exactly inspire most people's confidence.

He had spotted her, so Riley ignored her urge to drive on by. She pulled up to the curb and Ruhl climbed into the car.

He huffed, "Boy, I'm sure glad to get out of that place for the day."

Riley thought she understood why. On the phone just now, he'd said that his colleagues had laughed at his theory about Andrew Farrell's murder. Now she had a hunch that ridicule was a pretty routine part of his professional life.

Jared said in a shrill, reedy voice, "So—you said on the phone that we're driving to Birmingham. I guess we must be checking out the murder of that other rich guy there—Julian Morse, I think his name was."

"That's right," Riley said, a little surprised that Ruhl already had some idea of what they were up to.

As if picking up on Riley's curiosity, Ruhl said, "When you told me where we were going, I figured that must be the reason. Another rich guy brutally stabbed to death, just a week ago, and not all that far away—sounds like maybe some kind of pattern, huh?

I've got to admit, it hadn't occurred to me until I talked to you. But then, that's why you're the famous Agent Riley Paige, and I'm just a rookie nobody. You think of everything."

Then with a delighted grunt he added, "Hey, do you think maybe we're dealing with an actual serial killer? Wow, that would be great! I'd love that!"

Riley cringed a little. Of course she knew he was a rookie and anxious to prove himself, and naturally he was excited by the possibility of cracking a serial killer case. But hearing him say so aloud was rather grating.

"We'll see," she said. "Let's not get ahead of ourselves."

"So what's the plan?" he asked. "Do we check in with the Birmingham police as soon as we get there?"

Riley realized she hadn't taken the time to think through what she intended to do. But she figured that trying to bluff another police chief into thinking she was there on official FBI business might be pushing her luck.

"I don't think so," she said.

Ruhl let out a chirp of laughter.

"Oh, I think I'm starting to get it," he said. "You've gone AWOL again, haven't you? Yeah, you're kind of famous for going off the reservation, pushing the envelope of FBI protocol and all. I'll bet this isn't even an official FBI case. I'll bet you didn't even tell Chief Stiles what you were really up to. I just love this!"

Riley was getting irritated now. She didn't like Ruhl's apparent glee about her rule-breaking. Still, she had to admit …

He guessed right.

He seemed to be pretty smart, and she wondered if maybe he'd turn out to be useful after all.

She said, "Jared—may I call you Jared?"

"Sure. May I call you Riley?"

Riley suppressed a growl of annoyance.

"No, Agent Paige will be fine," she said. "Let me fill you in. I'd met Morgan Farrell back in February. When she called to tell me she'd killed her husband, I found it hard to believe. Then when you called me, it really piqued my curiosity, so I got myself down here to see what was going on. I talked to Morgan in her jail cell a little while ago, and now I'm all but sure that she's innocent. The problem is, *she* doesn't think so, and neither does the DA or even her own lawyer."

Jared nodded and said, "So you want to find Andrew Farrell's real killer. And you're thinking whoever killed Farrell also killed

Julian Morse. *But* … we can't talk to the Birmingham cops about any of this, because this isn't exactly a legit investigation, at least not yet. Which is kind of a handicap."

"You've got it," Riley said. "So—do *you* have any suggestions about how we should proceed?"

Jared thought for a moment.

Then he said, "Well, I suggest we just go straight to the crime scene, Morse's mansion, and see what we can find out on our own. We might have to bluff whoever we happen to meet there. But that's what you're good at, right? And I'll bet I can be pretty good at it too!"

Riley stifled another growl.

She was finding Jared more annoying by the minute.

And yet she couldn't think of a better plan than the one he was suggesting.

She said, "You'll find my laptop computer in the back seat just behind you. I want you to get online and find out everything you can about Morse's murder—every single detail that's been released to the media. We need to know as much as we can before we pay his house a visit."

Jared dutifully followed her instructions and soon began to relate everything he could find out about Julian Morse's death. The man's body had been found by a servant late one night, brutally stabbed to death when he was reclining beside his pool. No one was yet in custody, but the Birmingham police seemed to suspect a number of people—family members, servants, business partners …

It doesn't sound like he had any shortage of enemies, Riley thought as she listened to Ruhl.

The cops were strongly considering the possibility that the actual murder had been carried out by a hired killer.

Finally Ruhl managed to find the address for Morse's home.

As they drove westward past the vast amusement park outside of Atlanta, Ruhl began to ask Riley questions about her own career. At first she gave him polite but sometimes evasive replies. But when he started making nosy queries about her unconventional methods and her problems with authority, her answers became terse.

She was worried that the two-and-a-half-hour drive between Atlanta and Birmingham could get combative. But by the time they crossed the border into the state of Alabama, they weren't talking at all. This suited Riley just fine. Jared Ruhl wasn't exactly growing on her. And she was enjoying the scenery—long stretches of woodland broken up by small towns and farms.

Ruhl was fast asleep by the time Riley drove into Birmingham. She decided it was time for him to start earning his way.

"Wake up," she said sharply. "I could use some directions."

Ruhl directed her through the city, which he seemed to know pretty well. Riley had never visited Birmingham before. As she drove near a huge iron statue staring down on the city from a tall pedestal, she wondered whether it might be of some Confederate soldier.

"That's Vulcan," Ruhl explained. "Roman god of the forge. Birmingham began as a big steel center."

Riley remembered what Van Roff had said to her about Julian Morse—that he was the heir to a family steel fortune. So far, the two murder victims seemed to have at least one thing in common. They'd both been very rich.

Following the young cop's directions, Riley eventually drove into a very high-end neighborhood, where huge houses nestled among trees. When they arrived at Julian Morse's home, Riley saw that it was somewhat smaller than the Farrell mansion in Atlanta. When she'd visited Farrell the previous winter, she'd found the ostentation repulsive. This one didn't seem to be trying quite as hard to look wealthy.

Like the Farrell house, this one wasn't gated or guarded from outside. But both were in wealthy neighborhoods where an intruder would surely attract notice. A killer would have to blend into the community well or be very skillful at what he was doing.

She parked the car in front of the house, certain that security cameras were watching their arrival. When she and Jared approached the entrance and rang the bell, it was opened promptly by a tall, elderly man with a rather large belly. Clad as he was in an elegant black suit, at first Riley took him to be a butler.

Except for one detail. His spotted bow tie was slightly askew, as if to deliberately suggest a certain casualness.

The man looked them over carefully, especially scrutinizing Jared's uniform.

"May I help you?" he asked in a slow southern accent.

Riley took out her badge and said, "I'm Special Agent Riley Paige, FBI. My colleague here is Officer Jared Ruhl of the Atlanta police. We're here concerning the murder of Julian Morse."

The man's eyes widened.

"Oh, dear," he said. "You're not here to arrest me, I hope. I answered all the policemen's questions last week, and I thought they'd accepted my alibi. You see, I was in my own home playing bridge when my brother was killed."

"Your brother?" Riley asked.

"Yes," the man said. "I'm Roderick Morse, Julian's older brother."

Then he squinted and added, "But I would have thought you'd know that."

Riley squirmed a little inside and reminded herself …

Our plan is to bluff our way through this.

She just hoped that she and her new partner didn't blow it somehow.

Roderick Morse was glancing back and forth between Riley and Jared.

"I must say, this is rather odd," Morse said. "You, sir, are from Atlanta, and you, ma'am, must be based—where? The FBI is located in Virginia, I believe. Aren't you both rather far from your regular stomping grounds?"

Before Riley could speak, Jared started talking. Riley couldn't help holding her breath, worrying whether he might say something grossly inappropriate.

He said, "Maybe you heard that there was a similar murder in Atlanta—another rich guy by the name of Andrew Farrell."

"Oh!" the man said with a slight gasp. "Well, I assure you that I had nothing to do with that murder either."

Riley hastily said, "The killings were enough alike that we think they might be connected. That's why we're here. We'd like a look at the crime scene, if that's all right."

"Well, I don't see why not," Morse said. "Come with me."

As Morse led them into the house, Riley saw that instead of the ridiculously dramatic staircase and pale carpets of the Farrell mansion, this one featured sparkling marble floors, huge arched windows, and huge crystal chandeliers. She found it all just as overwhelming.

How could anybody possibly live in these places?

Morse kept on talking as they continued on through the house.

"I'm sorry to say that my brother and I were estranged during the last few years. But since he didn't leave an heir, it's up to me to settle the estate, which is why I'm here. This whole place and everything in it will have to be sold."

He let out a scornful chuckle and added, "I can't say that I'm the least bit sad about it. My tastes and my brother's were rather different. There's a whiff of the postmodern in this conglomeration of styles that doesn't agree with me. My own home reflects my own inclinations toward a good old-fashioned antebellum look."

He looked at Jared and said in a supercilious tone, "Antebellum means 'before the war,' by the way. I hope, as a fellow Southerner, I don't have to tell you which war I'm talking about."

Riley could see Jared bristle at his condescension.

"Yeah, I know which war." Jared grunted. "But weren't your folks in the steel business back when this town got started? That wasn't until after the Civil War, if I remember my history right—when the carpetbaggers moved in."

Riley was alarmed to see Morse's face redden with anger. She could tell that Jared had really hit a nerve. He was probably right that the Morse family hadn't arrived in Alabama until the Reconstruction years after the Civil War. They'd never been hifalutin plantation owners, never lived like a family out of *Gone With the Wind*.

Jared was turning out to be a sharp observer, but even so …

Saying what he's figured out isn't helpful, she thought.

She wished she could just tell him to keep his mouth shut. Fortunately, their host seemed to be keeping his ire in check—at least for now.

Morse said, "I suppose you want me to show you the actual location of the crime."

He led Riley and Jared through the house and out the back door into an outdoor recreation area with a swimming pool and an array of chairs and tables.

Riley felt a deep tingle as she walked toward a particular chair, where the cushions had been removed.

A familiar instinct was kicking in. It was a sense of the killer's mind.

Then, without consciously willing it, she stopped in her tracks.

It happened right here, she thought.

This was where he killed Julian Morse.

CHAPTER TWELVE

Riley breathed slowly and let that tingling sensation build up inside her.

That feeling was, after all, perhaps her most powerful gift as an investigator.

Of course, during the last week, the crime scene had been cleaned of every drop of blood, any sign that the murder had ever happened.

Even so, Riley was beginning to visualize the whole thing.

Morse said, "According to the police—"

"I know," Riley said, interrupting him.

She stared at the reclining chair and began to relate her impressions to Morse and Jared …

"It was night, and Julian Morse was alone enjoying some moments of quiet relaxation after his swim. Half-asleep, he didn't hear the intruder creeping up behind him—to directly where I'm standing right now."

Imagining herself holding a large knife, she crouched beside the chair.

"The killer leaned over and stabbed him from behind—right in the middle of his abdomen, if he had any idea what he was doing. In order to deliberately inflict multiple stab wounds, he didn't want the knife to get stuck between the victim's ribs."

Riley began to act out the killer's movements.

"He pulled the knife out, and Morse began to writhe. Morse opened his mouth to scream, but that first wound shocked him into silence. His diaphragm may have been pierced—if so, he could no longer breathe. He could only make a horrible choking sound. He began to writhe and flail his arms."

She breathed slowly, then said …

"The killer's adrenaline was already high, and for a moment he was alarmed by Morse's thrashing. I don't think …"

She paused to let the hunch sink in.

"I don't think he'd ever killed anyone before. He may have had a flash of self-doubt. 'Can I finish this?' he may have wondered. Suddenly the whole thing seemed a lot more difficult than it had a few moments before."

She felt more and more strongly what the killer must have felt

…

"He rallied his will and grabbed hold of the victim somehow, probably by using his free arm to seize him from under the chin. He plunged the knife into his body again and again …"

Riley felt slightly uncertain now. She hadn't seen the autopsy reports for either murder.

She knew that both of the victims had died from numerous knife wounds—but where had those wounds been inflicted? Just in the abdomen, or in all the surrounding areas, including legs and arms? Riley had a strong feeling that the killer had gone wild once he'd gotten started stabbing, randomly piercing the man's body all over the place.

But what had he done with the knife?

Had he escaped with it?

That was a detail that had been left out of the news stories.

Then she remembered something Morgan Farrell had said to her over the phone as she'd stood looking at her husband's body …

"The knife is lying right next to him."

Riley rose to her feet and spoke aloud again …

"He dropped the knife right here beside the chair. He may have stood looking at Morse's lifeless body, but only for a moment. Then he made his escape."

Riley turned to look at Morse and Jared.

Morse's face looked pale now.

He said quietly, "Well … that's considerable more gory detail than I heard from the police."

Riley suddenly felt awkward and self-conscious. She seldom carried out this disturbing exercise in the presence of civilians. It was hardly any surprise that Morse was shocked.

Jared let out a grim chuckle at Morse's discomfort.

He said, "That's because this is no ordinary cop. This is Special Agent Riley Paige of the BAU."

Riley noticed a note of pride in Jared's voice. He definitely seemed to be pleased with himself for working with her.

He'd better not get used to it, she thought.

Then Jared said, "But how did the killer get here in the first place?"

Riley looked up and noticed several security cameras pointing down into the pool area.

She said, "The first thing he did was disconnect the security system, including those cameras. Probably just a matter of cutting wires."

Morse said, "Yes, that's what the police said. Alas, Julian's system seems to have been woefully out of date, and it was easy to disconnect. A wireless system would have served much better."

Riley stood still and looked around the perimeter of the property. On the side nearest the pool was a wooded area. She could see a high chain-link fence there among the trees.

Riley pointed and said, "He went out over that fence, the same way he'd come in. See that branch hanging over the fence? Coming in, he climbed out onto it and dropped himself down right into this pool area."

Jared scratched his head and asked, "But wouldn't going back the same way be a problem?"

Riley walked toward the overhanging branch and looked at the ground under it.

"Not really," she said. "My guess is he's pretty agile, maybe even athletic. Look, you can see the soil is disturbed here. These indentations are from where he landed. Going out, he was probably able jump up high enough to grab hold of the branch."

She turned again toward Morse and Jared.

Morse's mouth was hanging open.

"Well," he said. "This has been a … stimulating exercise in ratiocination. Is there anything else I can help you with?"

Riley took another look around. She felt as though she'd gotten as much information from the murder scene as sheer intuition would allow. To learn anything else, she'd need access to police and coroner records—and that wasn't possible, at least not yet.

She said to Morse, "Thank you for your help. We'll go now."

Morse led Riley and Jared back through the house again. When they reached the front hallway, Riley stopped in her tracks when something startling caught her eye. It was something she hadn't seen before because it was off to one side, hanging over an ornate fireplace in a formal area.

It was a full-length oil portrait of a beautiful woman of indeterminate age. She was standing in an elegant strapless gown with one hand resting on an expensive-looking period table. She was buxom and curvaceous, but her figure was not what most struck Riley.

It was the expression in her eyes.

It reminded her of someone—and it only took a second for Riley to realize who that person was.

She'd seen that expression in Morgan Farrell's face.

The portrait artist had skillfully caught that look of

helplessness.

CHAPTER THIRTEEN

Riley stood staring at the portrait for a moment, studying that expression.

It was certainly troubling.

The truth was, this voluptuous woman bore almost no resemblance to the thin and waiflike Morgan Farrell …

Except for those eyes, Riley thought.

The look in those eyes was exactly the same—pleading, desperate, terrified.

Someone had deliberately decided to preserve those frightened eyes in an expensive portrait—someone who actually took pleasure in the woman's look of fear.

Probably not a whim of the artist, she thought.

Surely that expression had to be required or at least approved by whoever commissioned that portrait.

And Riley knew who that person must be—the man who had been murdered beside his swimming pool.

Her thoughts were interrupted by the sound of Roderick Morse's voice.

"I see you've taken an interest in the portrait. Rather lovely, isn't it?"

"Who is she?" Riley asked.

Morse said, "Charlotte Morse, Julian's wife—or widow, I should say."

Riley remembered the mention of a wife in the news clip that Van Roff had sent her, but her impression was that she was no longer in the picture.

"She doesn't live here, does she?" Riley asked.

"Oh, goodness, no," Morse said. "Charlotte and Julian were separated a good year or so ago. Nobody ever knew what it was about."

Still staring at the portrait, Riley asked, "Where can I find Charlotte Morse?"

Roderick Morse looked intrigued at Riley's question.

"She's moved into the Britomart Hotel, right here in Birmingham."

Riley asked, "Can you give me her contact information— phone, email, or whatever?"

Morse shrugged and said, "Aside from the name of the hotel, I'm afraid not. The woman has become rather a recluse, I fear. She and I have had next to no contact over the years—I don't remember ever even talking with her. I've only seen her at social gatherings. Still, I've always suspected that I'd like her better than I ever liked Julian."

Riley thanked Morse for his help, and she and Jared left the house.

On their way to the car, Jared asked, "What do we do next?"

"We need to pay Charlotte Morse a visit," Riley said.

"Why? Do you think she's a suspect?"

Riley didn't reply to his question as they climbed into the car. The truth was, she wasn't sure just *what* she was thinking at the moment. She doubted very much that the woman she'd seen in that portrait had killed Julian Morse, much less Andrew Farrell or anybody else. And yet …

That expression! Riley thought.

It had to mean something, although Riley didn't know just what.

Jared got out his cell phone and said, "I'll call the hotel, see if they'll connect me to her."

Riley remembered how quickly Jared had managed to antagonize Roderick Morse.

"Um … I don't think so," Riley said, taking out her own phone. "I'll take care of that."

"Why can't I do it?" Jared asked with a slight whine in his voice.

"Because I don't want you to piss anybody else off," Riley said.

"Aww, come on. I can be good."

Riley ignored him and found the number for the Britomart Hotel. When she got the front desk, she asked to speak with Charlotte Morse.

The male clerk purred in an elegant voice, "I'm afraid Ms. Morse isn't taking any calls. May I ask what this is about?"

Riley introduced herself and explained that she wanted to talk to Charlotte about her husband's death.

"I'll see if I can connect you," the clerk said.

Riley was put on hold and found herself listening to classical music for a few moments.

Then the clerk came back and said, "I'm afraid she's not answering her phone. She seldom does, actually."

"Are you sure she's in her room?" Riley asked.

"Oh, yes," the clerk said. "She never goes out at all these days."

"I'll be coming by to see her," Riley said.

Riley ended the call and started the car.

She said to Jared, "I need directions to the Britomart Hotel."

"Are you going to tell me what this is all about?" Jared asked as he found the directions on his own cell phone.

"When I know, you'll be the first to hear about it," Riley said as she started to drive.

*

Riley was impressed by the Britomart Hotel when she arrived and parked in front of the huge, old-fashioned building. She guessed that it must have been built more than a century ago, back in Birmingham's steel heyday.

Riley and Jared walked into the plush lobby and approached the front desk. The well-dressed clerk spoke in the same sophisticated voice she'd heard over the phone.

"Special Agent Riley Paige, I presume."

Riley showed him her badge and introduced him to Jared. The clerk tried to call Charlotte's room, but again got no answer.

The clerk said, "I'm sorry—perhaps you could come by some other time. I can leave her a message and she can get back to you."

Riley remembered something that Roderick Morse had said about Julian's wife …

"The woman has become rather a recluse, I fear."

Leaving it to Charlotte to get back to Riley was really out of the question. For one thing, Riley didn't anticipate staying in Birmingham a whole lot longer.

Still, she knew she didn't have the authority to push the issue.

Tread lightly, she told herself.

She said to the clerk, "I'm afraid this is very urgent to our investigation. And since it pertains to her own husband's death, I think she would want to talk to us."

The clerk glanced back and forth at Riley and Jared.

Riley held her breath again, hoping Jared wouldn't say something abrasive.

Finally the clerk nodded. "Follow me. I'll take you to her room. We'll see if she'll make herself available."

Riley and Jared followed the clerk into an elevator, which took them to the top floor of the building. When they stepped out into the hallway, Riley saw that there were only two room doors. She guessed that two enormous suites took up the entire floor of the building.

The clerk knocked gently on the door and called out, "Ms. Morse, this is Delaney from the downstairs desk. I'm terribly sorry to trouble you, but you've got visitors that I believe you'll want to see."

Riley heard a quiet woman's voice behind the door.

"Who is it?"

"A pair of law enforcement officials. One is from the FBI."

Riley heard the woman exclaim, "Oh, my goodness!"

The door opened, and inside stood a startlingly attractive woman wearing a kimono. She smiled in a warm, charming manner.

Riley was startled. Was this really the same person she had seen in the portrait?

This woman was markedly more full-figured—one might even say stout—but nevertheless quite beautiful.

And Riley didn't see even the tiniest trace of that fear in her eyes.

Has there been some kind of mistake? she wondered.

Had she come to see the wrong woman altogether?

She took out her badge again and introduced herself and Jared.

In a welcoming, musical voice, the woman said, "Do come in, the two of you. I'm curious to know what this is all about."

Riley and Jared followed her into the suite, which was even larger and more elegant than Riley had expected. Charlotte Morse invited them to sit down on an antique settee, then she sat in a chair facing them.

Riley took a moment to observe their surroundings.

This luxurious suite didn't seem as forbidding as the homes of Julian Morse and Andrew Farrell. Riley had found it hard to believe that anyone could live in either of those mansions. By contrast, this place seemed palpably lived-in. And yet at the same time, it seemed strangely sad and lonely.

It took her a few moments to understand why.

Everything here was very old—in excellent repair, but obviously well-used. The suite also had a slight mustiness about it—not an unpleasant smell, just another hint of its age. Countless people had surely stayed here during the many years since the Britomart Hotel had been built. Riley could almost feel their ghostly presence in the air.

She found herself thinking …

If this place could talk …

This room had seen many different kinds of visitors come and go—happy honeymooners, lovers on clandestine trysts, wealthy businessmen on errands far from home. Most of those people had shared one trait in common—and that was transience.

Wealthy as they had been, they were always on their way to or from somewhere else.

This suite had never been a home—only a temporary refuge. Even so, it was warmer and more welcoming than the family mansions.

Still smiling, the woman said, "I take it this must have something to do with my husband's murder."

Riley nodded and said, "There was a murder much like it in Atlanta the night before last. The victim was a wealthy man named Andrew Farrell. Perhaps you heard about it."

The woman shook her head slightly.

"I'm afraid not," she said. "I don't pay any attention to the news. I keep rather to myself these days."

Riley looked at the woman closely. She could see now that this *was* the same woman who had been in the portrait. It was just that she seemed to have gone through changes since that picture had been painted. Although she looked older, she now looked much happier.

Charlotte Morse tilted her head with curiosity.

"I'm not sure what this has to do with me," she said. "I'm sure the local police told you that I'm not a suspect in Julian's murder. I haven't left this place in—well, I don't know how long."

Riley wasn't sure what to say. But she kept thinking about the expression she'd seen in the portrait, and how much those eyes had reminded her of Morgan Farrell.

She was sure that the resemblance must be significant somehow.

She asked, "Ms. Morse, may I ask what led to your separation from your husband?"

Charlotte's smile faded, but only a little. She leaned slightly toward Riley and said …

"Agent Paige, take a close look at this face."

Riley did so, noticing that Charlotte wasn't wearing any makeup.

She looked about the same age as Riley—and like Riley, she had lines in her face that showed it.

After holding Riley's gaze for a few moments, Charlotte said …

"Does this look like the kind of face that would please a wealthy and powerful man like Julian Morse?"

Riley was startled.

Charlotte Morse was still a beautiful woman, and now she looked more *human* than she had in the portrait. Back then she had obviously taken great pains to appear flawlessly youthful.

Charlotte let out a slight laugh and said, "Fifteen years of monogamous marriage is a long time for a man like that. You might say that I outlasted my expiration date by a decade or so! Julian was more than ready to move on—although I've not heard that he found a suitable substitute for me by the time he died."

Then with a sigh Charlotte simply said, "Well …"

Then she shrugged and fell silent.

Riley didn't feel the slightest bit of sadness or bitterness in that silence. Instead, she sensed relief—and even a slight trace of bliss.

But why?

Choosing her words carefully, Riley asked …

"Ms. Morse … what can you tell me about your marriage? Were you … happy?"

Charlotte let out a musical chuckle.

"Happy! What an odd sort of idea! What could happiness possibly have to do with it? I was a good catch for him, and he was a good catch for me. But that was so long ago. He was in the process of divorcing me when … well, you know."

She gestured toward her surroundings and added, "This was all I was ever going to get from him—a nice place to live. His lawyers put together a brutal prenup when we first got married. Everybody said at the time I was a fool to sign it. I didn't care then, and I don't much care now. Belongings don't matter to me. This is enough for me."

Then with a glance down at her own full figure she added with chuckle, "And as you can see, I get plenty to eat. I don't have to worry about my figure anymore."

Riley almost asked …

"Was your husband abusive?"

But she quickly realized it was a foolish question. The fearful expression in that portrait had already told her the answer.

And the expression Riley saw right now confirmed it.

After fifteen years, Charlotte Morse was free from whatever awful tyranny she'd suffered in her own home from her own husband.

And she was perfectly happy about it.

Riley realized that Jared hadn't spoken a word since they'd gotten here. She was relieved, of course, that he hadn't said anything rude or insulting. She glanced at him and saw that he was listening raptly to everything that was being said and was gazing at Charlotte with complete sympathy. It seemed that Jared had been as charmed by her as Riley was.

Maybe he's not a complete nuisance after all, Riley thought.

Then Charlotte said, "I suppose you want to know whether Julian had any enemies. A better question might be, did he have any friends? No, none that I ever knew of. He liked to hurt and anger people. He did everything he could to keep everyone around him off balance and uncomfortable. He didn't like to see anyone happy, I guess because he was so unhappy himself deep down. I don't think he had any idea what friendship was. He certainly didn't know the meaning of love."

Then with a sigh she added, "I guess I didn't either. Maybe I never will."

Riley sat looking at Charlotte, wondering what other questions to ask.

But really, what could she expect Charlotte to tell her? This woman had no idea who had killed either her husband or Andrew Farrell.

Riley was accomplishing nothing by this visit except intruding on the only things Charlotte still had and treasured—her peace and privacy.

Riley thanked Charlotte, and she and Jared left the apartment.

On the elevator going down, Jared said, "I don't get it, Agent Paige. What was that all about? What did Morse's wife have to do with his murder? Weren't we just wasting our time?"

Riley stifled a sigh. Jared was through being silent. Still, it was a good question—and she really didn't know the answer.

When they got outside, she told Jared that they were headed back to Atlanta, and that she wanted him to drive. Maybe she could take a break and try to think things through.

As soon as Jared took the wheel and headed the car out of Birmingham, Riley's cell phone buzzed.

She groaned when she saw who the caller was.

It was her boss, Brent Meredith.

Oh, no, she thought. *This can't be good.*

CHAPTER FOURTEEN

When Riley took the call, she heard the familiar rumble of Meredith's voice.

"Agent Paige, is there something you'd like to tell me?"

She shuddered a little at the question. She could easily imagine her team chief's scowling dark features, which were daunting enough when he was in a good mood. And he sure didn't sound like he was in a good mood right now.

She stammered, "Sir, I—I can explain … whatever…"

Riley wasn't exactly sure what she should try to explain. Someone she'd crossed paths with must have complained about her being here. But which one?

"I sure hope you can," Meredith said. "I just got a call from Elmo Stiles, the police chief down in Atlanta. He said he was curious about what kind of investigation the FBI was conducting there, and just why we'd sent you down there to work on it. He said you hadn't exactly been forthcoming."

Then with a growl Meredith added, "Well, what was *I* supposed to tell him? I had no idea what he was talking about."

Riley fought down a sigh of despair. She had no choice, of course, but to tell Meredith the truth. Although she'd often played fast and loose with the rules, she tried to never lie to Meredith. He'd been her staunch ally through some pretty tough professional times, when people who ranked higher than he did had wanted to see her fired or worse.

She slowly began to describe everything, starting with when she'd met Morgan Farrell back in February. She also told him about coming to Atlanta and talking to Morgan in jail, and her growing certainty that the woman was innocent.

Meredith grunted, "A single murder doesn't exactly sound like an authentic FBI case."

"Well, as it turns out, there's been another murder," Riley said.

Without mentioning Van Roff by name, Riley explained that she had learned of Julian Morse's murder in Birmingham. The man had been killed under strikingly similar circumstances, just a week before Farrell's murder.

Meredith interrupted, "Don't tell me. You went to Birmingham to check it out."

Riley gulped and said, "Yeah, that's where I am right now."

"So … should I expect a phone call from the Birmingham police chief, wondering just what the hell you're doing there?"

"Oh, no," Riley said. "The Birmingham police have no idea I'm here."

As soon as the words were out of her mouth, she realized how bad that sounded.

I'm not making things any better for myself, she thought.

Choosing her words more carefully, she explained that she'd been to Morse's house and had also paid his widow a visit. She also told him that she was convinced that the two murders had been committed by the same culprit.

Then she said, "So you see, maybe we should make this case official after all. Two murders in two different states—doesn't that call for a Federal investigation?"

Meredith growled again.

"You know better than that, Agent Paige. The FBI is like the proverbial vampire. It's got to be invited in."

"Well, couldn't you call Chief Stiles back and—"

"The answer is no, Agent Paige. What you're telling me is still too flimsy for us to go throwing our weight around. By the way, when Stiles asked me what you were doing there, I told him I'd prefer not to discuss it. So I covered for your ass. You're welcome."

"I, uh, really appreciate that, sir."

"You'd better."

A silence fell. Riley braced herself for whatever might be coming next.

Was he going to demand that she come back to Quantico immediately?

Finally he said, "I hear you got your adoption case settled. Congratulations. It must feel good."

"Thanks," Riley said.

"So, I assume you're taking a little time off to rest and celebrate."

Riley started breathing a little easier. She felt pretty sure about where Meredith was going with this …

He's going to look the other way.

"That's right," she said. "I needed a break."

Another silence fell.

Then Meredith said, "Well, don't expect the company to reimburse you for any expenses. And I don't want to hear anything more about your activities—not unless you've got something that

I'll really want to know about. I'll expect you back in your office the day after tomorrow."

Without another word, Meredith ended the call.

Riley sat looking at her cell phone as she let a feeling of relief sink in.

Then Jared Ruhl asked, "So—that was the boss, huh?"

"Yeah," Riley said.

With a slight whine, Jared added, "Don't I deserve any credit? I didn't hear you mention my name once."

Riley heaved a deep sigh. The truth was, she had been so focused on Meredith that she hadn't given any thought to the young cop who was driving the car.

She said, "Believe me, I wouldn't be doing you any favors."

As Jared kept driving, Riley felt sure of one thing—she'd piqued Meredith's interest just enough to cut her some slack, give her a chance to learn more about this case.

But she only had one more day to accomplish whatever she could hope to do.

What could she possibly get done with just one day?

CHAPTER FIFTEEN

Tisha Harter sat in the huge recreation room staring at the game that was unfolding on an enormous video screen.

Guns were blazing, and explosions were going off all around her. Bad guys were popping up all over the place. Usually, Tisha had no problem handling the whole bunch of them.

But today, Tisha couldn't do anything more than fumble with the remote buttons. With an impatient groan, she gave up and logged out of the game.

For a moment, she just sat there and glared at her tightly bandaged right hand. Two of her fingers were wrapped together and her hand was covered with a foam support that extended all the way over her wrist.

She put down the remote and reached with her other hand for the glass of bourbon she'd poured for herself. She took a swallow, then grumbled aloud …

"That evil bastard."

She wasn't thinking about any of the villains in the game. She wasn't thinking about the nurse who had bandaged the hand, either.

She was thinking about her husband.

Edwin had broken her pinky finger just yesterday in one of his increasingly frequent outbursts of sadistic cruelty. He'd made her scream, which of course he enjoyed. He liked to inflict pain on people, especially on her. He'd been keeping her pretty bruised up lately, although until now he'd been careful not to leave any marks that couldn't be hidden by her clothing.

This was different—the first bone he'd actually broken. The live-in nurse who spent most of her time taking care of Edwin had set Tisha's finger and bandaged it. She'd told Tisha that it would have to stay in its splint for another four weeks.

She looked at the other wrist, with the gold bracelet he had bought after inflicting this latest wound. He always bought her nice things after doing bad things to her. It wasn't his way of apologizing—he never apologized to anybody. It was more of a transaction—his way of reimbursing her for services rendered, for allowing him to hurt her.

She used to almost think the nice trinkets were worth the pain, but things had gotten worse since he'd retired.

Why do I put up with it? she wondered.

She was no weakling herself. In her short life, Tisha had endured more than her share of hard knocks, and she liked to think of herself as being as tough as nails. She *could* fight back when Edwin got into one of his spells—and sometimes she did. But it always backfired. Edwin would call his blindly loyal security people to restrain her and lock her up somewhere until she calmed down. Not a single person in the house would ever come to her defense. They all did exactly whatever he ordered them to.

And now ...

Four weeks! she thought miserably.

She wouldn't be able to leave the house that whole time, since no one outside the mansion could be allowed see her injury. Normally, her freedom to go out and do as she liked was the one thing in life that still belonged to her—a precious liberty she took advantage of as often as she could.

She smiled a little as she thought ...

If only Edwin knew the kind of stuff I do when I'm away.

But now she was stuck right here, and she was going to be bored stiff for four whole weeks—especially now that she couldn't even take out her aggression by playing this damned game.

None of this was what she'd expected when she'd married Edwin four years ago.

She'd gone to unscrupulous lengths to land him. She'd been just twenty-one years old at the time, working as a bartender in one of the country clubs he'd belonged to.

She'd known Edwin to be her wealthiest patron. She also knew that his wife, Claudia, was an invalid in the last stages of cancer. So even while serving him drinks, Tisha had moved in on him with what she liked to think of as entrepreneurial zeal. Between watching TV and observing the women at the club, she'd learned to present herself in public in perfectly appropriate ways, but she also offered him youth, energy, and beauty.

He hadn't known, of course, about her checkered past, especially her run-ins with the law. He still didn't know about all that, and Tisha never intended to tell him.

It had been easy to seduce him, then keep an affair going until the wife died.

Edwin had proposed to Tisha the very day after Claudia's death, and they were married in a private ceremony just a few days later.

Everything had gone right on schedule as far as Tisha was

concerned.

But since then, her hopes had been dashed.

Taking another swallow of whiskey, she wondered …

When the hell is he going to die?

One of the reasons she'd targeted him for marriage in the first place was that he'd already had three heart attacks. Everybody knew that he loathed exercise and avoided anything resembling a healthy diet.

In fact, the staff of the country club where she'd worked had kept a betting pool going about when the old bastard was going to croak.

And that was what Tisha had been counting on. She'd made sure that he rewrote his will to cut out his three sons, leaving her as his only heir.

Whenever he died, she'd inherit a spectacular fortune.

These days his blood pressure was terrible, and so were his cholesterol levels. But he just kept right on living. The worst part of it was, he attributed his longevity to having Tisha in his life.

"You're a tonic," he often told her. *"You keep me young."*

Whenever he said that, she wanted to hit him with her fists.

In fact, she wished she could hit him right now.

And why shouldn't she?

She could find him, wherever he was in the house, and sucker punch him right in the face.

So what if she got punished for it?

In fact …

… why shouldn't she do something a whole lot worse?

She was feeling bitter enough right now not to give a damn about any consequences.

As her anger climbed up as a bitter taste in her mouth, she thought …

He's got no idea the kinds of things I've done.

He's got no idea what I'm capable of.

*

Edwin Gray Harter was wandering the hallways of his mansion looking at his vast collection of fine paintings—Picassos, Kandinskys, Braques, Klees, Pollocks, and other works. Combined, those paintings were worth several fortunes.

After all these years he was finally asking himself …

Do I even like this stuff?

81

All this modernism—he didn't even feel as though he understood most of it.

After all, his dead wife, Claudia, had been the art lover, not him.

She'd been the one who had told him what was any good, the stuff he'd want to buy. Not that she'd approved of his purchases, as she'd often told him when she'd still been alive …

"It's obscene."

Edwin kept the whole collection in the rooms and hallways here in his own private wing—a part of the mansion that no people except his personal servants were allowed to enter except with his permission. Even Claudia had seldom been permitted to come here. Now the same was true of Tisha.

He smiled as he recalled what Claudia had often said …

"Those paintings ought to belong to the world. They ought to be in a museum for everyone to see. It's all wasted on you. The whole thing is obscene."

He'd never been able to make Claudia understand—the whole point of this collection was to have things that the world wanted, but that nobody else could have for the simple reason that Edwin *owned* them.

He stood now looking at an especially chaotic abstract.

He couldn't even remember who the painter was, but for some reason right now he felt rather attracted to it, felt almost as though he could appreciate it.

The wild brushstrokes seemed to be deliberately meaningless …

Almost like my life.

A familiar bitterness was creeping over him.

Again he thought of the idealistic dreams of his youth. He'd betrayed those dreams over and over again. To make his fortune, he'd started with lucky investments in oil wells and Las Vegas casinos—and when luck hadn't been on his side, money laundering and other dubious endeavors had always taken up the slack.

And now he'd been a billionaire so long that he could barely remember ever being anything else.

He got tired of looking at the painting and walked over to a window. He stood gazing out into the night at the lighted golf course that stretched far into the distance. He used to like that view, with its hint of affluence and privilege. He'd also liked playing golf, had enjoyed the wheeling and dealing that took place on the course as much as the game itself.

But his interest in golf had soured, like so much else.

And then there was Tisha …

Tisha had been his final acquisition, his attempt to jump-start his waning enthusiasm for life.

When people asked him why a man his age had married someone so young, he'd told them …

"When you choose a dog, what do you look for? A puppy! Who wants an old dog that's already fixed in its ways? You want a puppy!"

He'd figured it would be the same with a wife. He could train her to be exactly what he wanted her to be. He hadn't been able to do that with Claudia, who had been thirty when he married her, and who had always been too much her own person for his tastes.

But now, as it turned out, he hadn't been able to do that with Tisha, either.

Some puppy, he thought.

Back when he'd known her as a bartender, she'd done a great con on him, presenting herself as cheerful and naïve and eager to please.

Not that she had completely fooled him. Naturally, he'd had her investigated, and he knew more about her dubious past than she realized. Still, he'd been taken in by that charming masquerade of hers, which had lasted until after she'd gotten him to rewrite his will. Then she started to reveal herself to be the vulgar piece of trailer trash she really was.

It was small wonder that he liked hurting her, liked hearing her yelp and scream in pain.

But he knew he'd gone too far by breaking her finger. Somehow, he sensed that she was going to get back at him for that.

She'd hated his guts for quite some time, of course. It didn't really bother him to know that she wanted him dead.

It didn't even bother him that she was already trying to kill him in her own subtle ways. He'd left her in complete command of his menu, and she made sure that he got daily toxic doses of fat and sugar and cholesterol—juicy red steaks and outlandishly sweet desserts.

The truth was, he didn't much care. He enjoyed the rich and toxic food, and after three heart attacks, he didn't figure he had much longer to live anyway.

And he wasn't the least bit afraid of dying. In fact, he rather looked forward to it.

After all, what did he really have to live for?

As he stood there gazing out the window, he felt his muscles cramping and aching.

Getting old is for losers, he thought.

Fortunately, there was still one deeply satisfying pleasure left to him in life, a way to ease his physical pain. He went through his bedroom and into his vast bathroom, where the hot tub lay already steaming. He felt the water with his fingers.

Perfect.

He took off his glasses and removed his hearing aid, set them on the bathroom counter, and took off his clothes.

Then he turned on the hot tub's massaging jets and climbed into the warm water.

He sighed and breathed slowly as relief flooded through his body.

As Edwin relaxed, he found himself slipping into reveries about the past, back when he'd been young and hadn't yet made his fortune and wanted to be an inventor. He'd studied electronics and hoped to change the world with his ideas and innovations. Instead, the whole information revolution, the great new age of computers and communication, had completely passed him by while he'd been moving money around, never making or creating anything of any use at all.

That brilliant and talented young man he'd once been now seemed like someone else, a stranger that maybe he'd like to meet …

… but who wouldn't like me very much.

Well, there was no point in getting nostalgic.

He knew he'd gotten exactly what he deserved in life, and he didn't feel the least bit sorry for himself.

He closed his eyes and let himself fall under the soothing, hypnotic spell of the bubbling heat and the friendly rumbling of the hot tub.

Then suddenly …

A deep, piercing pain stabbed just below his ribcage.

Another heart attack, he thought as the pain exploded through his abdomen.

This one hurt much worse than the others had.

Then he felt a sudden pressure on his chest and his face slipped down into the water. Sharp stabbing pains struck all over his abdomen.

He opened his eyes, which stung from the chemicals in the water, and saw blood billowing in the hot tub's bubbling water.

He waved one hand as though to wipe away the blood.

He tried to order the pain to stop, but coughed as water poured into his mouth.

Edwin Gray Harter's consciousness faded away as he sank into warm water that was stained with his own blood.

CHAPTER SIXTEEN

The next morning, Riley had no idea that everything was about to change. She was sitting in her hotel dining room drinking coffee, nibbling on a Danish, and feeling pretty defeated.

She was sure the murders of Andrew Farrell and Julian Morse were connected, probably committed by the same man. But Meredith had made clear to her yesterday that she was still on her own. Without official support, how could she follow up on her suspicions?

Should she approach Chief Stiles again, try to persuade him to contact the FBI and make this an official case? He surely knew about the murder in Birmingham, but he had never mentioned it to her. What would he do if Riley brought it up with him?

Probably just remind me that Morgan Farrell confessed, she thought.

Regarding the resemblance between the two murders, Riley guessed that Stiles would either chalk it up to coincidence or theorize that Morgan had deliberately copied the other murder.

Besides, there was one really big reason why contacting Stiles was a bad idea.

I lied to him about why I'm even here, Riley remembered. *Why should I expect him to trust me now?*

She wondered if she and Ruhl should have returned to Atlanta from Birmingham so hastily yesterday. Maybe she should have talked to the Birmingham police chief after all. Maybe she could have told him the truth about why she was there, asked him to allow her to investigate purely on her own.

Maybe she should drive back to Birmingham.

Or …

Maybe I should just give up and go back home, she thought.

She wished her partner, Bill Jeffreys, was here.

He'd surely know what to do.

Maybe she should give him a call. Or maybe she should call her other, younger partner, Jenn Roston.

Then she sighed as she thought …

And get them mixed up in this mess?

No, that wouldn't be fair. Meredith had shown considerable restraint in letting Riley continue to pursue the two cases on her own time. He'd be furious if Riley turned to any other FBI sources, especially Bill or Jenn.

As she mulled all this over, her phone buzzed. Riley growled under her breath when she saw that the call was from Jared Ruhl.

She'd dropped him off at his apartment building last night after they'd gotten back from Birmingham. She'd been careful not to say anything to suggest that their "partnership" was anything other than a one-day thing.

I guess he doesn't see it that way, she thought.

She took the call and was startled by the joy in the young cop's voice.

"Hey, Agent Paige! I've got great news! There's been another murder!"

"What are you talking about?" Riley demanded.

"It happened over in Monarch, just about thirty miles east of Atlanta. An old rich dude by the name of Edwin Gray Harter got killed in his hot tub."

Riley snapped, "And you call that good news?"

With a gleeful chuckle Jared added, "He was stabbed multiple times. That makes three rich men murdered in the same way within two hundred miles of each other. Now don't try to tell me they're all a coincidence!"

Riley's brain clicked away as she tried to process what she was hearing.

No, it sure didn't sound like a coincidence.

Still, she felt a bit queasy over Jared's delight at another death.

"When did it happen?" Riley asked.

"Just last night. The body was found no more than an hour ago."

Riley could hardly believe her ears.

An hour? she thought.

The murder could hardly be all over the Internet yet. Riley doubted that the media had even started to cover it.

"How did you find out so fast?" she asked.

"I've got my sources," Jared said.

"Sources? What the hell sources are you talking about?"

With a slight whine, Jared said, "Agent Paige, do we *have* to talk about all that now? We don't have much time. The cops there are expecting us."

Riley gasped aloud.

"What do you mean 'expecting us'?"

"Naturally I got in touch with the Monarch police chief. I told him we were on our way, because it was now an FBI case."

"But it's *not* an FBI case!" Riley almost yelled.

"Why not? With three murders, shouldn't it be? Oh, and I told the chief to keep the crime scene undisturbed—especially the corpse. Was that smart of me or what?"

Riley was nearly sputtering now.

"Jared, you shouldn't have called there until after you'd talked to me. Actually, you shouldn't have called at all. You should have let me make the call."

"Why? I figured time was of the essence."

Riley didn't know what to say. The truth was, it probably *was* a good thing he'd called right then, if it meant the crime scene would remain undisturbed.

At the same time, Jared couldn't keep on making calls and decisions like that on his own.

But how am I going to stop him? she wondered.

Sounding more and more excited, Jared continued, "I called into the station here in Atlanta, and I said I'm taking a sick day. Don't worry, I've got lots of them saved up. So. Who's going to drive us to Monarch? I've got a car, but I've been having some trouble with it lately, and I can't guarantee it'll get us there and back. You've still got that rental car, don't you?"

"Yeah," Riley said wearily. "I'll come and pick you up right now."

She ended the call. As she finished her coffee and Danish, she wondered …

Why can't I just tell that guy to get lost?

She really wasn't sure. But the truth was, he wasn't entirely useless. He'd had a few good insights yesterday, and now, somehow or other, he had found out about a new murder. And the truth was, Riley probably wouldn't have traveled here at all if it hadn't been for his first phone call telling her of his doubts that Morgan Farrell was a killer.

So despite how irritating and troublesome he generally was, Riley figured …

I guess I'd better not dump him—yet.

As she left the hotel and went out to her car, she thought …

Another murder.

She'd been right all along.

But she couldn't get smug about it. Now she had a new case to solve. And whether or not it was officially her case, she had to solve it before anyone else was killed.

CHAPTER SEVENTEEN

When Riley pulled up to Jared's apartment building, of course he was already standing on the sidewalk waiting for her. He climbed into the car and gave her directions for heading out of town and toward Monarch.

As she drove, Riley said firmly, "*Now* I want you to tell me how you found out about this murder."

Jared chuckled and replied, "Have you ever heard of a website called CrimeWidth?"

Riley tried to remember. She thought she'd heard someone mention that name—Bill, maybe.

Jared continued, "It's a violent crime alert streaming service, and it connects to police scanners all over the country. It's got an alert feeds page that keeps up with violent crimes in real time. They never miss a thing. That's where I heard about this new murder in Monarch."

She said, "So you just happened to be listening in when this new murder came up?"

Jared shrugged and said, "I listen to it when I can't sleep. And I sure as hell had trouble sleeping last night. It was a good thing I tuned in, huh?"

Riley's mind boggled at the idea of a public website that gathered so much real-time information about violent crime. She wondered whether it was a good idea for civilians to have access to such a tool.

Still, she had to admit it had been helpful this morning.

And Jared had been helpful as well.

*

It was only a short drive eastward from Atlanta to Monarch. As they entered the little town, Riley could practically smell the affluence in the air. Everything was posh and well-manicured, and the main street was lined with extremely high-end shops. It was all so sparkling and tidy that it hardly looked real to Riley. The storybook feel of the place was heightened when she noticed that some people here were riding around in golf carts instead of cars.

They continued along curving roads past entries to a couple of country clubs with enormous golf courses. In fact, it seemed to Riley as though the entire visible landscape was made up little except golf courses.

Then they made their way through a wealthy neighborhood of large homes until they reached the end of a cul-de-sac. There they found the modern stone mansion where Edwin Gray Harter had lived. Although the style was different, the sheer size of it reminded Riley of the homes of the other two victims. Like the others, this carefully maintained property wasn't gated and could be accessed from the street.

Definitely a pattern here, Riley thought as she tried to visualize how an intruder might have gotten in.

Right now, police cars and a medical examiner's van were parked outside the front entrance. When Riley parked and she and Jared got out of the car, she saw couple of uniformed men standing in the open doorway. One was smoking a cigarette as he stepped forward to meet them.

He said to Jared, "You must be the guy I talked to on the phone." Then he added to Riley, "And you must be the FBI woman he told me about. I'm Callum O'Neill, and I've got the bad luck to be the chief of police here in Monarch."

Riley immediately noticed that he had a really thick New York accent. He was a short, swarthy, black-haired man, almost comically compact and sturdy.

Sort of like a miniature football lineman, Riley thought.

After Riley introduced herself, O'Neill said, "You know, back in New York, I had to deal with lots of murders—drive-bys, gangbanger wars, mob hits, armed robberies gone bad, spouses killing each other, I can't tell you how much of that kind of stuff. I took this job here in Monarch to get away from all that."

With a growl of dismay, he added, "Fat chance of that, I guess."

He took the cigarette out of his mouth, tossed it on the ground, and put it out with his foot.

He said, "So this is now officially an FBI case, huh? I guess it's about time. Maybe if you'd gotten started earlier, the guy in there would still be alive. Small wonder folks in these parts don't much like Feds."

Riley winced a little. She decided maybe this wasn't the best moment to tell him this wasn't yet an FBI case—that in fact, he was going to have to call Quantico himself to make it official.

She simply said, "Show us the crime scene."

O'Neill led them into the house. Riley was increasingly struck by the general resemblance to the other victims' homes. This one, too, looked like some kind of gigantic showroom where no one had ever lived.

She noticed especially a common taste for immaculate white sofas. She wondered why anybody would want furniture that would show any wear or soil so easily. In her own home a thing like that wouldn't hold up for a whole day—not with two daughters and now a dog.

As Riley looked around, she imagined how much trouble the housekeeping staff must go to in order to keep everything so polished and pristine. She figured they must spend endless hours cleaning away any signs of human life.

They approached a dramatic staircase that wound up one side of the entry hall to an overhanging balcony. Riley could see that the stairs continued up even farther into the upper reaches of the house. Before Riley could start up the steps, O'Neill said …

"I wouldn't do that if I were you. I made that mistake myself when I first got here. Turns out nobody ever uses those stairs. I wish somebody had told me. I'm going wake up stiff and sore tomorrow morning."

He led Riley and Jared to the elevator, which they took to the third floor. When they stepped outside the elevator into a hallway, Riley saw that they were surrounded by paintings. Although she didn't know a lot about art, some of these were unmistakable. A couple of Picassos especially caught her eye.

Her mind boggled at how much must have been spent acquiring this collection.

Jared said, "Looks like Edwin Gray Harter was quite the art lover."

Although Riley didn't say so, she guessed differently. She sensed that this whole outrageously expensive collection was all about ostentatious wealth, not a love of art.

She shivered a little as she was hit with a strong gut feeling …

Love of anything *is in short supply in this house.*

Even all these expensive material possessions seemed somehow starved for affection.

Riley looked up and down the hallway.

"What kind of security is there up here?" she asked.

"None," O'Neill said. "I know, that sounds kind of perverse. But people on the staff tell me that this whole floor was Harter's private domain—and I do mean *private*. No security cameras or surveillance of any kind."

Of course Riley realized that the lack of any security footage was going to be a problem. But it also made the art collection seem even weirder to her. Harter had spent vast amounts of money collecting paintings he may not have even especially liked, but that no one except him was ever allowed to see.

She thought that Harter must have been a strange and empty man—probably both arrogant and pathetic.

O'Neill led Riley and Jared through a vast bedroom into an almost equally vast, white-tiled bathroom. Uniformed people were milling about, most of them hovering near an enormous hot tub.

The first things that caught Riley's eye were a tray and some broken china lying on the floor. Then she looked into the tub and saw the man's body there beneath the water. The water had turned pink with blood. At the bottom of the tub next to the body lay a large kitchen knife—obviously the murder weapon, again abandoned by the killer.

A rotund but remarkably nimble-looking white-clad woman came toward Riley. O'Neill introduced her as Sage Ennis, the county medical examiner.

"So, can we let out the water now?" Ennis asked in a sharp Southern twang. "We were told to leave everything like we found it until you got here, but this guy's already getting kind of ripe. I'd like him not to get too nasty before I have to do the autopsy."

Riley could definitely smell a disagreeable odor. She knew it was going to quickly get worse.

She took a long look at everything.

"You've got photos?" she asked.

"Of course we do, honey," the ME drawled. "I'll send them right over to you."

"OK," Riley said.

A member of the examiner's team opened the drain on the side of the tub, and the water started to run out.

Riley asked Ennis, "What facts have you been able determine so far?"

Ennis crossed her arms and said, "You're the FBI gal. What all can you tell *me*?"

Riley didn't like her tone of voice, but the attitude wasn't new to her. As O'Neill had just suggested, Federal officials of any kind weren't always especially welcome in this part of the country.

She's testing me, Riley realized.

Riley reached into the tub to feel the draining water.

"Still very warm," she said to the ME. "The murderer must have left the jets and heat running. My guess is they were still on when your people showed up and turned them off."

Ennis nodded.

Riley looked again at the tray and the broken china. She guessed that a servant had come into Harter's bedroom early this morning with coffee and a small breakfast. He or she hadn't found Harter in bed, but had heard the hot tub jets through the bathroom door. The servant had guessed that Harter was enjoying an early morning soak, then came in here and dropped the tray in horror when he saw the body.

Riley quickly reviewed what she already knew about the time sequence.

When Jared had called her, he'd said the body had been found no more than an hour before then. Riley had spent another hour picking up Jared and driving out here.

She looked at her watch and said, "One of Harter's servants found the body at about 6:30 a.m.—a male servant, since he felt free to come into the bathroom. That was Harter's regular time for breakfast."

Ennis tilted her head with interest.

Riley peered again into the tub. The water was draining away from the corpse now, and she could see it more clearly.

She said, "His body sank and stayed at the bottom of the tub. That means his lungs were full of water—he drowned while he was struggling with his assailant. Not that he wouldn't have died of his wounds pretty quickly. But if that had happened, there'd have been even more blood in the water."

Riley sniffed the sour air again and looked more closely at the corpse, which showed signs of bloating.

She wasn't trained in forensic medicine, but she'd seen and smelled more than her share of corpses in many different conditions—including quite a few that had been submerged under water of varying temperatures.

She reminded herself …

The jets and the heat were running until the cops and ME team got here.

The heat had somewhat accelerated the bloating and putrefaction processes. So the smell and the bloating gave Riley a pretty good idea of when the murder had happened.

She looked up at Ennis and said, "I'd put the time of his death at eleven thirty last night. What's your estimate?"

Ennis smiled, looking rather impressed.

"That's pretty much what I figured too," she said.

Riley stood looking silently at the body for a moment, trying to get a better sense of what had happened. She couldn't quite get a feeling for the killer's actual thoughts right now. But it was easy to see that Harter had been killed in much the same way as Julian Morse.

Harter had probably settled down in the tub facing away from the bathroom door. She spotted a pair of glasses and a hearing aid on a nearby counter. Over the rumble of the jets, he hadn't heard his assailant come inside. The killer had attacked him from behind, just as he had done with Julian Morse.

Riley could only be sure of one thing. There could no longer be the slightest doubt that the three murders were the work of the same criminal.

Riley looked at Ennis and said, "Your team can take the body away now."

Ennis began to give her people orders to remove the corpse.

Riley looked all around the bathroom and saw that Chief O'Neill's team was doing a careful and efficient job of examining the crime scene. O'Neill had obviously learned his forensic techniques well in New York. She felt sorry that his expertise was still proving to be so useful.

O'Neill stepped toward her and said, "What do we do now?"

Riley paused for a moment, then thought …

The wives.

She remembered again Morgan Farrell's persecuted look, and how similar Charlotte's expression had been in the portrait.

Although she didn't yet know why, Riley felt sure …

It means something.

Riley looked O'Neill in the eye and said, "Was Harter married?"

"Yeah," O'Neill said.

"Is she in the house?"

O'Neill nodded.

"I want to talk to her right now," Riley said.

CHAPTER EIGHTEEN

As Riley started to follow Chief O'Neill out of the bathroom, she noticed that Jared was leaning against a wall, looking pale. His mouth was hanging open.

He obviously had never seen a corpse in this condition before. At least the bloating and putrefaction must be new to him, and this might be the first time he'd encountered the smell.

Well, Riley knew that it could get a lot worse than this. She felt in no mood to coddle the young cop.

"Are you coming with us, or what?" she asked him.

Jared snapped out of his shock and followed Riley and O'Neill.

The three of them got into the elevator and went down to the second floor. O'Neill led them into a large recreation room with a pool table, a ping-pong table, and some other games.

A young blonde woman was sitting on a couch staring at a video screen.

To Riley's surprise, she was playing a video game, gunning down virtual villains. She seemed to notice the arrival of Riley, O'Neill, and Jared, but barely took her eyes off the screen.

"Look at this," she remarked with a note of satisfaction. "I'm getting pretty good with my left hand after all."

Riley saw that the woman was holding the remote in her left hand, and her right hand was tightly bandaged.

Right away Riley had a good idea of what had probably happened to that hand.

O'Neill spoke to her over the crackle of virtual weapons. "Mrs. Harter, we're sorry to trouble you in your …"

His voice faded. Riley was pretty sure he was going to say "your time of grief." But given how the woman was acting right now, that hardly seemed fitting.

Instead, O'Neill said, "An FBI agent is here to see you—Riley Paige."

The woman looked rather bored. She killed off a couple more of the game's attackers, then paused the program. Riley, Jared, and O'Neill sat down in chairs facing her.

Riley could see that, like the wives of the other victims, this woman was remarkably good-looking. Unlike the first two, she was comfortably dressed in shorts and a T-shirt. Most noticeably, she was extremely young.

There was something else about her appearance that unsettled Riley. She couldn't yet put her finger on it.

Riley said, "I haven't been told your name."

The woman crossed her arms and leaned back on a cushion.

She said, "Tisha Harter, formerly Brown."

Then with a grin she added, "Or *née* Brown, to put it properly. I always think it's kind of a funny word, *née*. Like the sound a horse makes. Of course, I know it's French for 'born.' I know some French, learned it on my own, no help from anybody. Also some Italian and Spanish."

Her grin widened as she said, *"¿Atraparon ustedes al asesino?"*

Riley's own Spanish was fairly good, partly due to having Gabriela in the house. She knew that Tisha Harter was asking if they'd caught the killer.

"Todavía no," Riley said. Not yet.

Tisha shrugged and said, "Well, it's like I keep telling everybody—*I* didn't do it."

She sat there looking from one face to the other, as if she couldn't imagine what else there might be to say about the matter.

Riley pointed to her bandaged hand and said, "Do you mind telling me how that happened?"

With a defensive look, Tisha tried to tuck her hand under her other arm.

"Yeah, I kind of do mind," she said. "Why do you want to know?"

Riley said nothing, just waited for Tisha to say something more.

Tisha said, "I'm clumsy. I tripped and fell."

Riley glanced over the young woman's taut, athletic body.

"You're not clumsy," Riley said.

Tisha's eyes narrowed, showing a flash of anger.

"What are you accusing me of?" she asked.

"Who said I'm accusing you of anything?" Riley said.

The woman locked eyes with Riley, as if to test which of them would blink first.

I can play that game, Riley thought, returning her gaze steadily.

The truth was, Riley didn't need to be told what had happened to Tisha Harter's hand.

Judging from the way it was bandaged, her pinky finger was

broken. And Riley had no doubt that her late husband had inflicted this injury. What intrigued Riley at the moment was Tisha's defensiveness about it. Riley was used to abused women who, for one reason or another, tried to cover or apologize for their husbands' cruelty. But something different was going on here.

Tisha Harter didn't want to admit that someone else had hurt her, either physically or emotionally. She wanted the world to think that she was much too tough for that.

And Riley sensed that her toughness was very, very real.

Again, Riley had a strange, uncomfortable feeling about this young widow, as if she were somehow familiar, someone she'd met before.

Riley continued to hold the woman's determined gaze, and for a long moment neither of them flinched.

Finally Tisha averted her eyes, looking a bit ashamed at being the first to break eye contact.

She said, "I can pretty much prove I was right here last night when it happened."

She pointed to security cameras in the corners of the recreation room and added, "Just check the security tapes. You'll see."

Chief O'Neill was just sitting there taking in all the comments. He'd had nothing to say, but suddenly Jared Ruhl spoke up.

"Do you have any idea who might want to kill your husband?"

Riley bristled a little, hoping Ruhl wouldn't say something tactless, but decided not to shush him.

The woman smirked and said to Jared, "Aside from me, you mean? Because I'm not going to lie to you, I really didn't like the bastard."

Riley could see Ruhl's eyes sparkle with interest.

He asked, "Are you going to benefit from his death?"

Tisha let out a sharp, short laugh.

"Oh, you bet I am. I'm going to inherit every last thing he owned. I'm not stupid, I knew how to handle him the minute I met him. And I always come out on top."

Tisha kept on talking, bragging to Ruhl about her resourcefulness. As Riley half-listened, those words echoed in her mind …

"I always come out on top."

With a slight shudder, Riley realized who Tisha reminded her of.

It was her own adopted daughter, Jilly.

The resemblance wasn't physical—Jilly was dark, while this

woman was a pale blonde.

The likeness ran much deeper than mere appearance.

Again Riley flashed back to that shocking night when she'd discovered Jilly in the cab of a truck, ready and willing to sell her body rather than go back to her abusive father.

If Riley hadn't shown up, what would have become of Jilly?

She'd have survived, Riley thought. *She's too tough not to survive.*

But what kind of life would she have gone on to live? Riley had tried not to think about it, but sometimes she couldn't help it.

If Jilly really had become a prostitute, Riley knew that drugs, violence, and disease would have taken their inevitable toll—as would the psychic scarring that came with such a life.

Jilly might have survived in the short run, but she would have lived a short and ugly life.

But now, as Riley watched and listened to this young woman, a different scenario began to unfold in her mind—one that really hadn't occurred to her before.

It was easy to guess at least some of the details of Tisha's life story.

Like Jilly, Tisha had surely suffered an abusive childhood, perhaps at the hands of her father. Maybe, as a young teenager, she had even tried her hand at prostitution. She'd also probably gotten caught up in other criminal activities of one kind or another.

But one day something had changed. Perhaps she'd looked in the mirror and realized how pretty she was—or at least how pretty she could be if she made some changes.

Also like Jilly, Tisha had always been smart, a quick learner. She'd given herself a crash course in making herself attractive to rich men. Although she'd surely dropped out of school and couldn't dream of going to college, she must have read lots of books to acquire knowledge and sophistication, and she'd found it easy to learn different languages. And she'd observed people carefully.

She'd found it easy to move in affluent circles and finally to catch the attention of a rich, elderly man like Edwin Gray Harter. As soon as she'd married him, she'd laid claim to his fortune, probably to the horror of his closest family members, especially his offspring.

Once Tisha had done that, Edwin Gray Harter couldn't die soon enough for her purposes.

Riley felt a deep chill at the thought that Jilly could well have wound up just like this tough, smart, but deeply bitter young woman who no longer could even imagine what it might be like to be happy or loved.

While Riley was thinking all this, Tisha had kept chattering boastfully about her hopes for her future now that she was a rich widow. Jared was listening with obvious distaste, but perhaps a touch of fascination too.

Then Riley noticed someone else entering the room. It was a tall, imposing woman wearing an expensive black pantsuit and a bowtie.

Riley asked Chief O'Neill, "Who is that?"

"I'll introduce you," O'Neill said.

Riley, Jared, and the chief got up and walked over to the woman, who stood firmly in the doorway with crossed arms and a haughty expression. She appeared to be in her thirties, and she projected an air of infallible authority.

O'Neill introduced Riley and then said, "This is Vivian Bettridge, and she's the chief, uh, butler here."

Bettridge stared at him and snapped disdainfully, "I believe I told you—my proper title is majordomo."

Riley was not at all surprised to hear the woman speak in an English accent. She'd struck Riley as British from the very first glance.

She continued speaking to Riley in a cold, efficient tone. "I am—or rather was—Mr. Harter's most trusted servant. I am completely in charge of the household—the staff, the finances, the day-to-day affairs."

Jared said, "Then perhaps you can explain what happened last night."

Bettridge's eyebrows rose sharply as she glared at Jared.

"I'm sure that I cannot," she said. "I believe that's the police's job."

Turning to Riley she added, "And the FBI's job too."

Riley detected a note of defensiveness in her voice. Riley guessed that Bettridge cared little about Harter's actual murder. All that mattered to her was that she not be blamed for letting it happen. Her professional reputation was at stake—and she didn't value anything in the world more than that.

Unless ...

Riley couldn't discount the possibility that Bettridge was the one person who really knew what had happened.

Riley turned to Chief O'Neill and asked, "What about the rest of the live-in staff?"

Chief O'Neill said, "I've had my people interviewing them since we got here."

Bettridge said, "And as I told you earlier, I hardly think that's necessary. I can assure you that nobody under my authority would ever have dreamed of doing such a thing."

Riley tilted her head with interest.

She said, "Then I take it nobody on the staff *disliked* Mr. Harter?"

Bettridge's lips curled into a supercilious smirk.

"What an odd sort of word to use, Agent Paige. To like or dislike—they're entirely irrelevant to the work we're all here to do. Every single one of my people is of impeccable integrity. I handpicked them all myself. We do our work and do it perfectly—nothing more and nothing less. The household functions like a well-oiled machine."

With a disdainful grunt, Jared said, "Well, *something* didn't seem to be functioning quite so perfectly last night."

Bettridge's expression darkened.

She said, "As I said—I believe it's your job to determine whatever that was."

Riley studied her face silently for a moment. The woman was so emotionally closed off, it was hard for even Riley to read her. She was also exercising textbook passive-aggressive behavior by shunting away all responsibility onto the police and the FBI.

Then she asked, "What about the security system?"

"It's the very best, completely state of the art."

"Unhackable?" Riley asked.

"I should think so," Bettridge said. "I researched it thoroughly, compared it with everything else on the market. It's called SafetyLinks. Perhaps you've heard of it."

Riley hadn't heard of it, but she didn't say so.

"And now, if you don't mind," Bettridge said, "I'd like to go see my staff. This has been rather an ordeal for them, as you can imagine."

Without waiting for permission, Bettridge headed toward the elevator.

Jared grunted again and said, "Well, isn't she a charmer?"

Riley turned to Chief O'Neill and said, "I want to meet with your whole team downstairs in five minutes."

O'Neill nodded and headed back into the bathroom.

"So what do we do now?" Jared asked.

"Give me a moment alone to think," Riley said.

Jared followed after Chief O'Neill.

Riley's head buzzed with ideas and suspicions.

She was especially curious about this supposedly unhackable, state-of-the-art security system.

And she knew just who to call for information about it.

She took out her cell phone and punched in a number.

CHAPTER NINETEEN

After a couple of rings Riley heard Van Roff's gruff voice answer the phone.

"Hey, Agent Paige. What's up? I take it you're in a sunny little golf-obsessed town in Georgia. Or more precisely, at the mansion of one late Edwin Gray Harter."

Riley was startled.

"How did you know?" she asked.

"Oh, I never give away the secrets of my trade."

Riley thought for a moment, then smiled as she remembered how Jared had found out about Harter's murder.

She asked, "Might it have something to do with a certain online service called CrimeWidth?"

She heard Van Roff gasp a little.

He said, "Uh … how did you guess?"

Riley laughed and said, "I never give away the secrets of my trade. Now don't tell me … you listen to CrimeWidth when you have trouble sleeping."

"OK, now you're just doing some spooky mind-reading number on me."

"Yeah, well, I'm known for that kind of thing."

Roff laughed and said, "When I heard on the alert feed about some rich dude getting knifed to death in Monarch, Georgia, of course I thought, 'Hmmm … same MO, probably the same killer. I'll bet Agent Paige is on her way to the crime scene right now.'"

"You'd have won that bet," Riley said.

In a husky growl Roff said, "I don't guess you called me directly from a crime scene because you adore the sound of my voice."

"Well, of course you *do* have such a lovely voice, but …"

Riley paused and thought for a moment.

"Our killer seems to have a pretty nimble way of getting around security. This time he got into the mansion despite a supposedly unhackable system called SafetyLinks. I wondered what you might be able to tell me about it."

Roff was silent for a moment.

Then he said, "I'll tell you what, let me get back to you about that."

He ended the call without saying another word.

Riley stood staring at her phone for a moment, feeling a little mystified. This didn't seem like Van Roff at all. She figured his knowledge of high-tech devices of all kinds was pretty much encyclopedic. Hadn't he ever heard of SafetyLinks?

She realized there was no point in just standing here waiting for the Seattle geek to get back to her. She hoped he'd come up with something useful soon.

Meanwhile, she had asked Chief O'Neill and his team to meet downstairs. It was time for her to join them.

Riley took the elevator down to the ground floor and found O'Neill and his people gathered together in the huge, pristine formal living room. Jared was there too. She wished they'd chosen some smaller sitting area elsewhere in the house, but everybody was already here, waiting for her. She couldn't help but feel a little amused to see uniformed officers trying to make themselves at home on snow-white furniture that looked like it had never been used.

Everybody looked distinctly uncomfortable.

Riley herself stayed on her feet. She said to Chief O'Neill and the group, "Does anybody here have any new observations or theories?"

O'Neill got to his feet. "Three of my people talked to the whole live-in staff, and I met with them all briefly. The place has got servants, cooks, maintenance people, and even medical personnel. They all had alibis, and most claimed to have been in their rooms when the murder happened. But they're edgy, and some of them are acting kind of odd."

Riley didn't say so, but the fact that they were "acting kind of odd" didn't especially surprise her. They were surely scared—partly from being close by when a murder took place, partly from being under suspicion themselves.

O'Neill hesitated for a moment, then said, "We're going to need some technicians to look at the security tapes, check on everybody's comings and goings. But I've got a weird feeling about everyone in this place—including the wife, and also that Bettridge woman—the butler or major-general or whatever she calls herself."

"Majordomo," Jared said.

"Right. This might sound weird but … nobody here strikes me as exactly innocent. I think this must have been some kind of inside job. Someone in this house is a killer, or at least someone inside let somebody from the outside get in unseen."

Riley was interested but skeptical.

"Explain," Riley said.

O'Neill paused again, then said, "This house seems to have ironclad security—at least everywhere except the third floor. I don't see how anyone could have broken through it from the outside. It would take someone who knew the system—and that would almost have to be someone who lived and worked here."

Riley's doubts were only increasing. But she'd learned from experience how to deal with local cops who weren't enamored of the FBI. It was best to hear them out as fully as possible.

O'Neill continued, "My theory is that more than one member of the staff was involved. Maybe it was some kind of team or conspiracy or something. Edwin Gray Harter sure didn't have any friends in this house."

Then Riley said, "You might be forgetting that two other men were killed in two other locations, apparently by the same killer."

"Or maybe *killers*," O'Neill said, starting to sound a bit defensive now.

One of O'Neill's cops nodded in agreement and said, "We haven't had a chance to run down where everyone in the staff was when the other men were killed. We've got some work to do there."

While O'Neill and the cop talked this over, Riley wondered …

Does any of this make sense?

It was partly a question of security systems. She still didn't know anything about the system in this house. She did know that security hadn't been a problem for whoever had killed Julian Morse. Just cutting the wires was all it took to disconnect the cameras around his swimming pool—it hadn't taken any hacking skills to accomplish that. And the truth was, she had no idea how difficult it might or might not have been to crack through Andrew Farrell's system.

She did have some personal experience with this kind of thing. Just last winter, the security system in her own townhouse had been disengaged by a man who then attacked April, Gabriela, and Blaine. She had put in a new system after that, but was still wary that it might not be impossible to breach.

She wished Van Roff would get back to her about SafetyLinks, and just how sophisticated it was. It still seemed strange to her that he'd ended their call so abruptly.

Meanwhile, she had to admit it wasn't impossible that one or more of the people in this house were involved in all three of the murders, but even so …

It seems like a stretch.

So far, no connections of any kind had turned up between the victims, their families, their employees, or their businesses.

Finally Chief O'Neill spoke to Riley directly …

"Look, Agent Paige, as far as I'm concerned, every single person who was in the house last night—including the wife—is a plausible suspect. We can check them all out, but that's going to take some time. Meanwhile every single one of them is a flight risk. I think we need to take all of them into custody."

Riley could hardly believe her ears.

She didn't yet know how large the household staff was, but rounding them all up and arresting them struck her as absurd. She could see by Jared's expression that he felt the same way.

She was on the verge of saying so when a synthesized female voice filled the room.

"Nobody move. The place is surrounded."

CHAPTER TWENTY

At the sound of the voice, Riley felt a sharp jolt of shock. Like everyone around her, she froze in place.

Then Vivian Bettridge charged into the room, her British composure completely gone.

"Could somebody tell me just what the hell is happening?" she yelled.

Everybody else broke into a clamor of explanations.

"What?"

"Who?"

Riley smiled as she began to realize what had happened.

When her phone buzzed and she took the call, she wasn't the least bit surprised to hear Van Roff's gravelly voice.

"SafetyLinks is hackable."

"And you just proved it," Riley replied.

"I did."

Riley said, "Could I put you on speakerphone so you can reassure my law enforcement colleagues? They're a little bit shaken up."

Van Roff laughed heartily.

"Sure, let me talk to them."

It took a moment for Riley to get the attention of the rest of the people in the room. When she finally overrode their exchanges of indignation and questions, she explained just who she had on the phone—an FBI technical wizard based in Seattle.

Then Van Roff spoke to all of them. "Folks, there's no cause for alarm. I just hacked the house's SafetyLinks security system. Of course I'm a genius, but believe me, it didn't take any brilliance to do it. In fact, as I poked around the system I found out something interesting in its records. Someone else hacked in last night and disabled it for a short time—someone outside the house, like me."

Riley couldn't help but grin at Bettridge.

She said, "So much for your thoroughly researched, state-of-the-art security system."

Bettridge's face reddened and she glared down at the floor.

Riley said to Roff, "Can you give me an estimate of what time the system was hacked?"

Roff let out a rumbling chuckle.

"An estimate? No, but I can tell you *exactly,* if that's OK. It was shut down at eleven fifteen p.m., then started again at eleven forty-five."

Riley saw Chief O'Neill's eyes widen.

Of course she knew what he was thinking.

Riley and the ME had determined the time of death to be about 11:30.

The security shutdown had given the killer enough time to get in, commit the murder, then get out again, restarting the security system in hopes that no one would notice that it had ever been shut down. And they might very well have gotten away with it.

Riley said to Roff, "Thanks, Van. You've been a great help."

Roff laughed again and said, "Don't mention it. It's always a pleasure getting to do some electronic breaking and entering."

The call ended, and Riley said to O'Neill, "Still want to stick by your theory that this was an inside job?"

Looking thoroughly abashed, O'Neill shook his head.

He said, "I'm obviously out of my depth here. The FBI is welcome to this one."

Riley was startled. She'd almost forgotten that Jared had told O'Neill over the phone that this was an FBI case—and that she'd let O'Neill go right on believing that.

A bit abashed herself now, she said to O'Neill, "Uh, could we talk privately for a moment?"

O'Neill looked surprised, but he willingly accompanied Riley to the adjoining hallway.

Riley said to him quietly, "The truth is, this isn't yet an FBI case—not officially, anyway."

O'Neill looked genuinely puzzled now.

"Then what are you doing here?" he asked.

Riley stifled a sigh. It wasn't easy to explain, but she did the best she could, and tried to be reasonably honest about it. She told O'Neill about how Morgan Farrell had called her after her husband's murder, then how she'd come to Atlanta after she'd heard from Jared Ruhl. She explained how Ruhl had noticed the similarity of Farrell's killing to the earlier murder of Julian Morse in Birmingham. Finally she told O'Neill how they'd found out about this morning's murder and had come straight here.

Riley wasn't surprised to see a look of dismay on O'Neill's face.

He said, "You weren't exactly on the up and up with me, were you?"

"No, and I'm sorry," Riley said. "I was just doing the best I could and following my own instincts."

O'Neill shook head. "Well, you've got good instincts, I'll give you that. What do we have to do to make this official?"

"You've got to call Quantico and ask for the FBI's help," Riley said.

She gave him the direct number to Brent Meredith's office, and he stepped away to make the call.

Riley felt relieved that detail would finally be taken care of. She could investigate officially, and she could get some help.

As O'Neill talked with Meredith, she began to process what she had just learned. She'd already known from how the killer had entered Julian Morse's property that he was physically agile and technically savvy enough to know which wires to cut to deactivate the security cameras. But now she knew that he was more than just savvy. She didn't think many people would be able to crack a system like the one in this house.

But that wasn't even the worst of it.

Above all else, he was ruthless and bloodthirsty.

And he had left no clue to *why* he was killing these particular men in such an especially brutal way.

Soon O'Neill came back and handed her his phone.

"He says he wants to talk to you," he said.

Riley was hardly surprised. She put the phone to her ear and heard the distinct rumble of Chief Meredith's voice.

"Agent Paige, I'm assigning you to an official FBI case involving three murders in the states of Georgia and Alabama."

Then he added with a note of irony in his voice, "Do I need to fill you in on any details?"

"No, not really," Riley said.

After all, she already knew much, much more about the murders than Meredith did—the reverse of the usual situation when he assigned her to a case.

Meredith made a scoffing sound, then said, "I'll get in touch with the authorities in Birmingham and Atlanta to let them know you're on the job. Meanwhile, what kind of help do you need to get started?"

"I could use a partner or two," Riley said. "Agents Jeffreys and Roston if they're available."

"Roston is working on another case," Meredith said. "But Jeffreys is right here in his office. I'll put him on it. I hear that you're near Atlanta. Jeffreys could fly right in to Hartsfield-Jackson

Airport, but the air traffic there always makes that complicated. I believe there's a small airfield just north of the city that we've used before—the Simon Tanner Airport, I think it's called. I'll tell him you'll meet him there."

Meredith ended the call, and Riley and Chief O'Neill rejoined the group in the living room. Riley gave instructions to the cops, and also to the residents of the mansion, telling them not to go anywhere for the time being and to stay available for questioning.

When she finally told everybody that she had to go meet her partner's plane, she noticed Jared Ruhl looking at her with a rather pleading expression that seemed to say …

"What about me?"

As helpful as Jared had been so far, Riley wanted to be free of him for at least a little while. But she didn't want to hurt his feelings.

She pointed to Jared and said to Chief O'Neill, "I'm leaving Officer Ruhl here to work with you. He's got as much expertise on this case as anybody else. You'll find him most helpful."

Riley was relieved to see Ruhl's face break into a smile at her flattering observation.

That'll keep him happy for a while, she thought.

The meeting broke up, and Riley headed to her rented car and called for GPS instructions to the Simon Tanner Airport. As she started to drive, she breathed a little easier knowing she'd soon be working with Bill again. She knew Bill kept his go-bag in his office, and he might well be boarding the FBI plane at that very moment. She'd be seeing him in just a couple of hours.

At the same time, Riley couldn't help but worry.

They had no description of the killer they were looking for. They didn't know whether he was settling personal issues or had a general hatred of extremely wealthy men.

This killer seemed to be tightening up the timeframe for his murders and they had no way to guess where he might strike next.

How could she know where to even start looking for him?

CHAPTER TWENTY ONE

When Bill emerged from the small BAU plane, Riley could hardly believe how happy she was to see his broad, strong, hearty face. As he came down the steps, carrying his go-bag and looking ready for action, she dashed forward to greet him.

As soon as his feet touched the tarmac, she gave him a big hug.

Bill laughed and said, "Hey, you act like we haven't seen each other in ages. It hasn't been that long."

"It seems like months," Riley said, leading him to the rented car. "Things have been really crazy here for the last day or so."

Bill looked around and asked, "Is it always this hot here?"

Riley remembered that the weather back in Virginia was milder. And of course, Bill was getting a blast of the heat after a couple of hours in air-conditioned comfort.

"Hot and humid," she replied. "And that pretty much describes the case too. It's a messy one."

Bill laughed again as he loaded his bag into the car.

"Yeah, from what Meredith told me, I'd kind of guessed that. So you went rogue again, did you? You should have called for my help."

"No, I shouldn't have," Riley said, thinking again of how she'd only have gotten Bill in trouble along with herself. "But I'm glad you're here now. And on a legitimate basis, too."

"I hope I can help," Bill said. "Believe me, the pressure's on back in Quantico."

Riley sighed and said, "Don't tell me—Carl Walder's on a tear about this."

Bill said, "Yeah, you know how he gets when rich and important guys get killed."

Riley certainly did know how he got. The incompetent, baby-faced Special Agent In Charge had always been a thorn in her side. He'd suspended and even fired her on more than one occasion. The fact that he'd always had to relent and put her back on the BAU team hadn't made him any happier.

As they climbed into the car, Bill continued, "Walder's heard of all three of the victims—even used to play golf with one of them, I can't remember which. He wants the case solved soon—preferably yesterday. He's threatening to send more BAU agents if

110

we don't get something fast."

"I just hope he doesn't come down himself," Riley said, starting the car engine.

Bill said, "So where are we off to now?"

"To the Atlanta police station. I need to check in with the police chief there. Just don't expect him to be very happy to see me."

As she drove, Riley filled Bill in on all that had happened during the last day and a half. Then they started tossing ideas back and forth. When Bill asked if any of the three widows had mentioned anything about their birth families, Riley realized that they hadn't told her anything of the kind. The idea surprised her.

"It's not so surprising," Bill said. "There's a certain kind of rich guy who doesn't marry for connections, just for control. They'd never choose a wife whose family might play any part in their lives. They also like knowing that their wives have nothing to go back to."

What Bill was saying made sense to Riley. The three widows she'd met had been strikingly different in their personalities, but they'd had one thing in common. They'd seemed strangely lost and rootless.

Bill added, "Of course, the wives make that bargain with their eyes wide open. They wind up financially better off than most people, probably better off than they've ever been in their lives. It's a trade-off."

"It doesn't sound like a very good trade-off to me," Riley said. "It makes me feel grateful to have a family to go home to."

Riley realized she also felt grateful to be exchanging thoughts with Bill again.

They pulled up to the police station and went inside, heading straight for Chief Stiles's office.

The chief rose from his desk, looking frustrated and perplexed as Riley introduced him to Bill.

He said, "I swear to God, you Feds have got me fit to be tied. I don't know what to believe anymore. First you come in here saying you want to talk to an incarcerated suspect about God-knows-what, and when I call your boss to find out what it's all about, he hems and haws and gets all vague about whatever is happening. Then this morning he calls me and tells me that the suspect I'm holding has been cleared and I've got to let her go, and he also says I'm now part of an FBI case involving three murders. What next?"

That's a good question, Riley thought. She wished she had

some idea herself.

She said, "Have you still got Morgan Farrell in custody?"

"You got here just in time," Chief Stiles said. "Now that she's cleared, her lawyer's here sorting things out with her. She'll likely be leaving any minute. Come with me."

Riley felt apprehensive as Stiles led her and Bill down the hall. After all, her last conversation with Morgan Farrell hadn't ended well.

She remembered the woman telling her in a bitter tone …

"Really, Agent Paige, this isn't kind of you."

Will things be better this time? Riley wondered.

Meanwhile, she had another question on her mind.

She asked Stiles, "How did Andrew Farrell's killer get into his house?"

"He hacked the security system," Stiles said. "Sounds like a pretty smart bastard."

Smart—and deadly, Riley thought.

Stiles escorted Riley and Bill into a conference room. Sitting at a large table were Morgan and her lawyer, a middle-aged man with receding hair and a double chin.

Stiles introduced Riley and Bill to the lawyer, Chet Morris. Riley remembered his name from talking to him on the phone yesterday. The call hadn't exactly been cordial.

Riley glared at him coldly and said, "I believe we're already acquainted."

"Somewhat," Morris said. "We talked a little yesterday, didn't we?"

"Yeah," Riley said. "I called to tell you that your client was probably innocent."

She managed to stop herself from adding …

"You didn't listen. You didn't even seem to care."

With a phony smile, Morris said, "Well, as it turns out you were right. I suppose I should thank you for the heads-up."

Riley asked, "May we sit down?"

Morris was obviously about to say no when Morgan spoke up.

"Oh, please do. I'm … well, this is all very strange."

Riley and Bill sat down at the table with them.

Riley looked at Morgan more carefully now. Instead of the orange jumpsuit, she was wearing slacks, a nice shirt, and some sandals—clothes that somebody must have brought her from home. Even so, she didn't appear ready to return to any kind of normal life. The circles beneath her eyes were dark and she still seemed weak and confused. Riley guessed that the woman still hadn't gotten any sleep to speak of, and she might not have eaten anything at all during the whole time she'd spent in jail. Her expression at the moment was one of numb perplexity.

Chet Morris peered over his reading glasses at a sheaf of legal papers and spoke to Morgan.

"As I was saying, your husband's mansion is now the property of his sons—Hugh, Sheldon, and Wayne Farrell. According to your husband's will, certain investment accounts will be transferred to you. You will be supported nicely …"

As Morris went into details about the accounts, Riley noticed that Bill was staring at the man with distaste.

Riley knew how he felt. She felt the same way.

Instead of coming here simply to get his client out of jail, Morris was taking this opportunity to tell her that the life she'd known and had become accustomed to was over. He was clearly eager to get this whole thing over with.

The cruelty was simply staggering.

But Riley understood the situation better than Bill could. She hadn't had a chance to explain the ugly tangle of connections—how Chet Morris worked for the same law firm that represented the murder victim, how he had even worked personally for Farrell, and how the DA himself had once been part of that firm. She hadn't yet told her partner that this lawyer had completely ignored the possibility that his client was innocent of murder.

Riley wouldn't be surprised if Morris was actually disappointed to learn that his client was innocent. It was probably quite inconvenient for him.

Riley didn't know much about law, but she couldn't believe all this was legitimate.

But she reminded herself that neither she nor Bill was here to protect Morgan Farrell from the web of legal manipulations that had been woven around her.

We're here to solve a murder case.

Chet Morris finished going over the financial information and moved on to another topic.

"I've got good news," he said to Morgan. "Your husband's sons are concerned about your current problems with alcohol and tranquilizers. So they've generously acquired accommodations for you at the Haverhill Dependency Center, an excellent facility just outside of Atlanta. They've even paid for your first six months there."

"What happens after that?" Morgan asked in a dull, apathetic voice.

Morris said, "Well, if you want to stay there, you should be able to meet your expenses with returns from the investment funds you've inherited. If not, you can do as you like."

Morgan said, "In other words, I'll be on my own after six months."

Morris shrugged and said, "Well, if you choose to look at it that way."

Riley wondered …

What other way is there to look at it?

She tried to tell herself that the money Morgan would be getting would probably be enough to allow her to live comfortably—possibly a lot more money than Riley herself would ever see.

But does she deserve to hear about it like this? Riley wondered.

Apparently finished with his business, Chet Morris started putting things in his briefcase.

He said, "If you'd like, I'll drive you directly to Haverhill right now."

Morgan seemed to think it over for a moment.

Then she said, "Am I absolutely forbidden to set foot in my home … their home … right now?"

Wincing a little, Morris said, "Certainly not."

"Well, then," Morgan said. "I'd like to stop by there, at least. Some of the things inside, my clothes I mean, actually *do* belong to me. At least I believe they do. I don't think that my … um, previous stepsons would actually want them. I'd like to pick a few things up."

The lawyer sputtered, "Certainly, my dear. No one is going to prevent your taking your personal belongings. In fact, I'll take you there right now."

"No, you needn't trouble yourself," Morgan said.

Then to Riley's surprise, Morgan turned to her and said, "Agent Paige, would you please take me there?"

"Of course," Riley said.

Morris hastily handed Riley a folder and said, "Well, perhaps you'll be so kind as to take Ms. Farrell to Haverhill afterwards. These papers will be all she needs check in."

The meeting ended, and Morris left the room. As Riley, Bill, and Morgan walked out into the hallway, Morgan said to Riley, "Thank you so much. I didn't think I could stand being around that awful man for another minute."

"Me neither," Bill growled, his face red with rage.

Riley realized that her partner was well aware that Chet Morris didn't have the best interests of his client at heart. She figured it was lucky that Bill hadn't taken a punch at the lawyer.

Riley had felt more than a little tempted to do so herself.

But she was glad that Morgan had made this choice. It would give her and Bill the chance to get a look at the scene of the second murder.

Morgan didn't have any belongings to pick up in the property room, so Riley and Bill accompanied her straight out of the building.

Morgan gasped and squinted when they stepped out of the cool interior into the hot, sunny day. But she didn't look fazed by the heat. She looked as though she suddenly understood something.

In a hushed, amazed voice she said …

"I'm free. And I'm innocent."

Riley realized Morgan had just grasped that fact for the first time.

As the three of them walked toward the car, Riley thought about the real killer.

He was out there somewhere, enjoying the same freedom, breathing the same air, looking at the same sunlight, and he was getting ready to kill again …

Unless we find him and stop him.

CHAPTER TWENTY TWO

Riley felt an unpleasant twinge of déjà vu as she stopped the car in front of the Farrell mansion. The last time she'd been here was to interview Andrew Farrell himself. It hadn't been an enjoyable experience.

And now he's dead, Riley reminded herself.

"I'd forgotten how big this place is," Bill commented, gazing at the building's impressive arches and columns.

"You can just park the car here in the drive," Morgan said from the back seat. She sounded tired, as though she'd lost the enthusiasm she'd displayed outside the jail.

At the front door, they were greeted by a tall, lean butler. Riley vaguely remembered him from when she'd been here in February. He'd been cold and officious back then, but now a warm smile spread across his face.

He took Morgan by the hand. "I'm so pleased to see you, madam. I was afraid you might not be coming here again."

"It's good to see you too, Maurice," Morgan said, giving him a small kiss on the cheek.

Maurice said, "I want you to know—I never for a moment believed that you were guilty of … you know."

Morgan chuckled softly.

"How odd," she said. "I was quite sure I was guilty."

Then with a glance at Riley, she added, "Luckily for me, others knew better."

She turned again to Maurice and said, "I won't be here long. I've just come by to pick up a few things."

Maurice's expression saddened, but he didn't look surprised.

He said to her, "I'm afraid you'll find things here to be in a … well, disagreeable state."

He led Riley, Bill, and Morgan into the massive entry room with marble floors and a broad, red-carpeted staircase. The room was chaotic, with servants coming and going with boxes and various belongings.

Huddled near the servant's path were three men poring over a list. Riley knew who they must be—Andrew Farrell's three sons. She remembered their father's chiseled, aristocratic features, and his supercilious expression. The resemblance of these men to their father was unmistakable, even though their faces were weak and characterless by comparison. They all had the same unkind, selfish expression.

Meanness runs in the family, Riley thought.

When Maurice announced the arrival of the visitors, the men looked up from their list at Morgan. Their lips twisted into contemptuous smirks. They didn't say a word to her.

Morgan stopped and smiled bravely. She told Bill and Riley, "These are my husband's three boys—Hugh, Sheldon, and Wayne."

Then she said to the sons in a cheerful voice, "Don't let me trouble you. I'm here to pick up just a few things. Don't worry, I won't steal anything that's not mine. You can check when I leave. Happy pillaging!"

Although all three hastily returned to their lists, Riley could swear she could hear at least one of them snickering in gloating contempt.

When she, Bill, and Morgan reached the hallway at the top of the stairs, Riley said cautiously to the widow …

"I know this is difficult—but my partner and I need to have a look at the crime scene."

Morgan's brave smile disappeared and she appeared to be gathering her strength.

"Of course," she said. "I'll take you there."

They walked past double doors that Riley knew led into Andrew Farrell's office. She'd interviewed him in there back in February.

She shuddered as she remembered how he'd boasted about cruelly provoking his youngest son to commit suicide by shooting himself in that very office, right in front of him. He hadn't been guilty of actual murder, but Riley had known real murderers who were less evil than Andrew Farrell.

Such a terrible man, she thought.

And from what Riley knew, the other victims, Julian Morse and Edwin Gray Harter, had been terrible men as well.

It was one thing they shared in common—aside from being very rich.

It felt a little strange to be seeking justice for three men she felt no sympathy for.

Morgan opened a door and led them into a sitting room, and from there into a huge bedroom. Riley saw right away that there was no hint that a crime had ever been committed here. Everything was sparkling, clean, and tidy.

Just then Riley felt Morgan's hand on her shoulder. Then Morgan's whole body began to slump against hers.

She's about to faint, Riley realized.

"Help me with her," Riley said to Bill.

They each took hold of one of Morgan's arms and led her back into the sitting room. They helped her to a chair, where they had her sit and put her head down.

Morgan murmured in a whimper, "I must have done it. If not me, then who … ?"

Riley murmured back, "You're innocent, Morgan. You didn't kill anybody."

Noticing the confused look on Bill's face, Riley whispered to him, "She's flashing back to the murder. She's still trying to grasp the fact that she's innocent."

Bill nodded.

Riley and Bill stood in front of Morgan for a few moments until she was strong enough to lift her head.

"I'm sorry," she said. "I don't think … I can't go in there."

"You don't have to," Riley said.

A short silence fell.

Then Morgan said, "I still want to get some of my things."

As she rose shakily to her feet, Riley took her arm again.

"I'll go with you," Riley said.

"You don't have to," Morgan said.

Yes, I do, Riley thought.

The woman was obviously too fragile to go anywhere in this house alone.

Bill said to Riley, "Go ahead. I'll take care of things here."

Riley wished she could stay and examine the crime scene with Bill. But she knew that he was as likely to uncover any evidence as she was.

She helped the still-shaky Morgan get up and go back into the hallway. They continued down the wide hall and around a corner to Morgan's own rooms.

*

Bill stood looking around the master bedroom for a few moments. The space was vast, and everything in it was gold and white, including the curtains draped around a huge canopied bed.

So that's where the man died, he thought. *Stabbed to death among his silken sheets and pillows.*

118

As he looked around the room, Bill began to feel an uncomfortable sensation in his stomach. He knew it wasn't because a murder had taken place here. He'd seen far too many crime scenes to be fazed by that.

Instead, it was a sense of disgust at the idea that anyone had ever lived here—had actually *slept* here.

No actual flesh-and-blood human being, anyway, Bill thought.

Like the rest of the house, the bedroom struck Bill as a setting where only some kind of automaton, an elaborate wind-up replica of a person, could really belong.

What kind of guy would ever feel comfortable here? he wondered.

How could he get any sleep?

The décor gave Bill a distinct hint about Andrew Farrell's personality.

Sleep wasn't what this room was all about. Comfort wasn't even what this whole house was all about.

The point was to be surrounded by as much proof of wealth as possible. For a man like this, ostentation substituted for comfort.

From what Bill had learned about the case so far, he thought Andrew Farrell probably didn't sleep much anyhow.

And apparently he didn't let the people who were closest to him get much sleep either.

He liked to keep people awake, exhausted, and off-balance.

As Bill walked farther into the room, he asked himself …

What exactly am I looking for?

Of course, he was sure he'd know it when he found it.

Although the police had surely examined the room carefully right after the murder, he knew that local cops often missed something—some sort of clue that a seasoned FBI agent like himself would pick up on.

He had a hunch that that was true right here and now …

All I've got to do is look.

*

Riley and Morgan continued on into Morgan's own private bedroom—a huge and luxurious room by Riley's standards, but noticeably smaller and more modest than Andrew Farrell's master suite. Like the rest of the house, the room was both fancy and impersonal, with everything arranged as if for a magazine photo.

Morgan seemed to have regained her resolve.

"The things I want are in here," she said, heading straight for a pair of doors. When Morgan swung the doors open, Riley almost gasped aloud.

The closet was a separate room by itself—as big as Riley's own bedroom. It was filled with a vast array of hanging outfits, and also with shelves, cabinets, and mirrors. In the center was a table with chairs.

Riley stood watching as Morgan began to finger various items of clothing.

Morgan said, "It's strange—to think that all this, at least, belongs to me. Until now, I'd always thought of everything in here as *his* property, as if I were only borrowing it. I guess that's because I always thought of *myself* as his property, just some sort of mannequin to show off all these wonderful clothes."

Riley's mind boggled at the sheer quantity of the wardrobe. But she understood what Morgan was telling her: a mannequin owns nothing. But now this woman who had played the mannequin role owned quite a lot of things.

She said, "Morgan, how are you going to move all of this? You'll need a van or a truck or …"

"Oh, no," Morgan said with a slight laugh. "I'll be selective. I don't want to take much. Andrew's sons can sell the rest of it off if they like. The truth is, I'll be glad to see the last of most of it. I always had to dress according to Andrew's taste, not my own, and there's not much here that I actually like. It'll be strange, though, deciding such things for myself again. I'd almost forgotten what that was like."

Morgan found a large wheeled suitcase and set it open on the table. As she started to put things into it, Riley gently asked her questions about her husband. Had he spent any time in Birmingham? Did he play golf in Monarch? Did Morgan know of any connection between Andrew and the other two victims?

Morgan brushed off all these questions and finally said …

"Honestly, why would you expect me to know anything about him? He never told me much, and the truth is, I never wanted to know much. I certainly never asked him a lot of questions. I tried to attract his attention as little as possible. My life was always better when he left me alone."

Morgan finished filling the suitcase with some of the simpler outfits, several jackets, and a few pairs of shoes. Then she walked over to a large safe and punched in the combination to open it.

Inside was an astonishing array of jewelry.

Morgan laughed aloud and said, "God, I can't believe I used to wear this stuff! So garish and vulgar! And Andrew always acted like he was being so generous for buying it for me, and I did my best to act grateful. Well, it *is* mine and it would sell for quick cash if I wind up needing it—enough to support me for a while."

Without even looking them over, she scooped up a handful of valuables and dropped them into a pocket of the suitcase. Riley's mind boggled at the thought of how much even that handful must be worth.

Enough to buy a house, I bet, she thought.

Morgan closed up the suitcase, then turned slowly around. Her expression was haunted as she gazed about the room.

Then she stood in front of a full-length mirror, looking at her reflection.

"It's over," she whispered to her reflection. "It's all over."

Riley sensed a world of ambivalent meaning in those words. A lot of things were over for Morgan Farrell—the tyranny of her terrible marriage, her husband's emotional and physical abuse, the duty to serve as his perfect toy, but also her life of luxury and security.

She was truly on her own now.

And Riley couldn't help but wonder …

Is she ready for this?

Does she even have any idea of how to live on her own?

Riley felt pretty sure that Morgan had lived a life of privilege for a long time. Her marriage had been just another chapter of all that. Now Morgan was leaving with quite a lot in the way of material goods—the returns from investment funds as well as the money the jewelry must be worth. Riley could imagine living the rest of her own life off that kind of money. Or at least sending her girls to a really good college.

But how well would Morgan manage?

Riley knew that Morgan had been a well-known model before her marriage. How easy would it be for her to get back into that scene if she wanted to? If she couldn't, how long would even a small fortune last her?

Riley's thoughts were interrupted by the sound of Bill's voice calling from the bedroom.

"Hey, Riley—are you in here somewhere?"

Riley could hear a note of excitement in his voice.

"Yeah," Riley called back. "Did you find anything?"

"I think so," Bill said. "Come have a look."

CHAPTER TWENTY THREE

Riley felt her heart quicken as she hurried out of the enormous closet to meet Bill. He was standing in the bedroom doorway, holding something in his hand.

"What have you got?" she asked.

"This," Bill said. "I checked the rest of the room, but it's been polished clean. No prints."

He handed her a simple ashtray made of blue-gray glass. In its bottom was the silver image of a man holding a spear in one raised hand. She recognized the Roman god Vulcan, but she was puzzled by the circle of scantily clad women dancing around the silver man.

"Where did you find it?" she asked.

"In plain sight," Bill said, smiling. "Sitting on a dresser right beside a Fabergé egg."

Morgan had come out of her wardrobe closet and was standing beside Riley. Her expression was puzzled as she looked at the object that Riley held.

"I don't understand," Morgan said. "Is this important?"

"Maybe so," Riley said to her.

"But it's just an ashtray," Morgan said.

Riley knew perfectly well why Bill had picked it up, but she let him explain.

"Precisely. Just an ordinary glass ashtray sitting next to a Fabergé egg and surrounded by all kinds of other expensive objects. Tell me, Ms. Farrell—was your husband the kind of man who'd normally keep something like this among a collection of priceless things?"

Morgan squinted at the ashtray. "Why, no," she replied. "Now that you mention it, I don't suppose so."

"Do you have any idea where it came from?" Riley asked.

"No. It isn't an antique and it doesn't look like any kind of collector's item. I suppose it could be from any ordinary store."

Riley couldn't picture either of the Farrells shopping at an "ordinary store." And yet, the ashtray was here, among their luxurious belongings. It was a thing of no value, except for whatever special significance it had to Andrew Farrell. Or to the killer. The thing wouldn't have been where Bill found it unless it meant something to somebody.

She wasn't surprised, though, that the police had apparently never noticed it. As far as they were concerned, this was just another object in a house full of objects.

She was glad Bill's keen eye had spotted the incongruity.

Bill said, "But there's nothing on it to say where it came from. No message. No trademark."

Riley pointed to the central image and said, "Well, I can tell you about him—that's a huge statue of Vulcan that stands on a hill in Birmingham."

Bill's eyes widened.

"Birmingham!" he said. "And the first murder was in Birmingham."

Riley asked Morgan, "Does this mean anything at all to you?"

Morgan shook her head silently. Riley noticed that she was slumping, and her face again showed that look of numb exhaustion.

Riley said to her, "Maybe we should get you out of here."

Morgan nodded and said, "Yes, if that's OK with you. I've got everything I need … everything I'll ever want from this place."

Bill wheeled her big suitcase out of the closet, and Morgan led them to the freight elevator. When they reached the first floor, they all made their way back through the front room. Andrew Farrell's sons were nowhere in sight. Riley guessed they were pillaging elsewhere in the mansion.

Maurice the butler hurried toward them, relieved Bill of the suitcase, and took it all the way out to the car for them.

Once the suitcase was loaded into the car, Riley pulled the glass ashtray out of her bag and showed it to him.

"Do you know what this is?" she asked.

The butler shook his head.

"My partner found it in the master bedroom."

With a haughty smirk, Maurice replied, "I can assure you, it was not part of the décor."

"But do you know where it came from?"

"I do not," Maurice snapped. Then he softened a bit. "The truth is that I very seldom went to … the master's quarters. No one was allowed to disturb anything there. Of course the day maids cleaned the room, but they have all been let go."

"All right," Riley said. "It's probably nothing. I'll get back in touch with you if I need to contact them."

Maurice gave a brief, courteous nod, and turned to Morgan. The two stood looking at each other awkwardly. Morgan stepped forward as if to give him another kiss on the cheek, but he waved her off. His lips were trembling, and Riley realized that the man was trying to keep from crying.

He shook Morgan's hand and managed to say, "Goodbye, madam. It's been an honor and a pleasure to serve you."

Morgan smiled and said to him, "I won't miss much about this place, Maurice. But I will miss you."

This comment seemed to be too much for the butler.

He choked back a sob as he nodded, then wheeled around and walked silently back to the house.

Bill got behind the wheel and started the car. Riley helped Morgan into the back seat, then got in front beside Bill. There was very little conversation in the car as they made their way through Atlanta to the Haverhill Dependency Center, just outside of the city.

When they arrived, Riley was surprised to see that the place looked like some kind of luxury resort, with several large houses nestled in an exquisitely maintained landscape.

The three of them went inside, Morgan carrying the folder her lawyer had given her and Bill pulling the wheeled suitcase. The lobby took Riley's breath away—a grand room with a high ceiling and huge windows framed by wood paneling. As Morgan got checked in, Riley picked up a brochure and browsed through it.

She could see that the treatments the place offered were all holistic, including yoga, meditation, hiking, acupuncture, Shiatsu massage, and others with exotic names Riley had never heard of. The kitchen offered the kind of gourmet menu that one might expect to find in an expensive restaurant. And of course, there was a swimming pool.

Trendy stuff, Riley thought.

There was no trace of anything resembling a twelve-step program.

She wondered whether all these features really added up to an effective treatment of addiction.

On the other hand …

Maybe I'm just envious.

She sure wouldn't mind spending some time here herself. Maybe they had something that would cut down on an addiction to work.

Soon Morgan was fully checked in. Clinic employees took her suitcase and led her away. Before she disappeared into a hallway, the thin, elegant woman turned and gave Riley a silent, grateful wave.

Riley felt an unexpected pang of sadness at the expression on

124

her face.

There was still something lost and waiflike about Morgan—something Riley doubted that all the treatments in the world could possibly cure. And now it occurred to Riley that most if not all of the clients in this place were surely as lost and sad as Morgan.

It felt strange to pity a woman who had the resources to spend months at a time in a place like this.

Maybe I don't envy her after all, Riley thought.

Riley and Bill got back in the rented car and found a place to have burgers. Riley pulled the ashtray out of her bag and turned it over, staring as though she should be able to find some hidden meaning.

"You know," Bill said, "that thing might not have anything at all to do with the case."

"I think you made a good catch," she said. "We need to follow up on it."

She realized that if others like this turned up at the other sites, they would be onto something. She would run the photo past the police chiefs in Monarch and Atlanta and Birmingham. She would also see if Flores and his team at Quantico could turn up anything on where the thing came from. She photographed the ashtray and sent the pictures off.

They finished their burgers, returned to the hotel where Riley was staying, and checked Bill into a room of his own. Riley sent cheerful text messages to April and Jilly. They had already sent her a string of messages accompanied by cute pictures of the little dog. Apparently Darby was settling in just fine.

It had been a long day—with a new murder that morning, then Bill's arrival, then getting Morgan out of jail, checking out the Farrell murder scene, and finally getting Morgan into her new quarters.

They were both tired, and intended to turn in early, but first they went down to the hotel bar for a drink. They were sitting in a quiet booth when Riley's phone buzzed. She wasn't entirely pleased to see that the caller was Jared Ruhl.

She answered and asked, "What's going on over in Monarch?"

She heard Jared let out a growl of irritation.

"I'm not in Monarch anymore. I'm back in Atlanta. After we got finished with the crime scene, the local cops just left me on my own, wouldn't even give me a ride. So I had to take a bus to Atlanta. Can you believe that? The nerve of those guys, dumping me like that!"

Riley couldn't muster a lot of pity for Jared over the inconvenience of a short bus ride to Atlanta. She could well imagine why the local police in Monarch might be eager to get rid of the rookie cop who was capable of being pretty obnoxious, but she didn't say so.

"Did anyone find anything new there?" Riley asked.

"Not a damn thing. It was a waste of my time. What's going on with you and your partner?"

Riley was tempted to tell him they'd found nothing at all. Maybe then she could be through with him.

But then she realized …

Fat chance of that.

Jared was surely going to find some way to nag her until she gave him something else to do.

Besides, she reminded herself that he had been useful from time to time. In fact, she probably wouldn't be here investigating this case if it weren't for him.

She said, "Jared, I'm going to send you an image. See if you can tell me where this thing came from."

She sent him the shot of the glass ashtray.

There was a silence, and then Jared said, "You should recognize that. I showed you the Vulcan statue in Birmingham."

"I know," Riley agreed. "But what are the dancing girls?"

Another silence followed.

Finally Jared said, "Uh … nymphs."

"Nymphs?"

Jared let out a snort of laughter.

"The Nymphs of Vulcan," he said. "It's a private gentlemen's club in Birmingham—you know, with exotic dancers and call girls and all, but really posh, really high class, with strictly private clientele, way out of my price range."

Then he stammered awkwardly, "Not that I … well, you know. The only reason I know about it is I hear guys talk, and they say stuff about …"

"Yeah, I understand," Riley said.

Jared's information excited her. If Andrew Farrell had belonged to a gentleman's club in Birmingham, perhaps Julian Morse had too. It wasn't even hard to imagine that Edwin Harter might have visited the same club. If any of that turned out to be true, it would be the first connection they'd found among the victims of this killer.

Jared also sounded fired up now.

"So, why are you interested in that place? Have you got some new clue leading there? Are you going there? When?"

Riley stifled a sigh. There was no point in trying to keep Jared out of this.

She asked, "Can you go with us to Birmingham tomorrow?"

"I sure can. Like I told you, I've got lots of sick days saved up."

"This is an official FBI case now," Riley told him. "I'm sure Captain Stiles will agree to assign you to me."

"I'll tell him you requested me."

"OK, then," Riley said. "We'll pick you up at your apartment tomorrow morning."

When she ended the call, Bill asked, "Who was that?"

Riley sighed and said, "That kid I told you about—the one who called me about Morgan Farrell, the guy I've been working with since I flew down here."

"So he'll be joining us tomorrow, huh?" Bill said. "I'm looking forward to meeting him."

Riley almost said …

You won't like him."

But she thought better of it. For all she knew, Bill and Jared might wind up getting along together perfectly. Instead she told Bill what Jared had just said about the ashtray.

"The Nymphs of Vulcan?" he said. "Well, we definitely need to check them out in person."

*

Early the next morning, Riley and Bill decided that Riley would drive the car to Birmingham. They went by Jared's apartment and picked him up, but they hadn't even gotten out of Atlanta before it became apparent to Riley that Jared was getting on Bill's nerves. Just as he had with Riley, the young cop asked all kinds of questions about Bill's investigative career. Finally Bill folded his arms and fell into a sullen silence, ignoring the sound of Jared's voice.

The drive seemed interminable, and Riley breathed a huge sigh of relief as the statue of Vulcan that towered over Birmingham finally came into view. They drove north of the business district until they arrived at the Nymphs of Vulcan gentlemen's club.

As they parked and walked toward the place, Riley was startled by its appearance. She'd expected a so-called gentlemen's club to be tacky and possibly rundown. But this building was a new and attractive piece of architecture, with smooth blue-gray slate walls and elegant designs suggestive of the nymphs in its name.

Riley and her colleagues weren't surprised to find that the business was closed for the morning. They knocked on the impressive and ornate front door until a tall, Nordic-looking, pale, platinum blond man came and let them in. His face seemed so plastic and nonporous that he looked more like a male mannequin than an actual human being.

When the man asked how he could help them, Riley and Bill produced their badges and introduced themselves and Jared.

Riley said to the man, "We were wondering if you'd ever had a client named Andrew Farrell."

The man shook his head and was obviously about to say no when Riley heard a woman's voice speaking from inside the club.

"Lars, who is that asking about Andrew Farrell? Send them on in here."

CHAPTER TWENTY FOUR

Riley felt a burst of anticipation as she followed the tall man named Lars into the club, with Bill and Jared close behind her. Whoever had called out just now seemed to have recognized Andrew Farrell's name.

Maybe they were about to get a break.

Inside, the club was spacious. It was even more impressive than the exterior, with the same smooth gray-blue surfaces. There was a high gallery looming above the bar and the tables, and a stage and runway with poles jutted out from one wall. Rising from the back of the stage was a majestic stairway that weirdly reminded Riley of the one in the Farrells' home—except that this one was smaller and more tasteful.

The place was dark now, but Riley could easily imagine what the place would look like with dancing lights and scantily clad silicone-enhanced women gyrating around those poles. Or perhaps dancing all but naked around someone decked out as the god Vulcan.

Riley quickly spotted a flash of color in that sea of dark, monochromic gray-blue. A youngish woman wearing a brightly printed silk kimono was sitting at a table with a computer in front of her.

The woman got up from the table to greet them.

"I'm Brynn Montgomery," she said. "Did I hear you say that you were FBI?"

With a laugh, she added, "You're not here to raid us, I hope! If you are, you might want to come back when there's more going on."

Brynn was a remarkably attractive young woman with a buxom figure that Riley was sure was much admired by the men who came in here. She had bright blue eyes and a slightly asymmetrical smile that projected a feeling of cheerful, world-wise irony. In her kimono and slippers, she seemed extremely comfortable and at home here. Riley also sensed a distinct air of confidence and authority about her.

Apparently Jared noticed this too. He asked her, "Do you own this place or something?"

"Own it? Goodness, no. But I'm flattered that you think I

might."

She gestured to the computer. "I guess you could say that I'm the brains around here, at least nowadays. I do the books and handle the advertising, most of the managerial work. And of course I've got …"

She paused and winked suggestively.

"I've got other duties, you might say."

Riley could imagine what "duties" she might mean.

Riley also sensed that what Brynn had said about brains was quite true. Perhaps she hadn't had much formal schooling, but she'd probably managed to learn a lot on her own. She was probably a lot more intelligent than the owner of this place, and most of the customers too.

Brynn invited Riley and her colleagues to sit with her at the table. Then she asked …

"So you were asking about Andrew Farrell. What's new with that cold-hearted son-of-a-bitch, anyway?"

Riley thought she heard an odd note of affection even in that insult.

"I'm sorry to have to break the news," she said. "He was murdered a couple of nights ago."

Brynn's eyes widened and she gasped slightly.

"Oh, my! How terrible! I didn't know. How did it happen?"

Riley told her without getting into specifics. She also told her that two other men had been killed under similar circumstances.

Then she asked, "Did you happen to know the other two men—Edwin Harter and Julian Morse?"

Brynn shook her head. Her wry smile was gone now, and she sat staring off into space.

Bill asked, "Were you close to Mr. Farrell?"

Brynn's smile flickered again as she lit a cigarette.

"Close? Yeah, I guess you could say that. Actually, I once had hopes that things might get serious between us—or at least as serious as a guy like that can be about a woman. But then he got interested in that model, Morgan Chartier, and he married her."

She chuckled softly. "I couldn't compete with a squeaky clean pedigree like hers. I've lived kind of a … well, colorful life, if you know what I mean. Not that I wasn't resentful when he hooked up with her. But one way or another, I knew it wasn't going to last. From everything I knew about Morgan, she wasn't a good match for Andrew. She just wasn't …"

Brynn seemed to be searching for the right word.

"Tough enough for him?" Riley said.

Brynn nodded.

"Yeah," she said. "He had … his ways, not all of them pleasant. A girl had to stand up to him, give back as good as she got."

Her voice dropped and her expression darkened. She flicked an ash from her cigarette into an ashtray that was identical to the one they'd found in Farrell's mansion.

Riley found herself feeling a certain admiration for this woman who was both smart and versatile—probably as skilled with money and figures as she was at adult entertainment and seduction. It was likely that Brynn had endured more than her own share of abuse over the years. But self-pity wasn't her style. Not that she'd gotten hard-bitten and cynical like Tisha, Harter's widow. Somehow, Brynn seemed to have gotten through it all without losing her spirit.

A real survivor, Riley thought.

Riley also got the distinct feeling that Brynn had something unspoken on her mind right now.

Riley asked, "Do you have any idea who might have killed Farrell?"

Brynn's brow knitted anxiously as she took another puff on her cigarette.

Then she said, "I could kind of get into trouble for saying this …"

Her face trailed away.

Jared said with a note of sharpness in his voice, "Things will be a lot better for you if you tell us."

Riley threw him an angry glare that said …

You're not helping.

Jared withered a bit under Riley's look. Riley hoped maybe he'd keep his mouth shut for a while. Threats weren't going to work on this woman.

Everything went quiet while Riley waited for an answer.

Finally Brynn said, "We've got a regular member here, Harrison Lund. Maybe you've heard of him."

"The name sounds kind of familiar," Bill said.

Riley also thought she'd heard the name, but she couldn't place it.

Brynn continued, "Harrison is an OK guy for the most part—at least with the girls. But our clients—men—don't like him. In fact, I think they're kind of afraid of him, although they never say that exactly. Once in a while he gets into an argument with one of our members, and it gets ugly. But he keeps his voice really low, so the girls and I can't hear what the argument is about. And afterwards …"

She paused for a moment, then said …

"Well, whoever he was arguing with usually stops coming here altogether. They even drop their membership."

Riley was starting to get an idea of what might be on Brynn's mind.

She said, "I take it he had an argument with Andrew Farrell."

Brynn nodded and flicked another ash off her cigarette.

"Yeah, and it was just a couple of nights before you say that Andrew was killed."

Riley's skin prickled with interest as she waited for Brynn to continue.

Brynn said, "Well, I asked Andrew what they'd fought about, and sure enough he wouldn't say. But he did tell me he wasn't going to let that bastard push him around. He seemed more angry than scared. He also wanted to have Harrison barred from the club. But … well, we're not exactly in a position to do that."

"Why not?" Bill asked.

Brynn shrugged. "Well, he's got kind of special privileges, on account of the fact that he's the architect who designed this place. The owner admires him and drops his name into conversations whenever he gets the chance."

Riley glanced around, again impressed by the elegance of the place.

Brynn shook her head and said, "Maybe I shouldn't have told you. No, I probably shouldn't have. Really, it was all about nothing, I'm sure—whatever it was that got Andrew so mad. Just forget I mentioned it."

Riley tried to reassure her. "We don't need to tell Lund that we heard anything from you. For all he'll know, we could have found out about him from any of your clients."

Brynn shuddered a little.

As if she thinks he'll know anyway, Riley thought.

Riley said in a gentle voice, "Brynn, what are your own impressions of Harrison Lund?"

Brynn inhaled and exhaled sharply.

"Like I said, he's OK with the girls, and they actually like him. But …"

She gulped and said, "He gives me the creeps somehow. I don't know why. I usually manage to stay away from him."

Riley sensed a world of unformed, wordless fears in her voice.

Riley thanked Brynn for her help and gave her an FBI card.

When she and her colleagues left the club, Bill commented, "So that was a nymph?"

"Well, why not?" Riley asked. "A nymph is a nature spirit, isn't she?"

Bill laughed. "I'd say that woman is more what you'd call a force of nature."

"Nature isn't always tame," Riley replied.

Then she turned to Jared and said, "I need for you to locate Harrison Lund for me."

Jared searched on his cell phone as they climbed into the car. Almost immediately he found the address for Lund's company, Lund Architects. It was only a short drive away.

As Riley started to drive, she remembered Brynn's words …

"He gives me the creeps somehow."

Riley had no doubt that Brynn was extremely intuitive as well as intelligent. If she felt some deep-seated dread of Harrison Lund, there must have been a good reason.

I've got to find out what that reason is, Riley thought.

CHAPTER TWENTY FIVE

Riley didn't like the way Harrison Lund smiled. The man rose from his desk as his assistant escorted Riley, Bill, and Jared into his office. The assistant had already told him who the visitors were via intercom.

Lund spoke in a friendly enough manner. "The FBI, eh? I was wondering when you'd show up." But his smile was absolutely reptilian.

Was he really expecting us? Riley wondered.

If he was, what could that mean?

Lund said, "Sit down, please. Make yourselves at home."

He had a thick southern drawl that reminded Riley of Julian Morse's brother, Roderick. But Lund's voice was smoother, darker, and somehow more sinister. He was about Riley's age, and he had a sardonic air about him. He wore an expensive double-breasted suit and had steel gray hair combed back sleekly.

Riley and her colleagues sat down in front of the desk, and Lund took his seat in the big chair behind his desk. Riley glanced around the huge office, with its wall-sized window overlooking downtown Birmingham. The dark slate walls and the wide, smooth surfaces definitely looked to Riley like the work of the same architect who had designed the Nymphs of Vulcan gentlemen's club.

Lund cradled his fingers together and looked at each of his visitors with an expression of cold but vaguely amused curiosity.

"So," he said, "what are you planning to do for me?"

Riley was startled by the question, and she was sure her colleagues felt the same way.

"I beg your pardon?" she said.

Lund tilted his head in what struck Riley as a mocking manner.

He said, "Well, I assume you're here on account of the three recent murders, aren't you? Andrew Farrell, Julian Morse, and Edwin Gray Harter—and there's a pattern there, isn't there? A pattern that led you to me."

Riley knew right away that he was toying with them. And she didn't much like it.

Jared spoke up.

"If you've got something to tell us, why don't you just come out with it?"

Riley was about to dart another silencing glare at him. But Bill beat her to it with a warning growl of disapproval.

Lund chuckled at Jared's comment.

"Oh, my," he said. "That sounds a bit hostile. I'm not sure I should entrust my life into your good hands. Because that's why you're here, isn't it? To make sure I'm well-protected? I'm certain that I'm on a pretty short list of potential victims in this area."

Laughing louder, he added, "The truth is, I'd feel a little hurt if I weren't on such a list. It sounds like your killer—whoever he is— has rather exacting tastes in murder victims. None but the elite and wealthy. And I'm certainly both."

Riley said, "We're not here to offer you protection, Mr. Lund. I think you've got that under control already. On the way through the building, I saw that you already have plenty of plainclothes security men on duty, toting concealed weapons. I'm sure you've got similar security at your home—although I should warn you that our killer is pretty smart at hacking electronic devices."

Lund leaned toward them.

He said, "Then I'm not sure I understand—what *is* your business with me today?"

Bill said, "We just want to ask you a few questions."

"For example?" Lund asked.

Riley locked eyes with him.

She said, "We would like to know where you were at the times of the murders."

Bill then told him the exact times and locations of the murders.

Lund leaned toward the intercom and called for his assistant. When the woman came in, Lund said, "Claudia, could you tell these folks about my comings and goings during the last couple of weeks?"

Claudia recited with rote efficiency an elaborate itinerary that included Zurich, Berlin, Paris, and London.

When she finished, Lund said to Riley and her colleagues, "Would you like Claudia to print up my reservations and hotel receipts and such?"

"That won't be necessary," Riley said.

It wasn't that Riley was by any means convinced that Lund was innocent. In fact, she was becoming more and more suspicious of him by the second. But she was also sure that his alibis would prove to be airtight. It would be easy enough for Flores to check out. Besides, she'd already considered the possibility that the three killings had been hired.

Riley held his gaze for a moment, then said, "Mr. Lund, did you personally know the first victim—Andrew Farrell?"

"Oh, yes," Lund said. "We were quite well acquainted."

Riley asked, "Didn't you have a falling out recently?"

Lund smiled that reptilian smile of his.

"Now that you mention it, I suppose I did. It was the night before I flew to Zurich—and if I'm not mistaken, two nights before Andrew was killed. And I suppose you know just where that falling out took place."

Riley carefully kept her silence.

Lund squinted at her inquisitively.

"What I would like to know is—how did you come by this bit of information?"

The question made Riley feel queasy.

She remembered Brynn's skeptical, worried look when she promised that Lund needn't know who had told her about the argument.

Had Lund guessed the truth—that Riley had talked to Brynn?

Riley steadied herself. She knew that almost everything this man said was calculated to keep her and her team off balance.

Don't let him get the best of you, she told herself.

She said, "What *I'd* like to know is, what was your quarrel with Farrell about?"

Lund clucked his tongue with disapproval. "I didn't like how Andrew treated the ladies at … a certain establishment, I suspect you know which one I mean. I'm rather old-fashioned that way— something of an anachronism, an old-school Southern gentleman. I believe in treating ladies with courtesy and respect. No matter who they are."

Riley remembered something Brynn had said about Lund …

"Harrison is an OK guy for the most part—at least with the girls."

Lund seemed to be a living, breathing contradiction—a misogynist with an inclination for exotic dancers and call girls who believed in treating those very women with some sort of faux gallantry.

Lund swiveled slightly in his chair and added, "I told Andrew I wasn't going to allow his behavior to continue."

Riley felt a chill at his words.

"So you threatened him?" she asked.

Lund laughed. "Oh, Agent Paige—now you're getting much

too personal. It was an ugly little quarrel, and I'd just as soon forget all about it. Can we change the subject, please?"

Riley felt stymied. Her questions seemed to be getting her nowhere. Lund struck her as clever and slippery—and also dangerous.

Fortunately, Bill spoke up. "Did you and Farrell share any other activities in common—aside from that 'certain establishment'?"

Lund shrugged and said, "Well, we played golf together from time to time."

"And where did you do that?" Bill asked.

"At the Cedar Creek Country Club, over in Monarch."

Riley's attention quickened at the mention of the town's name …

Monarch!

Riley remembered the golf course that had been visible from Edwin Gray Harter's house.

It might be the exact same club, she thought.

Lund continued, "Any golfer who can afford it goes to one or another of the Monarch clubs. Andrew didn't have a membership there, but I do. In happier times, I let Andrew play there on my membership."

Then with a sigh, he added, "A pity what happened to him."

With those words, Lund gave Riley a long piercing look.

She managed to suppress a deep shudder.

"I think that will be all," Riley said to him. "Thank you for your time and help."

Lund looked surprised and perhaps even disappointed that their little scene was over. As she and her colleagues headed on out of the building, Jared asked, "So what do you think? Did we find out anything back there?"

Bill didn't reply, and Riley didn't either.

But deep in her gut, Riley felt all but sure of something …

We were just talking to a cold-blooded killer.

CHAPTER TWENTY SIX

As Riley and her colleagues walked out of the building toward their rented car, she mulled over her impressions of Harrison Lund.

That he was an evil man she had no doubt.

But did she have any hard evidence against him?

Not so far, she thought.

Lund's cunning and intelligence worried her even more than his palpably evil nature.

When they reached the car, Jared commented, "We haven't eaten anything since we left Atlanta."

"I'll drive," Bill said. "Just direct me to the nearest hamburger joint."

Jared consulted his cell phone and directed them to a little café. They found a booth out of immediate earshot from the other customers and settled down to talk quietly.

"So what do you think about our interview just now?" Bill asked Riley as they waited for their sandwiches.

Riley paused for a moment, then said, "I'm all but sure he's a coldblooded killer."

Jared's eyes widened with surprise.

"Wow," he said. "How did you come to that conclusion?"

Before Riley could reply, Bill said to Jared, "Instincts. She's got good ones, the best in the business."

Then Bill told Riley, "I had a bad feeling about that one too. I'm glad it wasn't just me."

"So what do we do now?" Jared asked.

Before they could start discussing the question, a waitress came and took their orders. Then Riley's phone buzzed and she saw that the call was from Brent Meredith.

Riley glanced around. Their corner of the café was still clear of other customers, so she took the call and put Meredith on speakerphone.

Meredith sounded even more gruff than usual.

"Tell me you're making progress."

"We might be," Riley said. "We're not just sure just yet."

"Well, *get* sure, and fast. I'm catching hell here in Quantico. Special Agent in Charge Walder is breathing down my neck all the time now. He's furious that these murders are getting so much media attention, and he thinks we look incompetent. To make things worse, he knew one of the murdered guys."

Riley remembered Bill saying that Walder had played golf with one of them.

"Which one?" Riley asked.

"Julian Morse, the millionaire in Birmingham. They used to get together for drinks whenever they were in the same area."

Riley and Bill exchanged glances. Riley knew they were both wondering the same thing.

Bill said, "Did Walder mention having played golf with him?"

"As a matter of fact, he did."

Riley took a breath. "Did Walder happen to say which golf course they played at?"

"The Scofield Country Club, right here near DC. Why do you ask?"

Riley wasn't sure how to answer that question. Instead, she and Bill gave Meredith a verbal rundown of all that had happened since Bill had arrived. She also introduced Meredith to Jared Ruhl, who seemed uncharacteristically awestruck to be in on a conversation with an actual FBI team chief.

Finally Riley said, "And we just interviewed a possible suspect. He's an architect here in Birmingham—"

Riley broke off when the waitress appeared with their coffees.

"Hold on," Riley told Meredith.

"Here you are, sweetie," the waitress said cheerfully. "Sugar is there on the table. Do any of you want cream?"

Riley could hear Meredith's grunt of surprise.

"Where are you?" he growled.

"Getting lunch," Bill replied. "This place is pretty empty."

The waitress put the coffees down and left them alone again.

"All clear now," Riley said.

"Don't say another word," Meredith snapped. "Take me off speakerphone."

Wondering what Meredith was going to say, Riley switched off the speaker and put the phone to her ear.

Meredith asked, "Is the man you just interviewed Harrison Lund?"

"How did you know?"

Meredith fell silent for a moment.

"I need you to be very discreet with what I'm about to tell you. Don't share this with anyone but your two colleagues," he said. "One of our units has been investigating Harrison Lund for a couple

139

of years now. We're on the verge of proving that he personally hired the killings of five different men in three different countries."

Riley breathed sharply at Meredith's words.

She asked, "What were the motives?"

"Three seem to have been about business issues—trouble with zoning permissions, broken contracts, that kind of thing. But two of them seem to have been purely personal, petty quarrels possibly. In fact, all of them were probably personal at some level. We believe that he simply enjoys making hits with hired killers and getting away with it. He doesn't seem to know that we're closing in on him. We want to keep it that way."

Riley remembered something Lund had said …

"I didn't like how Andrew treated the ladies …"

Might that have been enough of a reason for Lund to want Andrew Farrell dead?

Riley's mind clicked away, trying to make sense of this new information.

She asked Meredith, "What was the MO for the five killings?"

Meredith said, "They were done the old-fashioned way—bullet to the heart, another to the head. Look, Walder's expecting me to update him right now, so I've got to go. I also have to notify the team that's working on the Lund case about your interaction with Lund. They need to know that. Keep me updated, OK? And close your case quick."

The call ended just as their sandwiches were served. Riley thought that her over-toasted grilled cheese sandwich helped explain why the café was so empty. She saw that Bill took a skeptical look at his burger, but both he and Jared chomped down on them hungrily.

While they ate, Riley quietly filled them in on what Meredith had told her about Lund.

Jared could barely keep his voice down from excitement.

"Then Lund's our killer," he said. "All we've got to do is close in on him."

Bill shook his head and said, "It's not that simple."

"Why not?" Jared said.

Riley suppressed a sigh and said, "Bill's right. Our killer's MOs don't match Lund's hits. I'm not saying Lund's not our killer. We can't be sure he's not. But there would have to be some good reason for him to start ordering his henchmen to brutally stab his victims instead of just shooting them."

Jared looked like he could hardly believe his ears.

140

"Lund's a sadistic asshole. Isn't that enough of a reason? He got bored, didn't get enough of a kick out of ordinary hits. So he dialed things up a notch, ordered nastier killings. Doesn't that make sense?"

Neither Bill nor Riley replied.

The truth was, it didn't make much sense to Riley, and she knew it didn't make much sense to Bill either.

At least my gut feeling about Lund wasn't wrong, she thought.

Lund was definitely a killer. But if he wasn't the killer they were looking for, she know they'd better leave it up to the other FBI team to bring him to justice. Although Riley couldn't discount the possibility that Lund had hired the latest murders, it didn't seem likely. She and her team needed to expand their search.

Jared said, "The truth is, they're *all* assholes. Lund's an asshole, and so were Morse, Harter, and Farrell. If Lund's not the killer, then I feel like rooting for whoever the killer really is. He's doing society a service. Why don't we just leave things alone? Don't we have worthier people to protect and serve?"

Bill looked at Jared with annoyance.

He said, "We all feel that way about some cases. It's kind of a dumb rookie thing to talk about it, though."

Jared's mouth dropped open with shock.

"Bill's right," Riley said. "Our job is to enforce the law, not try to be judge and jury. We've got a case to solve. And murder affects a lot more people than just the victims."

She gave Jared a hard look and added, "And if you're not all in with us, you'd better tell us now. Bill and I can get along without you."

Jared looked hurt now.

"Count me in," he murmured.

They ate in silence for a moment, mulling over what to do next.

Finally Riley said, "I'm interested in the golfing connection. We know that Farrell played golf with Lund at the Cedar Creek Country Club in Monarch. Julian Morse played golf too. Since he lived in nearby Birmingham, he probably played somewhere in Monarch as well. The whole area there is pretty much made up of golf courses. Edwin Earl Harter's house even overlooks one of them—and it might just be the Cedar Creek Country Club."

Bill said, "It sounds like you're suggesting we go there and ask some questions. I'm not sure how well that would work, though. Rich guys go to those places to get away from their regular lives. They keep things really insular in clubs like that. They don't like to talk to outsiders, let alone FBI agents."

Riley suddenly felt an idea forming in her brain.

She said, "You're right. But I think I know how to go about it."

"How?" Bill said.

Riley smiled at him and said …

"By stealth."

CHAPTER TWENTY SEVEN

Riley took a long, slow breath. She realized that Bill might not like the idea she was about to explain. But she was sure it was a good idea, and she really needed to talk him into it.

Squinting uncertainly over his burger at her, Bill asked, "By stealth? What do you mean by that?"

She said, "You just told me those clubs are insular, and that an FBI agent wouldn't exactly be welcome, especially asking a lot of questions."

"That's right," Bill said.

Riley shrugged slightly and said, "So you could go undercover."

Bill's eyes widened with surprise.

"Undercover as what?" he asked.

Riley said, "As a well-to-do golfer, just one of the guys there."

Bill frowned.

Nope, Riley thought. *He really doesn't like this idea.*

Riley continued, "Look, it wouldn't be the first time you've gone undercover."

"Yeah," Bill said. "But the last time was years ago, infiltrating a mob family. I was playing the part of a wannabe goon looking for a job as a hit man."

"So?" Riley said.

"This is different," Bill said. "I don't think I can pass myself off as …"

Riley chuckled and added, "As respectable?"

Bill squirmed a little and said, "Well, as rich, anyway. And I'd really blow my cover if I actually had to play any golf."

"You don't know how?" Riley asked.

"I've played, but I've never been much good at it. And I sure don't have time right now to hone my skills."

Jared was looking at Bill with interest.

"I don't know," he said. "You might clean up OK."

Bill smirked sarcastically. "Well, thanks for the vote of confidence."

Bill stared at what remained of his burger and added, "Besides, I'm not a member of any of the golf clubs in Monarch. We'd have to go through the management of one of those places to get me in.

That would take time."

Jared was starting to look enthusiastic.

"You won't need to be a member," he said. "You don't even need to play golf. All you've got to do is ride around in a golf cart."

Bill let out a snort of laughter.

"A golf cart?" he said.

Riley instantly understood what Jared was getting at.

She remembered how Monarch had looked when she and Jared had driven there—how the whole landscape seemed to be nothing but golf courses. She'd seen almost as many golf carts as cars in the town.

She thought …

This annoying little guy just might be right—again!

Jared continued, "The town's golf cart paths go everywhere."

She said to Bill, "Jared's got a point, Bill. You can get anywhere in Monarch in a golf cart, talk to anyone you want that way. You just need … well …"

Bill scoffed again.

"A set of golf clubs?" he said. "And a disguise? Good luck with that!"

Riley had to admit, that part was a tall order.

But Jared looked as though he thought otherwise.

"I've got an idea," he said to Riley. "Agent Paige, I know I got kind of queasy when I saw Edwin Harter's body in that hot tub. Even so, I got a good look at his corpse, especially when the ME's people were hauling it away."

Again, Riley caught his meaning instantly.

She said to Bill, "Edwin Harter was almost exactly your size and build."

"So?" Bill said.

Riley said, "So, a rich guy like Harter living in that area must have been a golfer. He surely has equipment and clothes—and a golf cart too, I'll bet."

Jared let out a sharp, cynical chuckle and added, "Yeah, and he sure won't be needing them now. You might as well make use of them."

Bill looked back and forth at Riley and Jared.

With a deep sigh, he said, "So do you think we can get our hands on that stuff?"

"There's only one way to find out," Riley said.

*

A few minutes later, Bill was driving Riley and Jared out of Birmingham and back toward Atlanta. Even though they could skirt around the city to get to Monarch, it would take them well over two hours to get there.

During the drive, they discussed their plans and agreed not to bother checking in with Callum O'Neill, Monarch's police chief. They really had no new evidence to offer the local police, and nothing to discuss with them. And they didn't want to explain what they were going to do.

It was another tedious ride, with Jared chattering even more than usual. Bill was especially grouchy and taciturn this time. Riley guessed that he still wasn't entirely sold on their plans.

Soon after they pulled into Monarch, Bill gaped at a string of golf carts traveling a wide path alongside the street. In the center of the little town, a parking lot near the stores was completely filled with golf carts. Bill laughed out loud at the sight.

It's making more sense to him now, Riley thought.

They parked the rented car in front of the Harter mansion, then went to the front door, where they were met by Vivian Bettridge.

Riley reminded herself not to make a mistake...

Remember, she calls herself a majordomo, not a butler.

Bettridge greeted Riley and her colleagues with her customary smirk.

"Our FBI friends again, I see," she said. "What can I do for you?"

Before Riley or her colleagues could say anything, they heard a woman's voice call from inside.

"Did I hear you say FBI, Vivian? Send them on in. I'm curious about what they want."

Bettridge led them into the dazzling interior with its immaculate white sofas. For a moment, Riley barely recognized the woman who had called out to them. It was Tisha Harter, but quite a change had come over her.

Riley remembered the sassy, insolent young woman in shorts and a T-shirt that she'd met before. Now Tisha was dressed casually but elegantly in comfortable slacks and a loose-fitting blouse. Even her sandals looked expensive. Her whole body language was different from when Riley had seen her slouching around insolently in the recreation room. Now she looked relaxed but poised, mature, sophisticated, and very much in charge—and very happy with herself.

Riley thought …

It's a new role for her to play—the "lady of the manor."

It was obvious that the young widow was thoroughly enjoying the part.

Riley also noticed that the cumbersome bandage Tisha been wearing on her right hand was now gone, replaced by a much less conspicuous flesh-colored one on her pinky.

Riley doubted the broken finger was really healed. Tisha probably just hadn't thought the bandage quite suited her new image and decided to do without it.

With elaborate graciousness, Tisha invited Riley and her colleagues to sit down and asked whether they might like Bettridge to bring them some tea or coffee. When they politely declined, she asked, "Tell me—are you making any progress toward finding my husband's killer?"

Riley said, "We're doing everything we can. We were wondering if maybe you could offer us some help."

"Oh, certainly. Anything I can do."

Tisha had been subtly flirting with Jared since they'd come into the house. Now she looked straight at the young cop, clearly expecting him—and not Riley or Bill—to explain what they wanted. Apparently falling under her spell, Jared did so, stammering from time to time like a timid schoolboy.

As manipulative as ever, Riley thought as Jared described what they had in mind.

Riley hadn't liked Tisha very much when she'd been here before, and she didn't like her now.

Nor did she trust her.

Tisha was beaming with girlish delight by the time Jared finished explaining their plan. Riley again glimpsed that less mature girl she'd met the last time she'd been here.

"Oh, that sounds … well, it sounds like fun."

Eyeing Bill flirtatiously now, she added …

"And I'm sure Agent Jeffreys here will look quite dashing in my husband's golf clothes."

Riley cringed a little at her tone of voice.

Tisha turned toward Bettridge, who had been standing dutifully nearby.

"Vivian, would you help this young man fetch Edwin's golf equipment—and his golf cart too?"

As Bettridge led Jared away, Tisha looked at Bill again. "Come with me, and let's get you all fixed up."

Riley followed Tisha and Bill into the elevator, which they took to third floor. Bill looked surprised as they stepped out into the hallway filled with incredibly valuable paintings.

With what Riley took to be feigned wistfulness, Tisha said …

"It feels odd, being free to come here on my own without Edwin's permission. This entire floor was his private domain, you know."

Tisha sighed and added, "Well, times certainly do change."

She led Riley and Bill into the dead man's vast bedroom. Of course Bill wanted to see the crime scene itself, so Riley took him into the adjoining bathroom and showed him the hot tub, which was now clean and empty.

Then Tisha held Bill's chin and turned his face from one side to another.

"Your hair could use a little work. It's just a tad too working-class."

As much as she disliked Tisha, Riley had to agree. Tisha found a pair of barber's scissors in a drawer. Riley made suggestions as Tisha ever-so-slightly trimmed Bill's receding hair around the edges and combed it differently. She tried not to giggle as Tisha patted the results into place with a styling gel.

Then the three of them all went into Harter's closet. It wasn't nearly as big as Morgan Farrell's closet in Atlanta, and there wasn't any furniture. But it was still a whole lot bigger than Riley thought a closet had any business being, with rows upon rows of racks exhibiting hundreds of outfits.

Tisha was having a great time now as she browsed the hanging clothes until she found her dead husband's sporting outfits. She pulled out a white polo shirt and white pants and found a pair of white golfing shoes. At a glance, it looked to Riley as if everything was going to fit Bill well—even the shoes.

Bill then exited into the bathroom while Riley and Tisha waited in the bedroom. When Bill emerged after a few minutes, Riley gasped at what she saw and thought …

Oh, my!

Bill truly was transformed, and he was incredibly good-looking in his all-white outfit.

Riley felt her face redden as she was suddenly reminded of just how attractive Bill really was. He was strong, lean, and solid, and she thought he could be a professional model the way he displayed those clothes. Even the touch of gray in his thick dark hair helped give him an air of seasoned sophistication.

Riley remembered how attracted she'd been to Bill when they first began to work together years ago, and how her attraction had flared up from time to time since then, sometimes with embarrassing consequences. And Bill had sometimes let her know that he felt the same way about her.

At the moment, Bill seemed self-conscious enough not to notice that Riley was blushing. He was carrying a white golfing cap in one hand, shifting it from one hand to the other, undecided whether or not to put it on.

Fortunately, Tisha seemed much too delighted by Bill's transformation to notice Riley either.

Riley forced her feelings down. Bill was recently divorced, and so was she—but she was just now striking up a relationship with Blaine Hildreth, a perfectly lovely man she knew better than to take for granted. She didn't dare spoil whatever was happening between them. To say nothing of the possible complications if FBI partners became romantically entangled.

Steady, she told herself. *Stay professional.*

She turned away and headed for the elevator. Bill and Tisha caught up with her and they all took the elevator back downstairs, where Vivian Bettridge was waiting for them. The majordomo was looking very happy with herself.

"Come on outside," she said. "I have something to show you."

Bill, Tisha, and Riley all followed Bettridge out of the house. In the driveway just outside, a red electric golf cart was scurrying around in circles. In spite of the bag of golf clubs in back, the vehicle looked more like an undersized sports car than a golf cart. Riley guessed it probably cost more than some ordinary cars.

Jared Ruhl was in the driver's seat, obviously having a great time.

Vivian Bettridge commented, "Mr. Harter hadn't golfed in years, but he did keep his equipment up to date and in excellent condition."

When he saw them, Jared pulled up nearby and stopped the whirring little vehicle.

He said to Bill, "Hey, Agent Jeffreys! You don't look half bad! Come on, we should get going."

Bill frowned and said, "What do you mean, we?"

Jared shrugged and said, "Well, I'm going to be your caddy, aren't I?"

Riley couldn't help but be amused by the suggestion—and by the scowl it provoked in Bill. The fact was, Jared really did look the part. Along with his regular summer clothes, he was wearing a caddy's bright red utility bib, which Bettridge apparently had found with the rest of the golfing equipment.

Bill growled, "Why do I need a caddy? I've already got a golf cart."

Tisha said, "Actually, Agent Jeffreys, having a caddy might be a good idea. The upscale golfers around here like to have both a caddy and a cart."

Jared added, "And I know what I'm doing. I worked as a caddy a couple of summers while I was in school."

"But I'm not even planning on playing golf," Bill said.

Jared shrugged and said, "Well, even so. You need to look like you *might* play golf."

Riley nudged Bill with her elbow and whispered to him, "Take him along, just for appearances' sake. Besides, you never know when he might prove useful."

Bill shook his head and walked toward the cart.

"OK. But move over, kid. I'm going to drive."

Jared grumbled, but he moved into the passenger seat, and Bill got behind the wheel. Riley stood there watching as the little vehicle whirred away. She hoped she wasn't sending Bill on a pointless excursion. Meanwhile, she needed to spend some time going over her own notes and information on this frustrating case.

As she turned to follow Tisha and Bettridge back into the house, Riley thought …

Three men, all very wealthy, all cruel—and all dead.

Why had the killer selected these particular men?

The golfing connection was tenuous and possibly meaningless, but so far it was all they had to work with. She hoped Bill's masquerade would help them find something more solid before another man wound up dead.

CHAPTER TWENTY EIGHT

Before Bill had driven very far along the carefully manicured paths, he began to feel a guilty pang. He had to remind himself that he had a job to do, and that he was dealing with a murder case.

I'm enjoying this too much, he realized.

Indeed, he felt like a college kid driving a new sports car. The only thing that bugged him was Jared's nonstop chatter. Pretty soon Bill said to him …

"I think a caddy is supposed to stay quiet until he's spoken to."

Jared immediately fell into a sullen silence. Bill couldn't get very concerned about whether he might have hurt the kid's feelings. He really liked how quiet the cart's electric motor was as they wound along a path beneath trees that arched overhead.

As he looked around, he saw that quite a few other people were out enjoying the shade on the hot summer day. Other carts whirred past them from the opposite direction, and there were some joggers out using the paths.

Pretty soon, Bill realized that a few of the golfers in carts and an occasional jogger were looking at him and Jared with curiosity.

What's up with that? Bill wondered.

He didn't really want to attract a lot of attention. The opposite would be better for his purposes. He began to wonder if maybe he didn't actually look the part he was playing.

Then three men in a canopied cart flagged him to a stop and pulled up beside him. Judging from their reddish faces and the goofy grins two of them wore, Bill guessed that they'd already been drinking a good bit.

One of the guys said to Bill, "Which club are you headed for today?"

Bill panicked a little. He felt stupid for not being prepared to answer such a question. But then, this wasn't the sort of undercover work he'd ever even thought about doing.

Fortunately, Jared spoke up.

"We're playing at the Cedar Creek Country Club."

Bill breathed a sigh of relief. Jared had remembered the one golf club Harrison Lund had mentioned when they'd interviewed him. Dutifully playing his role as Bill's caddy, he'd snatched the name of that club out of his head.

Bill thought …

Riley was right—the kid is of some use, after all.

Still, Bill worried—what if these guys were headed to the same course?

A guy who looked about Bill's age said, "Good luck with Cedar Creek. It's pretty hilly for my taste. You've really got to keep the ball in front of you and in play."

The youngest of the guys said, "Hilly? Buster, you're so full of shit your eyes are brown. There's nothing wrong with that course."

The oldest said, "There's a lot of water at the Cedar Creek. I don't like it much."

The youngest guy said, "Wusses, the both of you."

The oldest shook his head and said to Bill, "This guy gives me a lot of grief. I'm Zack Slattery, and I guess you could say I'm kind of the 'elder statesman' here."

The youngest snorted. "'Elder statesman'? What a crock."

Nodding to the youngest, Zack said, "This idiot is Louie Frazier."

The guy who was about Bill's age said, "I'm Buster Eades."

Bill quickly realized …

I don't need to lie about my name.

"I'm Bill Jeffreys," he said. "And Jared here is my caddy for today."

Louie squinted at Jared and said, "A caddy, huh? I don't remember seeing you at Cedar Creek or anywhere else around here."

Sounding characteristically defensive, Jared replied, "I've been around."

Zack peered at Bill curiously and said, "I take it you're not from around here, Bill. Where are you from?"

Better not say Quantico, Bill thought. They'd surely assume that he was involved with the FBI or maybe the Marines.

"The DC area," he said.

Zack asked, "What brings you around here?"

He quickly decided it might be strategic to bring Harter's death into the conversation.

He said, "I'm Ed Harter's cousin. I guess you probably heard that he passed away."

Louie let out a yelp of laughter, obviously amused by the euphemism.

"Yeah, I heard something like that," he said.

Zack glared at Louie and said, "Don't act like a prick, OK?"

Then turning to Bill again, Zack said, "I'm sorry for your loss. This must be a tough time for you." He nodded at the cart and added, "I thought I recognized that snazzy little cart. Harter used to drive it around here a lot. Hadn't seen him in recent years."

Now Bill realized why people had been looking at the cart. They, too, had recognized it. Bill wondered if maybe people had also recognized the clothes he was wearing.

He sighed and said, "Yeah, I hear that Ed pretty much quit golfing. Well, I can't say he and I were close. But I was asked to come down and help settle his affairs. It's all kind of a mess, if you want to know the truth. I thought I'd escape for a while, enjoy the outdoors."

Buster and Zack nodded sympathetically.

Then Zack said, "Hey, Bill—we're headed over to the Estes Golf Club for some brewskis. We're members there. Care to join us before you head on over to Cedar Creek?"

Bill smiled. This was exactly the kind of contact he'd been hoping for.

"Sure, thanks," he said.

Bill followed their cart about a mile to the Estes Golf Club, where they parked in a lot just for golf carts. Then they walked around the main building toward a pleasant little dining area with an open roof overlooking the course. As the men started to sit down at the table, Bill gave Jared a look warning him not to join them. Bill knew that caddies were excluded from these gatherings.

Jared obediently skulked away to a table on the edge of the eating area.

A waiter came by, and Buster ordered a pitcher of beer and three glasses. Bill wondered how much beer the guys had already been drinking today.

The beer was delivered and as they began imbibing, Buster asked Bill, "So what's your handicap?"

Bill felt unprepared again. The truth was, he was pretty much a bogey golfer—when he played golf at all, which wasn't often. But would these guys shut down on him if he said that?

He reminded himself that he wasn't planning to play golf today. He didn't have to be honest.

An average handicap might sound OK, he thought.

"Fourteen point seven," Bill said.

When the guys reeled off their own handicaps, Bill was glad he'd lied. They sounded like exceptional players.

Unless they're lying too, he thought.

152

Then Zack said, "Terrible thing about what happened to Harter. And I hear two other fellows were killed, probably by the same guy. Are the police anywhere near finding who did it?"

"I'm afraid not," Bill said, pleased at the opening in the conversation. "Were any of you friends with him?"

Louie shrugged. "I never actually met him."

Buster said, "Me neither."

Zack said, "I talked to him a few times. Never got close to him."

Bill asked, "Do you know anybody who did? Get close to him, I mean?"

Zack thought for a moment.

"Nobody I can think of. Harter wasn't much for making friends. He was kind of … I don't know …"

Buster scoffed and said, "He was really a snotty, superior son-of-a-bitch."

Zack chuckled. "Yeah, he was at that. I don't like to speak ill of the dead. But you won't find many folks around here crying about him."

Bill's interest quickened.

He asked, "Do you know anybody who might have wanted him dead?"

Zack tilted his head and said, "I can't think of anybody who cared enough about him to bother."

Louie rapped his knuckles on the table and said, "You know what? I think I know who offed him. It was that pretty young wife of his. I got a look at her a couple of times. Damn, but she looked fine."

Buster winked. "I'll say. And I bet she's a regular merry widow. I wonder if she's looking for … well, a little action. I wouldn't mind making myself available."

Louie laughed. "Be careful what you wish for. You might meet the same fate as Harter. Besides, you're a married man."

Buster grunted and said, "Don't remind me. Besides, it's not like that ever stopped me before."

Zack looked at Buster and asked, "How are things between you and Marilou these days?"

Buster swallowed a large gulp of beer, then said, "Not good. I'd be glad to be rid of her, except she'd find a lawyer to take me for everything I've got."

Zack said, "You a married man, Bill?"

Bill gulped a little. He really wasn't prepared for the

conversation turning personal.

"Divorced," he said.

Buster let out a grunt of disgust.

"Lucky man," he said. "You're well out of it."

Louie said, "I'll bet you're playing the field like some kind of Casanova."

Bill felt a sharp pang of sadness. He briefly considered covering his feelings by boasting about sexual conquests that had never happened.

After all, lying was what going undercover was all about.

But somehow, he couldn't make himself do it.

Instead, he said quite sincerely, "The wounds are still too fresh. I'd just as soon be alone for a while."

But he wondered whether what he just said was really true. Was he starting to enjoy working with Riley a little more than he should? Sometimes it felt like their old attraction might still be there, but then he thought that maybe he was just flattering himself.

Anyway, Riley had a boyfriend—a really good guy, actually— which put her off limits as far as Bill was concerned.

Meanwhile, the guys were watching his face, waiting for him to say more.

Bill sipped on his beer and said, "I guess Maggie didn't feel the same way—about fresh wounds, I mean. She's already remarried. Took our kids to another state. And I …"

His voice faded away as he choked up a little.

Why did I let myself get into this conversation? he wondered.

He was glad to hear Buster speak up.

"Marilou's still going to that damn group of hers."

Louie scoffed again.

"LifeGrasp, you mean?" he said. "God, I hated it when Jenny was going there."

Zack shook his head and said, "I was sure glad when Roberta gave up on it."

Bill felt a quickening of interest.

"Are you talking about some kind of support group?" he asked.

Louie chuckled cynically and said, "Yeah, the wives around here join up with it whenever they decide they're unhappy with their husbands—namely us. Seems like we all have to deal with it sooner or later."

Bill couldn't help but wonder …

Might Maggie have gotten some good out of that kind of group?

Could it maybe have saved our marriage?

Zack explained, "LifeGrasp's kind of a New Age fad. It can't end soon enough as far as the husbands around here are concerned. Its motto is something like, 'Every crisis is an opportunity for spiritual growth.' Roberta kept coming home with all kinds of damn fool ideas when she was going there."

Buster said with a growl of dismay, "All it's doing for Marilou is making her feel more superior. I'm not good enough for her anymore—not 'evolved' enough, she says."

Louie laughed harshly and said, "You do have kind of a caveman thing going for you, Buster."

Buster glared at Louie. "What's that supposed to mean?"

Still laughing, Louie said, "Well, maybe she'd think you were more 'evolved' if you didn't knock her around so much."

Buster's face reddened even deeper than it had been already.

He snarled at Louie, "You've got a hell of a nerve."

Louie shrugged. "Just saying," he said.

Buster said, "Don't tell me you never smacked Jenny."

"Only when she really has it coming," Louie said. "For you it's like some kind of sport."

Looking quite drunk now, Buster rose to his feet, scowling. Cursing, he cocked one fist back.

Louie leaped up, too, with both fists raised.

Before the two could start swinging at each other, Bill had instinctively gotten up and moved between them, separating them.

Buster turned his fury on Bill and took a swing at him.

Bill deftly grabbed Buster's arm and twisted it behind his back.

Seeing that, Louie stepped back and sat down, looking thoroughly intimidated.

Zach laughed and said, "Hey, Bill, you've got some good moves there. Where did you pick those up?"

Bill suddenly felt flustered.

Damn, I almost blew my cover.

Then he said, "I'm a former Marine."

"Thank you for your service," Zach said. "Sit back down, let's all relax."

Still looking surly, Buster sat back down, but Bill stayed on his feet.

He felt a strange tingle.

All this means something, he thought.

Finally he said, "Listen, guys, thanks for the beer. I ought to get going."

Zack looked embarrassed.

"I'm sorry for how the guys are acting," he said. "They'll be better now. Don't let them drive you away."

"Oh, it's not that," Bill said. "It's just …"

It's just what? he wondered.

He took a few dollars out of his billfold and put it on the table.

Then he said, "Here's for the tip. Maybe I'll see you guys around."

Bill strode away from the table toward where Jared had been sitting and watching the group.

Bill said to him, "Come on, we're leaving."

Jared got to his feet. "Hey, don't *I* get a tip?"

"No," Bill said.

His head was buzzing after the conversation about the support group.

"What's going on?" Jared asked as they trotted toward the lot where the cart was parked.

Bill didn't reply.

The truth was, he didn't yet know.

But he was sure of one thing …

I've got to call Riley right now.

CHAPTER TWENTY NINE

The feeling was familiar, and Riley always hated it—especially when more lives might be at stake.

"We're getting nowhere." she said into her cell phone.

"Yeah," Van Roff replied.

She was sitting alone in the Harters' huge living room talking with the Seattle computer nerd. They'd been brainstorming possible connections among the victims, and also among the victims' wives. Van had run a few unproductive searches.

Finally he said, "Listen, I'd better get back to my regular work. The boss might come around any second."

"OK," Riley said. "Let me know if you get any ideas."

She hung up and sat quietly for a moment.

Then, in a whisper, she repeated what she'd said to Roff …

"We're getting nowhere."

Just then her cell phone rang. She was excited to see the call was from Bill.

"Have you got something?" she asked him when she took the call.

"I don't know. Maybe you can tell me. I just had beers with three guys complaining about their marriages, and how their wives went to a support group called LifeGrasp. A lot of angry wives around here seem to go there. At least two of the guys I talked with sound like abusive husbands. So I'm wondering …"

Bill's voice trailed off, and Riley finished his thought.

"Maybe this is the connection we're looking for."

"It's a long shot, I guess," Bill said.

"Maybe not," Riley said.

"But what does it mean?" Bill asked.

Riley thought for a moment.

Two words that Bill had just said really caught her attention …

"… angry wives …"

She said, "Bill, I'm wondering if maybe …"

Her voice trailed off, but Bill finished her thought …

"You're wondering if maybe the killer is a woman."

Riley hesitated, then said, "I guess it sounds kind of crazy …"

"Not so crazy," Bill said. "She'd have to be strong, but not extremely strong."

Riley thought about how the killer had deftly dropped from a tree limb in order to get into Julian Morse's pool area, and had also successful deactivated two security systems.

"She'd have to be exceptionally agile," Riley said. "And she'd have to have excellent hacking skills."

Bill said, "A woman could have those abilities as easily as a man."

Riley's mind raced as she tried to process this new idea.

She said, "Bill, you should have seen and heard Morgan Farrell when I talked to her in jail. She was absolutely convinced she had murdered her husband. She was sure she'd stabbed him again and again and again. She'd truly been desperate enough to kill. She couldn't have killed the other two and I've never believed that she killed her husband, but she was sure that she could have."

Bill said, "Maybe another woman could have been disturbed and angry enough to kill Farrell and the other two victims. But do you really think this support group, LifeGrasp, might be some kind of connection? Maybe it even provided some kind of encouragement to a killer?"

"I'm not sure. The men were killed in different locations. Linking them to a single group might be kind of a stretch. But even so …"

Her voice trailed off again.

Then she said, "Let me check a few things out. You just keep doing what you're doing. You still might get a good solid lead. And you'd better get in touch with Chief O'Neill, let him know that there are at least two domestic abusers in Monarch that he needs to look into."

"I'll do that," Bill said.

They ended the call, and Riley sat thinking for a moment.

She remembered again what Bill had said about LifeGrasp …

"A lot of angry wives around here seem to go there."

A while ago Vivian Bettridge had told her to call out if she needed anything. Riley called out her name, and right away the majordomo entered the room.

Riley said to her, "I really need to talk to Tisha again."

Bettridge nodded and went away. After a few moments she came back with Tisha, who sat down near Riley.

Riley asked Tisha, "Are you familiar with a women's support group called LifeGrasp?"

Tisha shrugged and said, "Sure, it's really a popular thing around here. Believe me, there's no shortage of women in Monarch who need that kind of help."

"What about you?" Riley asked.

Tisha smirked resentfully.

"Do I look like the kind of woman who needs group therapy? I'm not a loser like them. That kind of thing isn't for me, thanks. I can take care of myself. I'm tough."

Riley felt a flash of discouragement.

So much for that possible link among all three of the wives, she thought.

But even so, she couldn't dismiss the idea that she was finally on to something.

She asked, "What more can you tell me about LifeGrasp?"

Tisha shrugged again.

"Only what I hear. I do know there's more than just the one clinic here in Monarch. It's kind of a franchise. I know there are clinics in some other locations."

Riley felt a renewed tingle of interest.

She asked, "Like maybe in Birmingham? Or even in Atlanta?"

Tisha said, "I don't see why not. But the main clinic is right here in Monarch. Sort of the corporate headquarters, I guess you'd call it."

Without another word, Riley got up and hurried out of the house to be by herself. Then she reached into her purse and found the brochure she'd picked up at the Haverhill Dependency Center. She found its phone number and called its main desk on her cell phone. She told the receptionist her name and asked to speak with Morgan Farrell. The receptionist paged Morgan, who seemed eager to take the call.

"Agent Paige! I hadn't expected to hear from you so soon—or maybe even at all! How are you? What's going on?"

Pacing in the driveway in front of the mansion, Riley said, "Morgan, I need for you to tell me something. Did you ever belong to a support group connected to a company called LifeGrasp?"

Riley heard Morgan gasp a little.

"As a matter of fact, I did. How did you know?"

Riley asked, "Where was the clinic you went to?"

"Why, right here in Atlanta, of course. But we didn't call it a 'support group.' It's a 'process group,' a way to achieve positive goals even when going through traumatic times. We learned ways of coping with depression and anxiety. But there was more to it than that. It was all about finding self-fulfillment. The LifeGrasp motto is, 'Every crisis is an opportunity for spiritual growth.'"

"When did you go there?" Riley asked. "For how long?"

"Oh, for about six or seven months, late last year and early this year. I'd love to have stuck with it. But Andrew put a stop to it. He didn't like what it was doing for me—didn't like the ideas and notions I got there, he said."

Morgan sighed and added, "He just couldn't deal with the possibility of me becoming empowered."

Riley thanked Morgan and ended the call.

Then she found the number for the Britomart Hotel. The male clerk who answered her call remembered Riley's recent visit, so he put her through directly to Charlotte Morse's room. Right away Riley asked Charlotte whether she'd been part of a LifeGrasp process group.

Charlotte said, "Oh, yes, and it did me a world of good. It was the reason I got strong enough to leave Julian. He was furious, of course, but by then I didn't care."

"Do you still go there?" Riley asked.

"Oh, no. The whole group agreed that I was making wonderful progress on my own. It was time to cut the cord, so to speak. Really, I don't know what I would have done without LifeGrasp."

Riley thanked Charlotte and ended the call.

She was tingling all over now, more and more certain she was on the right track. There was some connection between that organization and the murders.

She headed straight to her car. She knew where she needed to go and whom she needed to talk to.

CHAPTER THIRTY

Riley's hopes were rising as she parked in front of the house with the dignified sign that read LIFEGRASP COUNSELING, INC.

This could be it, she thought. *This could be the break I've been looking for.*

In fact, she was feeling sure that she was on the right track.

She got out of the car and walked toward the house. Other than the sign, it didn't look like a business at all. It was just an attractive, wood-frame, three-story house in a neighborhood with houses much like it.

When Riley walked through the front door, a little bell tinkled to announce an arrival.

She found herself in an almost alarmingly peaceful space. What had once been a large living room had been painted in muted, pastel colors, with mildly surrealistic paintings hung from the walls. There was a scent of incense in the air, and droning music that featured wind chimes was playing quietly.

A woman rose from the front desk as Riley came in.

"How can I help you?" the woman asked, smiling prettily.

Riley produced her badge and introduced herself.

"I need to speak with whoever's in charge here," she said.

The woman suddenly looked concerned.

She picked up her desk phone, punched a button, and said, "Eleanora, a woman is here to see you."

She glanced up at Riley and added in nervous whisper, "She says she's from the FBI."

A few moments later, another woman seemed almost to float into the room. She was about Riley's age, and flamboyantly dressed in a puffy, colorful peasant dress. She had large hands that seemed to just love making large gestures. She also had an enormous, glowing smile and deep green eyes.

She immediately inspired Riley with a gut-level feeling of dislike.

Riley reintroduced herself, and the woman said ...

"FBI! Oh, my! This must be serious!"

"I'm afraid so," Riley said.

"Well, I'm Eleanora Oberlander, founder and CEO of

LifeGrasp Counseling. Come on, let's find somewhere we can talk."

Riley followed her upstairs into an enormous room that looked like it had once been two or three smaller rooms when people had lived here. The same music was being piped in, and this room also smelled of incense.

The hardwood floor was scattered with rolled-up yoga mats, and chairs were stacked against the walls. It was easy for Riley to see that this was where at least some of the process groups were held.

The woman unrolled a couple of mats and invited Riley to sit down with her.

Riley was used to interviewing people who asserted their dominance one way or the other, often by placing themselves physically above her. Riley was sure that Eleanora was doing the same thing right now in her own way, by making Riley sit on the floor instead of fetching them a couple of chairs.

As Riley sat down cross-legged on the mat, she realized that her feeling of dislike was starting to morph into outright suspicion.

Eleanora said, "Now do tell me what this is all about."

Riley said, "I'm working on a murder case."

Although the woman's expression changed a little, Riley couldn't read her reaction.

"Oh—murder. How terrible! Does this have to do with those three prominent men who've been murdered recently?"

"It does," Riley said.

"But what can that possibly have to do with LifeGrasp?"

Riley considered her words carefully.

Then she said, "We're starting to think that the murderer could be a woman. An abused wife, possibly, or someone who knew they were abused. Someone who is very angry."

Eleanora's eyes widened, and so did that disarming smile of hers.

"Surely you don't think that LifeGrasp is some kind of connecting factor," she said. Then her green eyes narrowed and she added, "That sounds downright silly to me."

Riley's suspicions were rising. Something about Eleanora Oberlander really bothered her.

Is it possible that this is the killer? Riley wondered.

Or were her persistent suspicions triggered by something else entirely? She felt sure that something was wrong here.

Riley said, "Two of the murdered men's widows have attended

your company's sessions. Morgan Farrell went to your clinic in Atlanta. Charlotte Morse went to the one in Birmingham. Did you get to know either of those two women?"

Eleanora tilted her head curiously.

"Agent Paige, are you accusing *me* of something?" she said.

"I'd just like you to answer my question," Riley said.

A silence fell between them.

Finally Eleanora said, "There is such a thing as therapist-client confidentiality, you know. Do you have a warrant to go poking into such matters?"

"Not yet," Riley said. "I could get one very quickly."

It was a bluff, of course. And Riley could tell by Eleanora's expression that she wasn't falling for it.

Eleanora rose to her feet.

"Well, I think you should do that," she said. "And in the meantime, if you don't mind, I have quite a lot of important business to attend to."

Suddenly, Riley's suspicions took a much clearer shape.

She knew now exactly what she'd mistrusted about Eleanora.

She got to her feet and stood facing the woman.

She asked, "Tell me, Eleanora—this business of yours is properly certified, isn't it?"

"Why, of course. I myself am a certified clinical psychologist. I can show you the certificates if you like."

Riley could see a growing discomfort in Eleanora's face.

Now she's *doing the bluffing,* she realized.

Riley asked, "Where did you get your doctorate, Eleanora?"

Riley could see movement in Eleanora's throat as she gulped a little.

"Thiebert University," she said.

"I've never heard of it," Riley said.

"I'm surprised," Eleanora said. "It's a very prestigious institution."

"I'm sure it is," Riley said, maintaining a tone of calculated politeness. "I ought to look it up, just out of personal curiosity."

Eleanora's smile disappeared entirely—and Riley was sure she knew why.

Thiebert University was nothing but a diploma mill.

And LifeGrasp wasn't legitimately certified for any kind of therapeutic practice at all.

Riley knew she had Eleanora completely stymied now.

"Why don't we sit back down, Eleanora?" Riley said.

She and Eleanora both sat down on the yoga mats again.

Riley said, "And now I'd like you to answer my question—did you get to know Charlotte Morse or Morgan Farrell?"

"I'm afraid I didn't," Eleanora said. "But that's really not unusual. Although I frequently sit in on group sessions, I do very little hands-on therapy myself, and I'm constantly traveling among our clinics. I'm responsible for the quality of the overall program. My employees take care of the individuals who come to us for help."

Riley felt sure that Eleanora was telling the truth now.

"Besides," Eleanora added, "our clients seldom go by their real names."

"What do you mean?" Riley asked.

Eleanora shrugged slightly. "One of the first things we do when a client shows up is … well, tap into her mythic identity, as we like to put it. We give her a list to choose from, and she adopts a name of some goddess or female mythic figure—Ariadne, Freya, Niobe, Isis, Ishtar, Kuan Yin, or what have you. And that's the name she goes by in our sessions."

Riley said, "But surely you keep track of the women's real names."

Eleanora blushed a little.

"Um, sometimes yes, sometimes no. I'm afraid we're a little careless about that. Besides, some of our women are drop-ins who pay in cash and only come to a few sessions, then disappear again. Our records are rather … spotty."

Riley felt a wave of discouragement.

How was she going to get any hard information in a place this poorly organized?

She thought for a moment, then said, "Surely your team of therapists report to you about what's going on in their groups."

"Of course," Eleanora said.

"Have any of them happened to mention …"

Riley paused to consider …

What is it I want to ask, exactly?

Finally she said, "Have any of your therapists mentioned clients who've recently adopted *warlike* identities? Goddesses of destruction, maybe?"

Eleanora said, "We've got a few of those on our list. My team mentioned a few recent clients who chose those kinds of names. One woman called herself Anut, after the Egyptian war goddess. Then there was one who took the name of the Hindu warrior Durga.

Oh, and I can remember one from a few sessions I sat in on right here. A woman called herself Brunhilda—you know, the Norse Valkyrie maiden."

"Valkyrie?" Riley asked.

"Yes. The Valkyries chose which male warriors were to live and die in battle."

Riley's interest was piqued.

"What can you tell me about her?" she asked.

Eleanora chuckled and said, "Well, she was a tough young thing—pretty, but tough. Her husband was abusive, but she refused to get all weepy with self-pity about it, like so many of other clients. 'I always come out on top,' she liked to say."

Riley felt a flash of recognition.

I've heard someone say those very words recently, she thought.

Then Eleanora squinted and said, "On the other hand, maybe she wasn't so tough. Or at least not very honest. The last time she came here, she had a broken finger. The therapist was sure her husband had broken it, and so was I. But she denied it. She said she was clumsy, that she'd tripped and fallen."

Riley almost gasped aloud.

She knew perfectly well who this "Brunhilda" was.

But Tisha had flatly denied ever coming to LifeGrasp.

She lied to me!

CHAPTER THIRTY ONE

Riley was furious at herself as she drove back to the Harters' mansion.

I should have known, she thought.

I should have paid attention to my instincts.

After all, she had been wary of Tisha's amoral cunning since she'd first met her. She'd also been keenly aware of the young woman's intelligence, her enormous capacity to learn things on her own. Riley had no doubt that if Tisha was interested in disabling security systems, she could have taught herself the necessary hacking skills. Or at least, she could have found out where to learn what she needed to know.

Judging from Tisha's appearance, she also could be nimble enough to have gotten into Julian Morse's pool area. She was certainly strong enough to stab someone multiple times. And Riley also believed that Tisha could have been angry enough to carry out the murders.

Riley worried while she drove. Was Tisha Harter even still there in the mansion?

She might well have realized that Riley was on her way to LifeGrasp to ask questions. Might Tisha have already fled, fearing arrest?

Riley knew that Tisha was shrewd and chameleon-like.

If she chose to disappear, how hard would it be to find her again?

And how could she be stopped from killing again?

I should have arrested her already, Riley thought.

But for what? Until just now, there had been no probable cause.

Would it be best to phone now and make sure the woman was still at home? And that she would stay there?

No, Riley decided. It was only a few minutes' drive. There was no reason to raise an alarm.

When Riley arrived there and rang the doorbell, Vivian Bettridge answered the door, Riley charged inside right past her.

"Where's Tisha Harter?" she demanded.

Bettridge was visibly alarmed by Riley's agitation.

"She said she doesn't want to be bothered for the rest of the day," Vivian said.

Riley felt a twinge of relief.

It seemed that Tisha hadn't fled the mansion.

She spoke sharply to the Bettridge, "I asked you, where is she? I need to see her right now."

Bettridge appeared about to protest, but the expression on Riley's face stopped her. Looking truly intimidated now, she said, "Upstairs in the rec room. But …"

Riley didn't wait to hear the majordomo's weak objections. She hurried into the house and took the elevator to the second floor.

When Riley got to the rec room, she found Tisha dressed as casually as when she'd first met her, again killing opponents in the violent video game. Gone was the more mature, sophisticated persona on display just a little while ago. The "lady of the manor" had reverted to the sullen, hostile young woman she really was.

Tisha looked up from the game as Riley strode into the room.

"Agent Paige! What the hell? I told Vivian I wanted—"

Ignoring the protests, Riley ordered, "Get on your feet."

With a stunned look, Tisha got up from the couch. She looked like she didn't know whether to fight or to run.

Riley said, "Tisha Harter, you're under arrest for lying to an FBI agent—and also on suspicion of murder in the first degree."

Riley took out her handcuffs and recited Tisha's Miranda rights.

Tisha protested loudly as Riley slapped the cuffs on her.

"This is stupid. You don't have anything on me. I didn't do anything wrong. And you can't prove I did anything wrong."

Riley was leading her out of the rec room toward the elevator now.

"Yes, I *can* prove you did something wrong. You lied to me, in violation of Section 1001 of Title 18 in the US Code. Martha Stewart was jailed for that. Do you think you can get by with something she couldn't?"

As they took the elevator down, Tisha was still cursing and complaining. Then she fell silent and looked like she was thinking hard, turning various possibilities over in her mind.

Finally she asked meekly, "What did I lie about?"

When they reached the ground floor, Riley just said "Come on" and marched Tisha into the living room.

Then she heard Bill's voice.

"Riley! What the hell—?"

Riley saw that Vivian Bettridge was just then escorting Bill and Jared into the mansion. The two were still in their undercover outfits, but had apparently finished their investigations for today.

She told him, "I'm arresting Tisha Harter."

"For what?" Bill said.

"For lying to me, for starters. That will hold her for a while. But don't worry, we won't have any trouble proving that she's also a murderer."

Bill said, "Riley, no, please listen—"

Riley interrupted, rapidly telling Bill about her visit to LifeGrasp and how she'd learned that Tisha Harter had deliberately lied to her.

Finally Bill interrupted her, almost shouting.

"Riley, stop! She's not the one we're looking for. Tisha is not a serial killer!"

Riley's mouth dropped open. She was speechless.

Bill said, "Remember when you told me to call Chief O'Neill about those two domestic abusers? While I had him on the phone, he filled me in on how his investigative team was progressing. They've been doing good work. He told me they'd studied the security tapes for inside this house."

Riley stammered, "But—but the security system here was hacked when Harter was killed. There wouldn't be any video record—"

"Not for Harter's murder, no," Bill said. "But the tapes show that Tisha Harter was definitely here at home when the other two murders took place. She couldn't have killed those men, Riley."

Riley felt sick to her stomach.

What kind of mistake did I just make?

Tisha was glaring at her now.

She said, "You're crazy, Agent Paige. Do you know that?"

Riley realized that she had no choice but to uncuff the woman. Arresting her now would just be a waste of valuable time.

As she did so, she said, "I *know* you lied to me about LifeGrasp. That was you being crazy, not me."

"So what if I lied?" Tisha said.

"So what?" Riley snapped. But then she felt herself softening up. This wasn't the first or last mistake this young woman would make, and surely not the biggest one. It wasn't worth taking her in over.

Riley said tiredly, "It's a crime, Tisha. What were you thinking, lying to an FBI agent? Why did you do that?"

Tisha shrugged and said, "I was embarrassed, OK? I was feeling weak and helpless when I went there. And I don't like feeling like that. I like to think I can deal with anything, no matter how rough things get. I sure as hell didn't want to admit I'd gone there. Especially not to a tough chick like you."

Riley felt thoroughly mortified now. She had no doubt that Tisha was telling the truth—at least about this. And from what Bill had just said, Tisha obviously was not the murderer.

When she was freed from the cuffs, Tisha rubbed her wrists.

"I've got half a mind to sue your ass for what you just did," she said.

Riley suppressed a growl of annoyance.

She wanted to say …

Go ahead and try.

She knew she had Tisha dead to rights for lying to an FBI agent, if nothing else. Tisha couldn't make a case against her for attempting a false arrest.

But now that she knew the truth, questions started crowding into Riley's mind.

Trying to calm herself, Riley said, "Tisha, you might have important information. Did anyone in the LifeGrasp group stand out to you? Someone especially angry? Someone who took special interest in your situation?"

Tisha snapped, "If you think I've got anything more to say to you, you're even crazier than I already thought."

Tisha turned and walked away. Riley took a couple of steps to follow her, but Bill's voice stopped her.

"It's no use, Riley. You aren't going to get any answers from her, at least not now. Come on. Let's get back to Atlanta."

Feeling thoroughly defeated, Riley followed Jared and Bill out of the house.

I just blew it, she thought. *I completely screwed up.*

Meanwhile, she knew they were losing valuable time.

There was a serial killer at large who might well have already targeted another victim.

CHAPTER THIRTY TWO

During the short trip from Monarch to Atlanta, Riley was struggling with despair and embarrassment.

She wondered …

When am I going to get something right about this case?

Bill was driving, filling her in what he and Jared had been doing since the last time they'd talked. He said that rest of their little undercover mission had been unproductive. They'd extended their golf-cart trip to the various courses in the area, questioning people pretty much at random. But they'd done no better than the more organized computer searches the FBI had been making. Nobody had turned up any connection among the victims that might point to a killer.

In fact, they hadn't gotten any useful information at all.

Riley then shared more details about her use of the one bit of information Bill had passed on to her—that a lot of local wives participated in group sessions at LifeGrasp. That slim lead had only resulted in her disastrous attempt to arrest Tisha Harter.

When she finished, Jared wanted to get into the conversation.

He asked, "Isn't it still possible that one or more of the widows is guilty? Or even all of them? Maybe they met at LifeGrasp and wound up conspiring together, agreeing to kill their husbands in exactly the same way so that the murders looked like the work of a single killer."

Jared barely paused for breath before he took another tack.

"Or maybe they even traded murders. You know, like in that Hitchcock flick, *Strangers on a Train*."

That sounded farfetched to Riley, but she didn't dismiss it out of hand.

But Bill shot down that theory.

"The women seem to have all gone to different LifeGrasp clinics," he said. "We've got no reason to think they ever met each other."

Riley added, "Besides, I'm all but sure that neither Morgan nor Charlotte has the kind of computer skills needed to hack security systems. And my instincts tell me that neither one of them has got the makings of a killer."

Jared let out a snort of laughter.

"Your instincts, huh? How good were your instincts working when you slapped the cuffs on Tisha Harter back there?"

Riley felt both stung and angry.

She said, "You'd better watch your mouth, Jared."

Jared seemed completely unfazed by her comment.

He said, "Or maybe the women were brainwashed into killing by all that New Age crap at LifeGrasp. You know, like in *The Manchurian Candidate* …"

As Jared ranted on about the mesmerizing effects of incense and droning music, his ideas went off the rails of plausibility altogether. Riley and Bill were both relieved when they dropped him off at his apartment building and drove on to their hotel. They each went to their rooms to freshen up before getting back together for dinner.

While she was alone in her room, Riley took the opportunity to call Van Roff again. She wanted the computer geek to hack into LifeGrasp's business records. Of course he said he would be delighted to do so.

She then asked him to check credit card payments to see if he could locate any clients who might have gone to more than one of the LifeGrasp clinics. Roff turned up nothing, which didn't surprise Riley. After all, Eleanora Oberlander had told her that many clients paid in cash. If the murderer really had been a LifeGrasp client, she would have known better than to leave a credit card trail that led to her.

Riley thanked Roff and ended the call.

She sat on the edge of the motel room bed wondering …

Is there anything else I can do right now?

The whole day had gone so terribly wrong. Was there anything she could do to salvage some hope of solving this case?

Her cell phone rang, and she saw that the call was from home.

She answered and heard Jilly's crying voice.

"Mom, April's up to something awful! You've got to make her stop!"

Riley stifled a sigh. The last thing she wanted to deal with was a sibling spat right now.

"What's wrong?" Riley asked, trying to sound patient. "What did April do?"

"She wants to get a kitten! I keep telling her we can't, but she won't listen."

Suddenly Riley's head hurt.

She almost asked, *"Why can't April get a kitten?"*

But she stopped herself.

So far, nobody had talked to her one way or the other about a kitten. And she certainly hadn't had time to think the possibility through. If she wasn't careful, she might agree to something she'd be sorry for later.

Riley groaned and said, "Is your sister there?"

"Yeah, I'll get her."

She heard Jilly stomping away, then the sound of the two girls speaking sharply to each other.

Finally April got on the phone.

Riley asked, "April, what's going on with you and your sister?"

"Oh, Mom, Jilly's being crazy and selfish."

"What's this she said about you wanting a kitten?"

April sounded on the verge of tears now.

"My friend Addie has a cat that just had a litter. Addie's given all the kittens away except one. If I don't take it, Addie's mother will take it to the pound. And you know what's liable to happen to it then! They'll kill the poor thing!"

Riley's headache was getting worse by the second.

She said, "April, I really need for both of you girls to—"

April interrupted, "Mom, if you could see this kitten, it's so cute and adorable! She's black and white and fluffy, and she purrs so loud when you pet her! She just breaks my heart! Look, I'll send you a picture."

"Don't," Riley replied hastily. "Just give me a minute."

Riley fell silent, trying to think this new crisis through.

Finally she decided that she had to ask the obvious question …

"April, why does Jilly think you can't get a kitten?"

"Because of the new puppy! Jilly's got this stupid idea that you can't have a dog and a cat in the same house. She says they'll never get along. But really, I just think she doesn't want me to have a pet of my own. She wants Darby to be the only pet in the house. She's just being selfish."

Riley was starting to feel angry with both girls now.

She said, "April, you've been so responsible and grown up lately. Can't you figure out some way to handle this on your own? Or wait until I get back?"

"It can't wait, Mom. It's today or never. They'll take the kitten to the pound tomorrow."

Riley tried to sort through what she was hearing.

Why does this seem so difficult? she wondered.

Of course, she knew that getting another pet was a big decision under the best of circumstances.

And these definitely weren't the best circumstances.

Riley heaved a long sigh. "Put Jilly back on the phone."

"But Mom—"

"Just do it, OK?"

Jilly was still crying when she got back on the phone.

Riley said, "Jilly, where did you get the idea that cats and dogs never get along?"

"I don't know. Everybody says so."

"Well, that's not true—at least not all the time. Sometimes, if they start out living together as puppies and kittens, they grow up to be best friends. Doesn't that sound nice?"

Riley heard Jilly gulp down a sob.

"I guess," she said.

Maybe I'm getting somewhere, Riley thought.

"Jilly, you were really, really happy to get Darby back, weren't you?"

"Yeah."

"Was April upset when you came home with Darby?"

"No. She was happy too."

Riley took a long breath. "Well, would it be so hard for you to be happy for April about getting a kitten? Doesn't that seem fair?"

A silence fell. Riley held her breath and waited.

Was Jilly going to throw a typical teenage fit about this, accuse Riley of always taking April's side?

Finally Jilly said, "I guess it's fair."

Riley breathed a sigh of relief.

"OK, then. I want you to go tell April that you're really happy about her getting a kitten. Can you do that for me?"

"Sure," Jilly said.

"And tell her I love both of you and miss you."

"I'll do that. Love you too, Mom."

The call ended, and Riley sat on the edge of the bed trying to sort through what had just happened.

She realized …

I just told the girls they could have a cat.

Exactly how that had happened, she didn't really know.

She headed to the bathroom to get herself ready to meet Bill for dinner.

*

173

While Bill was in his room alone, he used his cell phone to find a local restaurant. He'd been worried about Riley ever since the episode with Tisha Harter. She'd seemed more upset than she usually got over a setback. Bill figured they both deserved the comfort of a nicer-than-average dinner on the FBI's credit card.

He drove Riley to a pleasant little steakhouse that he'd found online. They ordered steaks and red wine and talked about the case. By the time their food arrived, Bill had to agree with Riley that they were truly at an impasse.

Riley said, "I can't believe I was so stupid, trying to arrest Tisha Harter like that."

"Stop beating yourself up, Riley," Bill said. "At least we know now that there was some connection among the three widows. It might still mean something. Maybe the killer really is a woman."

Riley just let out a growl of discouragement.

Bill fumbled around trying to think of something encouraging to say.

"Maybe the women hired a killer," he said.

"Those weren't professional hits, and you know it."

Bill didn't reply. The truth was, he knew that Riley was perfectly right.

He'd never dealt with a female killer who was that violent, and he'd never heard of a hired killer going crazy with a knife like that.

He and Riley tossed around a few more lame ideas over dinner, then gave it up entirely. By the time they finished eating, Riley wanted to go over to the restaurant's bar.

Bill started to worry. Riley had already gone through a few glasses of wine and he knew that she could overdo it from time to time. But he didn't want to make her feel worse by making a fuss about it.

At the bar they both ordered bourbon. They drank silently for a few moments until Bill said, "You know, it's really my fault. I shouldn't have made such a big deal out of those guys complaining about their wives. I should have known better than to think that amounted to anything."

Riley shook her head and sighed.

"No, I've been off my game from the start," she said. "I keep getting gut feelings that lead us nowhere. First I suspected that architect, Harrison Lund. Now I've made this stupid mistake with Tisha Harter. And for a few moments back at the LifeGrasp headquarters, I half-believed Eleanora Oberlander was the killer. How could I be so consistently wrong?"

As Riley called to the bartender for another bourbon, Bill said, "But Riley, you weren't really *wrong* about any of those things. Your gut was right about Harrison Lund. The FBI is already investigating him for murder, even if he's not *our* murderer. And you had good reason to get suspicious about that Oberlander woman—she's a phony therapist running a faked-up business. And Tisha Harter really did lie to you. You weren't wrong about that either."

Riley was staring bitterly into space.

"I'm losing it, Bill. My instincts are all scattershot. I can't focus anymore. I'm burning out."

Bill shifted uneasily on his bar stool.

He said, "Riley, there's not an agent in the BAU that doesn't feel this way from time to time. You've felt this way before—and don't tell me you haven't. I've been there too, so I know."

Something was dawning on him …

I'm kind of feeling the same way right now.

He'd always relied so much on Riley's instincts that he'd forgotten how to listen to his own …

Or maybe whatever instincts I ever had are just plain shot.

He took a long, slow breath.

The last thing Riley needed right now was for him to chime in with his own worries.

Instead he said, "It passes. It always does. You know it does."

Riley swallowed the rest of her bourbon and ordered another.

I'd better make sure this is her last, Bill decided.

Riley sipped her new drink. "Yeah, I guess you're right, Bill. You know, sometimes I think self-doubt and despair are part of the process. They happen on every case, then they go away. Why do you think that happens?"

Bill shrugged again.

"Maybe it's just how we keep ourselves sharp. It keeps us from getting overconfident. It makes us work harder."

Riley chuckled a little.

"Well, it sure is a pain in the ass," she said.

Bill laughed as well.

"It sure as hell is," he agreed.

They were both quiet for a few moments.

Then Riley said, "You know, maybe I did solve *one* problem a little while ago …"

She went on to tell Bill about how she'd dealt with an argument between her two daughters over a kitten, and whether the family

175

could have a kitten along with a puppy.

When she was finished, Bill chuckled again.

"You're a great mother, Riley."

"I dunno," Riley said. "The truth is, I think maybe I got had."

"What do you mean?"

"You know. Conned. Tricked. Hoodwinked. If it had just been April calling to ask me if she could have had a kitten, I'd probably have said no, and that would be the end of it. But both of them blubbering like that really had me over a barrel. Maybe they really planned the whole thing. Maybe they really played me."

Bill laughed harder now.

"Well, either you're just being paranoid, or your girls are getting along together just fine. You should be happy about that. And is there anything so bad about getting a kitten?"

"Naw, I like cats."

Bill suddenly felt a wave of melancholy.

"Riley, don't take your kids for granted. I wish I still had problems like that."

Riley looked at him with intense sympathy. She reached over and took hold of his hand.

"I'm sorry, Bill. I keep forgetting. I shouldn't go talking about family like that."

Bill said, "Don't go second-guessing yourself. I want you to talk about that stuff. I want to know about whatever is going on in your life."

As he squeezed her hand back, he felt again a familiar attraction to her. It was always there, deep in the background, and it surfaced from time to time.

And he was absolutely sure that she felt the same way.

We'd better be careful, he told himself.

With considerable effort, he let go of her hand.

Riley was slurring her words a little.

"It's just that … Bill, I'm so comfortable with you. It's so easy to talk with you. It's so easy to laugh with you. You make everything seem OK. And I can tell you absolutely anything."

Bill felt himself tense up. He knew he'd better not say he felt exactly the same way about her.

He said, "I'm sure it's the same with Blaine."

Riley looked almost surprised at the mention of Blaine's name. Then she knitted her brow in thought.

Bill hoped she wasn't going to say it *wasn't* the same with Blaine.

If she did, he wasn't sure what he himself might do or say.

But Riley was silent and he finally said, "I think we should call it a night."

Riley nodded. Bill helped her off the barstool and out to the rented car. When they got back to the motel, he walked her to her room door. She took his hand again and looked into his eyes.

She said, "Bill …"

As he returned her gaze, Bill flashed back to an awful incident last year.

Riley had phoned him in a state of drunken despair, and he could still hear her words as if it were yesterday …

"I think about you, Bill. And not just at work. Don't you think about me, too?"

Riley had wanted to begin an affair while Bill was still struggling to keep his marriage and family together.

That phone call had almost wrecked his relationship with Riley—both professionally and as a friend.

We can't go down that road again, he thought.

He let go of her hand and patted her on the shoulder.

"Let's both just get some sleep, OK?" he said.

Riley nodded again, took out her key, and went on into her room.

After the door closed, Bill headed for his own room.

This case is really getting to Riley, he realized.

He tried to shake off his concern as he walked into his room.

He reminded himself …

There are things I just can't fix.

CHAPTER THIRTY THREE

Riley was sitting cross-legged on a yoga mat on a hardwood floor in a very large room.

She was in a circle of maybe twenty women who were seated the same way.

Or are they real women? *Riley wondered.*

They all seemed to be absolutely motionless. Riley saw that none of them even seemed to be breathing. They seemed more like mannequins than real people.

Suddenly, the air was pierced by a cry of despair.

Riley turned and saw that the woman sitting next to her had come to life and had burst into tears.

"He's a monster," she said. "My husband's a monster."

She kept on sobbing, and the same thing happened to the woman sitting on Riley's other side ...

"He's a monster," she wailed. "My husband's a monster."

In a matter of seconds, grief and anguish shuddered through the whole circle of women.

They were all crying out, not in unison but in a chaotic cacophony ...

"He's a monster. My husband's a monster."

Riley's eyes quickly fell upon one woman who wasn't crying and wailing.

She was sitting directly across from her, but Riley couldn't see her clearly. Of all the women there, only she seemed to be in shadow.

But a faint light revealed that the woman's lips were moving.

She was saying something, but Riley couldn't hear it over all the wailing.

One by one, the women in the circle seemed to become aware of the woman in the shadows.

One by one, the others fell silent.

They all stared at the woman in the shadows.

They all listened.

"It's all right," she whispered. "I can fix it ... "

Little by little, the words she was saying became clearer ...

"I can make everything better ... Just trust me ... Just wait ... You'll see ... Everything will be better ... "

Now the women were all listening to her in rapt silence. They seemed to be taking comfort in those words.

And indeed, the voice sounded soothing and gentle.

But Riley shuddered at the sound of that voice. She heard something that none of the other women could hear.

It was hatred—insane, murderous hatred and fury.

She wanted to warn the others not to trust the woman ...

I've got to make them understand.

She opened her mouth but no words came out.

*

Riley's eyes snapped open.

Where am I?

She looked around and saw that she was lying in bed in a hotel room.

Most of the clothes she'd worn yesterday were scattered on the floor. She'd slept in her underwear.

She struggled to remember. She knew she'd had too much to drink last night.

She remembered feeling that old attraction to Bill.

Had they ...?

No. She remembered that Bill had led her back to her room but had left her there.

Riley felt a flood of gratitude that he had handled things so well. She was sure she wouldn't be able to deal with the terrible complications of an affair with her best friend and her developing relationship with Blaine.

Why, she wondered, *can't I ever just have just a simple happy relationship?*

Was it because she was so good at her job?

But now she wasn't doing much of a job. She had a sense of dread that this killer wasn't finished.

She groaned and sat up in bed. Sunlight was peeping through the crack between the closed curtains.

She had to get up. Everybody would be expecting her to tell them what they were going to do next. But she didn't really know what to do next.

They couldn't just wait around for another death.

Before Riley could shake herself completely awake, wisps of sounds and images began to run through her mind. She remembered women wailing. She remembered someone saying, *"I can fix it ..."*

She realized she'd a nightmare. And like many of her nightmares, it had told her something.

She shuddered. But she forced herself to remember what she could of it.

There had been a circle of women sitting on yoga mats …

One woman had been speaking …

That was it!

She had to throw aside her self-doubt.

She had to trust her instincts …

The killer really is *a woman.*

She really does *go to LifeGrasp meetings.*

And somehow, LifeGrasp was the key to finding and stopping the killer.

Riley scrambled out of bed and headed for the bathroom. She needed a quick shower. She needed to get dressed and call Bill.

She knew what she was going to do today.

CHAPTER THIRTY FOUR

Riley had a strong sense of déjà vu. She was sitting cross-legged on the yoga mat with her eyes closed, just as she had in her dream last night. This time, it was all too real.

This was the third meeting she'd attended today. Her nostrils felt positively saturated by the smell of incense, and she was sure she'd never get that droning New Age music with wind chimes out of her head.

She found herself remembering something Jared had said yesterday …

"Maybe the women were brainwashed into killing by all that New Age crap at LifeGrasp."

Riley was wondering if that was such a ridiculous theory after all. She knew that some kinds of meditation could be helpful to agents, especially for relieving stress. She used a form of meditation to get in touch with her own insights. But this program was way too flowery to work for her. The elaborate directions, the persistent music, and the pungent smells were becoming a distraction rather than an aid.

She was supposed to be visualizing herself in her own dream refuge or sanctuary—sitting beside a running stream, or walking along a misty beach, or sequestered in the safety of a cave illuminated by firelight …

Or some such place.

Instead, she kept trying to visualize a serial killer. Her mind was on the case and nothing but the case.

So, she acknowledged to herself, *the problem with all of this might just be me.*

She hoped that attending these meetings wouldn't be a waste of time.

But she was starting to have her doubts.

After last night's nightmare she'd felt sure that the killer must be a frequent visitor at these meetings. When she'd talked to Bill about it over breakfast, he'd pointed out that the women whose husbands had been killed had gone to three of the four LifeGrasp centers.

That left one LifeGrasp center unaccounted for—the one located in Marshfield, a wealthy suburb of Atlanta.

She and Bill had agreed that the killer must surely be going to the Marshfield clinic next, looking for signs that some woman's husband deserved to die.

Bill had approved of Riley's plan to go undercover to all of today's Marshfield meetings. Right now, Bill and Jared were parked a short distance down the street, not so patiently waiting for Riley to come out and tell them what she'd found.

If I find out anything.

The first two of the meetings had been a bust as far as she was concerned.

A few of the women in attendance complained of unhappy marriages, but none had indicated the kind of physical or emotional abuse that might attract the killer. A few were actually trying to come to terms with serious issues such as life-threatening illnesses. Some were dealing with serious problems such as opioid or alcohol addiction or eating disorders. But most of these women seemed to be struggling with general feelings of malaise and ennui.

As Eleanora Oberlander had explained to Riley, all the women had adopted names from myth and legend. Riley herself had chosen the name Penelope simply because it was the first mythic name that popped into her head.

Riley hadn't yet had anything to say at the meetings, and she hoped she wouldn't have to. She preferred to stay as inconspicuous as possible so she could focus on what the other women were complaining about. If she did get stuck talking, she figured she could share some of her own real-life problems—a messy adoption, a messier divorce from an unfaithful husband, and the seemingly hopeless task of juggling work and family.

LifeGrasp's one-size-fits-all solution was supposed to fit every situation. That solution was a long process of self-realization and inner transformation.

Riley was, of course, skeptical—especially knowing as she did that even LifeGrasp's CEO and founder wasn't a certified therapist.

But she couldn't deny that most of the women were apparently benefitting from the LifeGrasp experience …

Or at least they think *they're benefitting from it.*

Some of those who spoke were eloquent about the gains they'd made. And maybe that was all that mattered.

Maybe for some of them LifeGrasp really was all that it was advertised to be.

It sure had better be, she thought.

She herself had paid for each of the sessions in cash, and they were damned expensive. She couldn't imagine spending so much money on something like this on a regular basis. She was glad the FBI was going to reimburse her.

Eventually the therapist in charge of this meeting, who called herself Minerva, spoke to the group in a gentle voice, coaxing the women out of their visualized sanctuaries and back to the reality of the large meeting room.

Like everybody else, Riley opened her eyes on Minerva's final command.

Then she sat looking around the room. Darkness was falling outside, so the room was lit by candles.

As she had at earlier meetings, Riley felt a bit disoriented.

There had been some changes since she'd closed her eyes.

There were still about thirty women sitting in the circle. But some who had been here before had left, while a few others had just arrived. LifeGrasp meetings seemed to be somewhat porous. Women came and went pretty much whenever they liked.

Minerva said …

"Now who would like to share first?"

A woman on the opposite side of the circle from Riley raised her hand. She called herself Demeter. She started talking about her feelings of abandonment by her grown children.

Riley fought down a sigh …

Still no luck.

When Demeter finished talking, the leader encouraged the rest of the group to offer the woman their affirmations. The women purred out kindly thoughts and wishes, assuring Demeter that she was strong and self-sufficient. Soon Demeter was crying—tears of happiness, Riley felt sure.

Then a Latina woman who called herself Mayahuel began to talk about her feelings of guilt for having married into prosperity, while others in her family remained poor and struggling. She tried to help them out however she could, she said, but it never felt like enough.

At Minerva's coaxing, women assured Mayahuel that she was a beautiful soul who fully deserved of her good fortune, and that she had nothing to feel guilty about.

Another woman spoke about how she'd given up her dream of becoming a concert pianist, and yet another about how she and her husband were unable to have children, and …

This is pointless, Riley thought.

She was about to get up and walk out of the meeting when a

woman who called herself Hecate held out her arm and showed a long scratch on her wrist.

"This happened this morning," she said, her voice trembling with emotion. "Harlan did this to me. He's getting worse and worse. He bruises me and burns me and cuts me and does all kinds of terrible things. Oh, he always apologizes afterward, but I'm sure he has no idea … how deeply he hurts me."

Riley listened with keen interest.

Maybe this is what I've been waiting for, she thought.

Hecate's voice started to become more shrill and desperate.

"I don't know … if I should say this …"

Minerva told her gently …

"You can talk to us about anything, Hecate. You know that."

Shaking all over now, Hecate said, "I'm so angry. I want to do something terrible. I think I want to …"

She choked down a sob while the rest of the group waited for her to continue.

"If he does anything like this again, I'll kill him. I don't thing I can stop myself. You know, some wealthy men have been murdered lately. They're probably cruel to their wives, just like Harlan is to me. Their wives probably did it. I don't blame them. In fact I …"

The woman fell silent, too overwhelmed to continue.

Then Riley heard a voice from nearby.

"Oh, Hecate, I know this is hard, and you feel helpless. But you won't be trapped in that pain forever. In fact, this agony won't go on much longer. Things will be better before you even know it. I promise. I know."

Riley looked and saw that the woman was the fourth woman sitting to her left. She must have arrived while Riley's eyes had been closed.

Riley recognized her immediately.

She called herself Eris, and she'd shown up during both of the earlier meetings. Riley had been curious enough about her to look up that name and find out that Eris was a Greek goddess of strife and discord.

But aside from introducing herself at the other meetings, Eris hadn't said a word.

Until just now, Riley thought.

Eris was brightly dressed in an outfit that matched her mane of red hair. She had a warm smile that reminded Riley of Eleanor Oberlander, except that Eris seemed much more sincere.

Eris continued to speak comfortingly to Hecate, in an almost eerily soothing voice, assuring her that somehow, as if by magic, her problems would soon be over and she'd no longer be trapped.

Minerva, the group leader, stood outside the circle smiling, apparently pleased by Eris's words of comfort and optimism. As for Hecate herself, her anger seemed to melt away, and she smiled through tears of joy.

Then another woman spoke up. She called herself Aura, and Riley had noticed earlier that her arm was in a sling.

She looked at Eris and said, "Oh, I believe you, Eris. You're such a wise soul. I feel like I can believe anything you say."

Some of the other woman murmured in agreement. It seemed that Eris was not a total stranger to this group, and that many of the women who came here were quite enchanted with her.

The woman who called herself Aura pointed to her injured arm.

"I've been lying to people about this," she said to Eris. "I've been saying that I slipped and fell. But my husband, Emil, did this to me. I'm terrified of his rages, but I don't dare talk about it to anyone outside this group. Please tell me, Eris—should I just keep on lying? What else can I do?"

Eris smiled at Aura. When she spoke, her words had a joyful, triumphant ring.

"Trust me, Aura, you won't have to lie to anybody much longer. You will be free of all this very soon. I promise you."

Riley felt a prickle of realization as Eris continued speaking words of comfort.

Eris is the killer, she thought.

She simply has to be.

And the killer fully intended to fix both these women's problems—by murdering their husbands.

CHAPTER THIRTY FIVE

Riley could barely contain her excitement as she sat through the rest of the meeting. The other women who spoke complained about nonviolent issues, such as the challenges of child rearing and their general despair at the state of the world.

Eris showed no interest in those other women or their problems. She didn't say another word.

When the meeting broke up, the women mingled in groups as they headed out of the house. Riley tried to get close enough to Eris to talk to her, but she was quite popular, with a cluster of women gathered tightly around her.

Not that it mattered …

What would I say to her, anyway?

That I know she's a killer?

Riley was nowhere near proving anything of the kind. She needed to find something solid to act on.

When Riley got outside, she kept her eye on Eris and the two women that Eris had comforted, Aura and Hecate. Aura, the woman with the broken arm, headed toward a BMW where a driver was waiting for her. Hecate walked toward an Audi, and Eris toward a large Mercedes.

Riley didn't want the women to notice her writing anything down, so she glanced at the three license plate numbers and made a mental note of each. She'd trained her short-term memory to hold such information in her head, at least for brief intervals. Then as she walked away from the house toward where Bill and Jared were parked, she took out her notebook and jotted the numbers down.

She jumped into the seat behind Bill and Jared and pointed down the street.

"Follow that Mercedes," she said. "I'll explain in a minute."

As Bill started to drive, Riley called up Van Roff on her cell phone. As usual, the technical wizard sounded pleased to hear from her.

She told him, "I need for you to track down the owners of three vehicles and get back to me about them. Here are their license plates …"

She read off the numbers to Roff, then told him she was most interested in whoever owned the Mercedes.

186

When she ended the call, Bill glanced back at her. "Who were you talking to?"

Riley reminded herself that Bill didn't know about her clandestine use of Roff as a font of information that might not be as quickly available from more official sources.

Now's no time to tell him, she thought.

She simply said, "A friend."

Bill shook his head and sighed. Riley knew he'd figured out instantly that she was breaking the rules again.

He knows me too well, she thought.

Fortunately, he also knew better than to ask her nosy questions.

Bill was skillfully following the Mercedes at a safe distance. Riley appreciated that he knew what he was doing. The driver wouldn't realize she was being tailed.

As they drove, Riley explained what was going on—that she believed she'd spotted the killer and the wives of two potential victims.

"So what's the name of the suspect—the woman we're following?" Bill asked.

"She calls herself Eris. I don't know her real name."

Jared griped, "What do you mean, you don't know her real name? What *do* you know about her, anyway? Just that she *sounds* suspicious? Are you taking us up another blind alley or what?"

Riley grunted under her breath. She was about to tell Jared to shut the hell up when they saw the Mercedes pull into the driveway of another posh residence—a pretentious pseudo-classical mansion with white columns. Bill drove past the house as if he were continuing on down the street. Then he turned a corner and parked where they could see the house through an iron fence.

It was dark outside now, and Riley was pretty sure their car wouldn't be noticed from the house. The front of the building was well lighted, and Riley and her colleagues watched as the woman got out of her car, walked between the white columns, and entered the front door.

Jared was complaining again. "So what the hell do we do now? Just sit here waiting for her to do … well, what, exactly? Agent Paige, have we got any kind of a plan?"

Riley suppressed a growl of anger. But the truth was, she knew that Jared had a point.

She didn't have a plan—not yet.

What *were* they going to do?

So far, the situation didn't even have the makings of a stakeout.

Riley's phone buzzed again, and she was relieved to see that the call was from Roff.

"I've got some names and information for you," Roff said. "The woman in the BMW's name is Victoria Slattery, married to a Marshfield lawyer named Emil Slattery. It looks like she's been treated for some mysterious injuries recently …"

Riley said, "Most recently a broken arm, I'll bet."

"You'd win that bet," Roff said. "The woman in the Audi's name is Nora, and her husband's a bestselling author you might have heard of—Harlan Ford."

Riley felt breathless with expectation.

The name was familiar to her. She thought she might have read some of his books at one time or another.

"What about the last woman?" she asked Roff.

"Well, this is the really interesting one. Her name is Adrienne McKinney—a name not totally unfamiliar to those of us in my area of expertise. Her husband was a brilliant software engineer and entrepreneur named Knox McKinney."

Riley's ears pricked up at Roff's use of the past tense.

"Was?" she asked.

"Yeah, he was murdered a couple of years ago. Caused quite a stir in the geek community. I was sure shocked about it."

Riley was tingling all over.

"Murdered? By whom?"

"Bradley Cruickshank, a disgruntled employee who claimed that McKinney had stolen an idea from him. He just walked into McKinney's office and shot him. The last I heard, Cruickshank was still on death row in the Georgia Diagnostic and Classification Prison in Butts County. Adrienne inherited McKinney's fortune, naturally. She hasn't remarried."

Riley heard Roff take a deep breath.

He said, "Here's what I think you'll find most thought-provoking. Adrienne was once a promising programmer in her own right, although she kind of disappeared under her husband's shadow after they got married. She also had a reputation for hacking skills."

Riley gasped aloud.

Hacking skills!

That meant Adrienne could have hacked the victims' security systems.

"But she didn't kill her husband?" Riley asked.

"Apparently not. There was no doubt who killed him. And no sign she or anybody else put the guy up to it."

Riley's mind buzzed. What had it meant to Adrienne that her husband had been killed? Had she been devastated? Or had the murder in some way set her free?

She remembered all too clearly the woman's eerie calmness when she'd said …

"Things will be better before you even know it. I promise. I know."

Riley was still certain that the woman who called herself "Eris" was the killer, but she was no closer to being able to prove it.

Riley thanked Roff, who said, "Is there anything else I can do?"

Riley couldn't think of what to suggest, but she didn't want to lose the gifted hacker's input.

Finally she said, "Be creative."

Roff rumbled with laughter.

"I can do that," he said.

Riley ended the call. She wasn't surprised both Bill and Jared were staring at her with interest.

Jared asked, "Just who the hell do you keep talking to?"

Before Riley could say anything, Bill snapped, "Shut up, Jared. It's none of your business."

Again, Riley was grateful that Bill understood that the less said about it, the better.

Jared sat there with his mouth hanging open.

Then he asked quietly, "What do we do now?"

Riley said, "I've just learned that Adrienne McKinney has hacking skills. That's enough cause to pay her a visit."

Then she pointed at Jared and added sharply, "But you're going to keep your mouth shut and let Bill and me do that talking. Otherwise, you wait right here in the car."

Jared nodded, looking thoroughly cowed.

"Got it," he said.

Riley and her colleagues got out of the car and walked up to the front entrance. When they rang the bell, they were met by a young woman dressed in a black and white maid's uniform.

"How may I help you?" the maid asked, looking surprised to see visitors.

Riley and Bill pulled out their badges and introduced themselves.

The maid's eyes widened.

"Oh, my!" she said.

Bill said, "We need to talk to Adrienne McKinney."

The maid shook her head.

"I'm sorry, but … Mrs. McKinney isn't here."

Riley felt a burst of alarm.

She was sure she'd seen the woman get out of her car and walk into her own house.

Bill said, "Ma'am, it's illegal to lie to FBI agents."

"I'm telling the truth," the maid said.

"So where is Mrs. McKinney?" Jared asked, disobeying Riley's order to keep his mouth shut.

The maid shrugged a little.

"I don't know," she said. "She just told me she was going out for a drive."

Riley snapped, "But her car's still in front of the house."

"She took her van, like she often does," the maid said. "She keeps it in the garage out back. There's an exit to another street. She likes to take drives in the van at night."

Riley demanded, "Can you describe the van? Do you know the license number?"

The maid stammered, "Y-yes, but … I'm not sure if I should …"

Bill spoke forcefully. "Ma'am, this is extremely urgent. An FBI matter. For both your sake and Mrs. McKinney's, you'd really better cooperate."

The maid hastily described the van—an ordinary white Ford—and recited the license plate number.

Bill had his cell phone out and was taking down the information. Riley knew that he was forwarding it straight back to Quantico. But how long would it take for the FBI to get the local police mobilized to look for the car?

While Riley was puzzling over what to do next, her cell phone rang.

Once again, she saw that the call was from Van Roff.

When she answered, Roff said …

"I got something hot for you."

CHAPTER THIRTY SIX

As Adrienne crept softly and quietly through the house, she recognized a familiar change coming over her.

She no longer felt like the kindly woman who called herself Eris, that part of herself who comforted other suffering women in LifeGrasp meetings.

Her feelings of warmth and goodwill were giving way to …

Fury, she realized.

She could feel wrath beginning to flood her body.

She thought she became something different when she felt like this.

She was sure that she became one of those mythical Greek spirits of vengeance called Furies—wild, violent women who avenged terrible wrongs.

They were said to have snaky hair, like Medusa, and wings like bats.

She knew the Greek word for such a creature was *Erinys.*

That's what I am now, she told herself.

An Erinys.

A Fury.

Like a true Fury, she had to sublimate her rage just enough to keep her head clear. The important thing was to carry out the task at hand.

To do that, she had to stay quiet and unnoticed, so she moved slowly through the silent house.

Although that poor woman who called herself Hecate hadn't said much until today's meeting, Adrienne had noticed her many small injuries. She had no doubt at all who had inflicted them.

So Adrienne had been preparing for tonight's task for several days now.

She'd hacked municipal records to find this house's blueprints, so she knew the interior well. And of course, she'd been fully prepared to hack the house's security system from her van.

SafetyLinks! she thought with contempt.

Just like Harter's house!

Didn't people know how easy that system was to disable, even from afar?

She was pleased with how deftly she'd thwarted the system.

The doors had unlocked on command. She'd found it easy to slip inside and locate an appropriate knife in the well-outfitted kitchen.

Now she would grant yet another woman the freedom that the Furies had granted her. That young man who had killed her husband hadn't realized that he was setting her free. He'd thought he was acting out of his own grievances. But she was sure that Bradley Cruickshank had merely been a tool of the Furies, an unknowing male *Erinys* who had taken away her tormenter.

After Knox was gone, Adrienne had realized that she owed the Furies a debt of gratitude. She had to do for other women what that young man had done for her.

She moved across the open living area to the stairs and began to ease her way upward.

*

Riley hung on for dear life as Jared drove crazily through the streets.

She could see that Bill was similarly unnerved as he sat in the front passenger seat.

He was now on the phone, notifying the local police that a violent crime was likely in progress.

Jared had insisted on driving, and with good reason.

He knew the streets of Marshfield well enough to find the address they were looking for.

And they couldn't get there a moment too soon.

Maybe it's too late already, Riley thought.

She tried to push the thought out of her mind …

It can't be. It just can't be too late.

A few moments ago, Van Roff had told her what he'd done to be "creative." He'd hacked into the security systems of the other two houses—not to disable them, but to monitor them.

And sure enough, the security system at one of the houses went down.

Roff was absolutely sure that it was the work of a skilled hacker.

Riley had tried calling the house to warn its occupants, but she'd only gotten an answering machine.

She snapped at Jared …

"Drive faster!"

Jared snapped back …

"Do you want to get there alive or what?"

As they neared the address, Riley saw that the house wasn't as large as the other mansions, but it was impressive and comparatively tasteful. Sure enough, a white Ford van was parked on the street near the house.

There was still no sign of any police.

Riley tried to fight down her worry, but she couldn't help but wonder …

Did the cops take Bill's call seriously?

She also knew that suburban cops could sometimes be slow to answer emergencies, especially at night. But she thought they'd respond to a high-end neighborhood like this.

As Jared entered the driveway, Riley said to him, "Check the van, see if she still might be in there."

Jared said, "OK, but what are you going to do?"

While the car was still in motion, Riley jumped out.

She heard Bill call out to her …

"Riley!"

But Riley was already running to the front entrance. She pushed the door, which opened easily. She found herself in a dimly lit, open, modern interior. No one was in sight.

Where should we look? she wondered.

Then she spotted a flight of stairs.

*

Adrienne moved down the wide upstairs hallway to where she knew two large bedrooms were located. The doors were on opposite sides of the hall.

She paused for a moment.

Hecate had mentioned a couple of meetings ago that she and her husband were now sleeping in separate bedrooms. The *Erinys* was sure that both the husband and wife were in their rooms asleep …

But which room is which?

Which one is he *in?*

She smiled, rather amused by her little conundrum.

It was nothing to get worried about, after all.

If she peeked through the wrong door and found the woman asleep, she'd simply sneak away to the other room.

She reached for the knob of the door on the left and gently turned it.

Harlan Ford wasn't a deep sleeper, so he was easily awakened by the light footsteps moving across his bedroom floor.

He was pleased by the sound.

Nora slept in the bedroom across the hall these days, but …

She must have had a change of heart tonight.

She must have come over here to join him.

He'd been lying on his side facing away from the door. When the footsteps stopped at the edge of his bed, he turned over to greet her.

"Nora," he said in a welcoming voice and holding out his hand. "Join me."

But the silhouetted figure had raised her arm, and something metallic glinted in her hand.

Then the arm plunged down fast and he felt a sharp and shocking pain.

She's gone crazy! he thought.

She wants to kill me!

*

Damn it! Adrienne thought as she landed a clumsy stab in the man's shoulder muscles.

She hadn't reckoned on having her prey wide awake.

The other men had been either fast asleep or deeply relaxed when she'd delivered the first blows that had incapacitated and subdued them.

She pulled the knife back and climbed onto the bed, prepared to lunge again.

"Nora!" the man cried. "What are you doing?"

Adrienne screeched back at him, "I'm not Nora. I'm an *Erinys*. I'm Nora's avenger."

The man was twisting and struggling wildly now.

His arms flailed, intercepting the swings of her knife, and although she knew that he must already be bleeding badly, she was displeased with how this was unfolding.

Nevertheless, she told herself …

In a few moments he'll be dead.

That's what matters.

*

Nora snapped awake at the sound of her own name being shouted …

"Nora!"

… followed by words she couldn't understand.

It was her husband. Yelling from across the hall in his bedroom.

Then she heard a woman's voice roaring with anger.

What's going on? Nora wondered.

She scrambled out of the bed and rushed out of her room into the hallway. She flung open the door that led into Harlan's bedroom and switched on the light.

For a moment she was sure she was hallucinating. Her husband had often said she imagined things.

So had her therapist.

Could what she saw now really be happening?

Harlan had tumbled from the bed. He was writhing on the floor, bleeding badly.

A knife-wielding woman stood spread-eagle above him as if ready to strike, her face wild with hatred.

Nora recognized that mane of red hair.

All at once, she knew this was real.

"Eris!" Nora yelled.

The woman looked up, distracted by Nora's voice.

Some of the hatred faded from her face and was replaced by sheer confusion.

Then she pointed the knife toward Nora.

"Stay back," Adrienne hissed. "I'm not Eris now. I'm doing this for you."

The look of hatred returned as she raised the knife again.

"No!" Nora yelled. "Eris, stop!"

The woman froze in place and stared back at her.

Nora felt a massive shock of realization.

She suddenly understood something terrible and heartbreaking.

The abuse she thought she'd suffered at her husband's hands— he hadn't done any of that at all.

He'd been trying to convince her of the truth all along, and so had Dr. Ridge.

The bruises, burns, cuts, and scratches …

I did them to myself!

And through it all, despite his own pain and confusion, Harlan hadn't stopped giving her his love and support.

That realization gripped her with a feeling of shame and sorrow.

She burst into tears and screamed …

"Harlan never hurt me. He's never hurt me once since I met him. He's the kindest soul I've ever known."

Eris's widened with perplexity.

She looked down at Harlan, and then again at Nora.

"You're either lying or stupid," she said.

Nora threw herself across the room and against the woman she knew as Eris before the knife could plunge down again.

*

Riley heard an uproar as she dashed up the stairs.

As soon as she reached the hallway she saw the light from an open door.

She rushed into that room and was baffled by what she saw.

A man lay bleeding and barely conscious on the floor, and two women were struggling over him, trying to wrest a knife out of each other's grasp.

One woman was wearing a nightgown, and the other was dressed in black.

Riley recognized both of them.

She knew perfectly well which was the killer.

But in this wild tangle of bodies, she didn't dare use her weapon.

Instead, she rushed forward and forced the women apart.

The woman in black had the knife in her hand.

She slashed horizontally at Riley.

She knows how to handle a knife, Riley realized.

In a fight, slashing motions would cause the most damage.

But Riley knew how to thwart her. She dived sharply against the woman's legs, toppling her to the floor.

Riley and the woman rolled together several times until Riley managed to pin her arms down. Riley looked up in time to see Bill crouching over the man's body, working to stop his wounds from bleeding.

Nora was weeping, trying to help him.

Gasping, Riley said to the woman she was holding down…

"Adrienne McKinney, you're under arrest."

As Riley read Adrienne her rights and put her in handcuffs, she finally heard approaching sirens.

It's about time, she thought.

She saw Jared step into the doorway. He stared around the room with his eyes wide and his mouth hanging open.

"Damn," Jared said.

CHAPTER THIRTY SEVEN

Riley joined in the general laughter at how the puppy and the black and white kitten were dealing with each other.

April said, "At least Marbles isn't hissing at Darby today."

Jilly added, "And at least Darby isn't trying to hide under the furniture."

They were all on Riley's back deck, along Blaine and his daughter, Crystal. Bill, who was taking a well-deserved leave from work, was there too. And of course Gabriela had served everybody delicious snacks, this time balls of deep-fried batter called *buñuelos*.

They were all enjoying the confrontations between the two little animals. Though still a puppy, Darby was larger than the kitten that April had named Marbles. Nevertheless, Darby had been thoroughly frightened of her smaller housemate—at least until today.

Now the situation appeared to be changing. Darby wasn't backing away at Marbles' stalking approach.

She was holding her ground.

And now, when Marbles raised her paw to swat at Darby's face, Darby did something she hadn't done before.

She raised her own paw and pushed it against Marbles' head.

The kitten fell backward into a startled heap.

The whole back yard echoed with laughter now.

"Way to go, Darby!" April shouted with glee.

And in another instant, the two animals were playfully wrestling with each other, obviously enjoying their mock-battles.

Jilly looked up at Riley with a grin.

"Wow, you sure were right, Mom!" she said. "They're great pals now!"

Like everybody else, Riley had already laughed until her lungs hurt.

But as her laughter waned, a feeling of melancholy began to creep in.

She and Bill had returned from Georgia just yesterday, and she wasn't sure which of the two women she pitied more—the murderer, Adrienne McKinney, or Harlan Ford's troubled wife, Nora.

The truth was, Riley could almost understand Adrienne's

madness, especially now that she knew more about her awful story. When she'd been a young and immature computer prodigy, she'd married much too hastily, and realized too late that her husband had been attracted to her for her youth and beauty, not her mind. Much worse, the man was a depraved abuser—by all accounts more vicious than Harter, Farrell, or Morse, all of whom had been murdered for their cruelties.

When her husband was killed by a disgruntled employee, something in Adrienne's mind finally snapped. She fancied herself some sort of righteous scourge against abusive men. Riley wondered if this was one killer who might mount a successful insanity defense. In any case, she would never be free again.

Nora Ford, on the other hand, hadn't been the victim of a man at all, but of some mysterious illness that ravaged her brain. A therapist who treated the woman after her ordeal told Riley that Nora had some kind of terrible breakthrough when she saw her husband's life in danger. But that breakthrough was but the awful beginning of a long struggle to regain her mental health. Would she ever recover from the guilt of knowing that her own delusions almost killed the man who most loved her and cared for her?

Riley sighed and thought …

At least it's all over.

Riley had no doubt that the three widows, Morgan, Charlotte, and Tisha, would persevere nicely. They were all young and beautiful and had plenty of resources now that their husbands were dead.

And they're sure not going to do a whole lot of grieving.

Things had also worked out well for Jared, who had become something of a celebrity among Atlanta cops for the part he'd played in solving the case. Riley had to admit that he'd done some excellent work.

Not that I'm going to miss the obnoxious little guy.

All three of the girls were now on the floor playing rambunctiously with the kitten and the puppy. Bill and Blaine were deep in amiable conversation.

Riley breathed a sigh of relief that Bill had gently rebuffed her advances that night when she had felt so down.

Finally Bill looked at Riley and said, "I'd better be going."

"You don't have to," Riley said.

Bill looked over at Blaine, then at Riley.

He grinned as if to say …

"Yes, I really should go."

As soon as Bill left the house, Riley scooted her chair next to Blaine's and held his hand.

Blaine said to her, "What do you want for your birthday?"

Riley was startled. She'd almost forgotten that she was going to turn forty-one in just a few days.

"Anything," she said, "but no surprises."

Blaine looked a little embarrassed. Then he nodded silently toward the kids.

Riley immediately realized what he was trying to tell her. The kids and Gabriela were planning a surprise party—and there was nothing she could do to stop them.

"Oh, no," Riley said to Blaine.

"Oh, yes," Blaine said.

Riley chuckled a little at her own mild discomfort.

Everything's good, she thought as she watched the happy scene. Riley knew she didn't always manage everything well, but sometimes she did all right.

She cared, and these people all knew that she cared.

So why did she feel a pang of sadness?

Riley knew the reason perfectly well.

She often felt that happiness like this must be terribly fragile in such a cruel and violent world.

But then she wondered …

Was it really?

Or was it possible the joy she was witnessing right now was stronger than she had believed?

Riley hoped so with all her heart …

If only I could know.

ONCE DORMANT
(A Riley Paige Mystery—Book 14)

"A masterpiece of thriller and mystery! The author did a magnificent job developing characters with a psychological side that is so well described that we feel inside their minds, follow their fears and cheer for their success. The plot is very intelligent and will keep you entertained throughout the book. Full of twists, this book will keep you awake until the turn of the last page."
--Books and Movie Reviews, Roberto Mattos (re Once Gone)

ONCE DORMANT is book #14 in the bestselling Riley Paige mystery series, which begins with the #1 bestseller ONCE GONE (Book #1)—a free download with over 1,000 five star reviews!

After lying dormant for 10 years, an elusive serial killer strikes again, leaving few clues—and the only way for FBI Special Agent Riley Paige to catch him in the present is to solve the riddles of the past.

Women are turning up dead, and in this dark psychological thriller, Riley Paige realizes she is in a race against time. The murders of the past were too perplexing to be solved back then. Can Riley solve them 10 years cold? And connect the dots to the present-day crimes?

When Riley finds her personal life in crisis, playing cat and mouse with a brilliant psychopath may just be too much for her. Especially since there is something that is just not sitting right with this case....

An action-packed thriller with heart-pounding suspense, ONCE DORMANT is book #14 in a riveting new series—with a beloved new character—that will leave you turning pages late into the night.

Book #15 in the Riley Paige series will be available soon.

NOW AVAILABLE!

A NEW SERIES!

WATCHING
(The Making of Riley Paige—Book 1)

"A masterpiece of thriller and mystery! The author did a magnificent job developing characters with a psychological side that is so well described that we feel inside their minds, follow their fears and cheer for their success. The plot is very intelligent and will keep you entertained throughout the book. Full of twists, this book will keep you awake until the turn of the last page."
--Books and Movie Reviews, Roberto Mattos (re Once Gone)

WATCHING (The Making of Riley Paige—Book One) is book #1 in a new psychological thriller series by #1 bestselling author Blake Pierce, whose free bestseller Once Gone (Book #1) has received over 1,000 five star reviews.

22 year old psychology major—and aspiring FBI agent—Riley Paige finds herself in a battle for her life as her closest friends on campus are abducted and killed by a serial killer. She senses that she, too, is being targeted—and that if she is to survive, she must apply her brilliant mind to stop the killer herself.

When the FBI hits a dead end, they are impressed enough by Riley's keen insight into the killer's mind to allow her to help. Yet the killer's mind is a dark, twisted place, one too diabolical to make sense of, and one that threatens to bring Riley's fragile psyche crashing down. In this deadly game of cat and mouse, can Riley survive unscarred?

An action-packed thriller with heart-pounding suspense, WATCHING is book #1 in a riveting new series that will leave you turning pages late into the night. It takes readers back 20 plus years—to how Riley's career began—and is the perfect complement to the ONCE GONE series (A Riley Paige Mystery), which includes 13 books and counting.

Book #2 in THE MAKING OF RILEY PAIGE series will be available soon.

Blake Pierce

Blake Pierce is author of the bestselling RILEY PAGE mystery series, which includes fourteen books (and counting). Blake Pierce is also the author of the MACKENZIE WHITE mystery series, comprising eight books; of the AVERY BLACK mystery series, comprising six books; of the KERI LOCKE mystery series, comprising five books; and of the new MAKING OF RILEY PAIGE mystery series, which begins with WATCHING.

An avid reader and lifelong fan of the mystery and thriller genres, Blake loves to hear from you, so please feel free to visit www.blakepierceauthor.com to learn more and stay in touch.

BOOKS BY BLAKE PIERCE

THE MAKING OF RILEY PAIGE SERIES
WATCHING (Book #1)
WAITING (Book #2)

RILEY PAIGE MYSTERY SERIES
ONCE GONE (Book #1)
ONCE TAKEN (Book #2)
ONCE CRAVED (Book #3)
ONCE LURED (Book #4)
ONCE HUNTED (Book #5)
ONCE PINED (Book #6)
ONCE FORSAKEN (Book #7)
ONCE COLD (Book #8)
ONCE STALKED (Book #9)
ONCE LOST (Book #10)
ONCE BURIED (Book #11)
ONCE BOUND (Book #12)
ONCE TRAPPED (Book #13)
ONCE DORMANT (Book #14)

MACKENZIE WHITE MYSTERY SERIES
BEFORE HE KILLS (Book #1)
BEFORE HE SEES (Book #2)
BEFORE HE COVETS (Book #3)
BEFORE HE TAKES (Book #4)
BEFORE HE NEEDS (Book #5)
BEFORE HE FEELS (Book #6)
BEFORE HE SINS (Book #7)
BEFORE HE HUNTS (Book #8)
BEFORE HE PREYS (Book #9)

AVERY BLACK MYSTERY SERIES
CAUSE TO KILL (Book #1)
CAUSE TO RUN (Book #2)
CAUSE TO HIDE (Book #3)
CAUSE TO FEAR (Book #4)
CAUSE TO SAVE (Book #5)
CAUSE TO DREAD (Book #6)

KERI LOCKE MYSTERY SERIES
A TRACE OF DEATH (Book #1)
A TRACE OF MUDER (Book #2)
A TRACE OF VICE (Book #3)
A TRACE OF CRIME (Book #4)
A TRACE OF HOPE (Book #5)